COLD LOVE FROM A THUG

SHONTAIYE MOORE

SYNOPSIS

One phone call was all it took to dismantle a relationship that Serenity Smith had spent the last seven years building with her fiancé Yosohn Thomas. One phone call that confirmed everything she'd known for years: that he was a lying, cheating, two-timing dog. Embarrassed, hurt, and fed up, Serenity does the only thing she can think to do. She leaves, forcing Yosohn to get his act together.

Although Yosohn knows he isn't perfect, he loves Serenity with all his heart. While he regrets cheating on her, his biggest regret was cheating on her with a chick that just can't seem to let go. For Jocelyn Rodriguez, Yosohn is like an addictive drug that she can't get enough of. She's hooked. And just like a drug addict craving a high, she'll do anything to get her next hit.

Despite loving one another endlessly, Serenity and Yosohn are torn further and further apart by lies, obsession, and deadly secrets. Will the two of them make it, or will their relationship be destroyed by the people closest to them?

CHAPTER 1

S erenity hopped out of the king-size bed that she shared with her fiancé Yosohn. He was also up but he was too stunned to move. He had heard Serenity arguing on the phone and knew exactly who it was on the opposite end. He made a silent vow to fuck Jocelyn up when he saw her. He hated a messy broad, and Jocelyn had outdone herself on the messy tip when she called Serenity's direct line to start some drama in their household. He wondered how she had even gotten the phone number. He would get to the bottom of that later. Right now, he had to do damage control. Their argument had been heated, ending when Serenity hung up on her. He was praying to God for the miracle that she left it at that; however, when Serenity raced to his phone on the nightstand, he knew shit was about to get real. Serenity immediately began searching for the number that had just called her.

Yosohn regularly erased his calls, but like a bloodhound searching for a scent, Serenity still managed to find a total of thirteen incoming and outgoing calls to the number. She also found a few texts between him and Jocelyn. One read: *Why you not answering the phone?* His response was: *Chill my shorty with me.* Some were explicit, but many of them were: *what you doin'? Are you coming over?*

With each message her eyes scanned, Serenity grew angrier. Here she was thinking that things were good between the two of them and it was all a lie. They were even going through fertility treatment to expand their family, and here he was cheating on her. Yosohn watched as Serenity angrily scoured his phone. He got up out of the bed to take it.

"Yo, give me my phone. Whatever she told you was a lie." He quickly motioned towards her, but as soon as he reached down to try and take his phone, Serenity leaned back and threw it into the wall. The forceful impact caused it to bust, leaving an ugly dent in the paint. Yosohn watched as it slid to the floor in pieces.

"You're a fucking liar!" Serenity shrieked. "Who was that?" She demanded to know, her body trembling. She waited for Yosohn to respond, but all he could do was stand there quietly with a blank face. He wasn't sure what to say. He had just woken up and wasn't prepared to answer those type of questions. He wanted to say he didn't know, but as furious as she was, he didn't want to dare insult her intelligence.

"Ren, please." Yosohn begged. He looked away and took a deep breath before pausing. He hoped the moment of silence would calm her. "Just calm down for a second so I can talk to you," he plead while he bit down on his lips and struggled to come up with an answer.

"Yosohn, please don't beat me in the head with the bullshit. The bitch just told me on the phone that she was fuckin' and suckin' you. How did she even get my fuckin' number? Huh?" she asked. "Is this what it is now? This where we at wit' it?" Serenity questioned; her beautiful maple-brown eyes desperate for an answer.

She was far from a fool. No random bitch would have the balls to call her line at 7 o'clock in the morning and disrespect her at that magnitude. *Is Yosohn with you? If he is, wake him up?* The brief conversation played in her head over and over. She couldn't believe the audacity of the bitch. When Serenity asked who she was, she would reply, *I'm the bitch that's fuckin and suckin' yo' man.* It was crystal clear she knew that Yosohn was in a relationship. It just seemed as though she wanted her presence to be known to more than just Yosohn. Serenity had no doubt that whoever the broad was that called her, wanted *Serenity* herself to know just exactly who she was.

Serenity's heart pounded in her chest. It was taking everything in her just to breathe. Despite doing her best to calm herself down, it wasn't working. Suddenly, a thought ran across mind. If Yosohn wanted to act like he didn't know who the chick was that was calling her phone, then she was going to find out herself. After all, the bitch did just call *her* phone. As angry as she was, she didn't even think to even try and call the number back.

Without saying a word, she stormed over to the nightstand where she'd laid her phone down. After snatching it up and swiping to her call log, she found what she was looking for. The chick hadn't even bothered to block her number.

"Please don't do this, Ren," Yosohn begged, walking towards her as soon as he realized what she was about to do. His heart raced in his chest when he saw Serenity press down on the exposed digits. He had no doubt that Jocelyn was about to blow his shit up. He should have cut her off a long time ago; she was way too unpredictable. He raced towards Serenity and tried to snatch the phone from her hand; unfortunately, she was too quick. She gripped the phone tightly and made a dash into their private bath and slammed the door shut, locking it.

"Fuck you, Yosohn!" she called out from the opposite side of the door. She stared down painfully at her phone and waited for the call to connect.

Yosohn rested his head against the outside of the door. He was so close … yet so far. If he could just grab her phone and break the bitch in half. He heard the phone begin to ring and prayed to God that Jocelyn didn't pick up.

A few seconds later, the call connected, and Yosohn could hear Jocelyn's sultry voice coming from the speaker.

"Hello," Jocelyn answered. She had been waiting. She had Yosohn and his precious Serenity right where she wanted them. Now all she had to do was pour more gasoline on the fire she knew was blazing in their home.

"Listen, this is uhh, Serenity … Yosohn's fiancé. Look, I'm not calling you to go back and forth. I just want some answers," she admitted honestly. "You do too, or you wouldn't have called me." Serenity sat on the bathroom floor with her back against the door. She sighed and continued. "Obviously, you knew about me, so what I really want to know is how long y'all been fuckin'?"

"I've been messin' with Yosohn since April." Serenity did a quick calculation in her head. It was November so he'd been cheating for seven damn months.

"He told me about you, but he made it seem like y'all was having problems and he was leaving soon," Jocelyn lied. He had actually stated the opposite. However, since she had Serenity on the phone, she was going to tell her anything to split them up.

"He's basically between there and here, obviously lying. I tried to cut him off, but he wouldn't let me. Said that y'all was about to be over. Like a fool, I believed him." Jocelyn continued to lay it on thick, pretending to be the unknowing mistress. She could hear the distress in Serenity's voice. She wanted her to feel the same pain she felt on the regular.

4

"So, he fuckin' you and me? Do y'all use protection?" Serenity asked, temporarily ignoring the other hurtful lies. She couldn't handle all the shit Jocelyn was telling her, but she had to know that part.

"Never. He pretty much over here doin' the same shit he doin' over there: playing house with both of us believing he in a relationship with just us. I had to know the truth, so the first chance I got, I went in his phone while he was sleeping and gotcha number. And honestly, I apologize for coming off the way I did when I first called you, but I was mad. I shouldn't have taken that out on you.

"Don't even worry about it. But trust ... I'll be sending him and his shit to you," Serenity said before hanging up. There was nothing more left to say or hear. She'd heard all that she needed to. Yosohn was getting the fuck out *or* she was leaving. Either way, she wasn't about to share no bed with a dog ass nigga. She was either his all ... *or* his nothing.

Serenity stood up from the floor and pulled back the door to go back into the bedroom. She wasn't surprised when she saw Yosohn standing right outside of it. He had heard the brief conversation between the two women. Jocelyn hadn't told her everything, but what she did say was more than enough. He could see the pain and fire in Serenity's eyes. She didn't say a word. She simply began packing her shit.

"Ren? What are you doing?" Yosohn asked, moving quickly behind her. She had walked into her closet and Yosohn could hear her unzipping her suitcase and subsequently tearing clothing down from hangers to shove into it.

"I'm leaving yo' ass," she said calmly as she continued to load up her suitcase. "I done dealt with too much shit over these past years. All the illegal shit. The court cases. The bitches. You might have become legit, but you still can't seem to keep ya fuckin' dick in ya pants. You never gon' change, and I'm tired of sitting around hoping and praying you will."

She spoke low and calm, which scared Yosohn but also saddened him at the same time. She was hurting and it was all because of him. Tears glistened in the corner of her eyes. He had to figure out a way to make it right. He didn't want her to leave him. He couldn't let her leave him. He loved Serenity and her daughter. They were his life. He didn't have any family. They were it. They completed him. If she walked out on him, she would literally be taking his whole life from him.

"Ren, please don't do this," Yosohn begged, standing behind her. He reached down and grabbed her hand to stop her from packing. She quickly snatched it back in repulse.

"Don't fuckin' touch me!" She stormed out of the closet and headed back into the bathroom. She just needed a minute to calm down. She was tired, and her heart ached so bad if felt like it was going to explode. She felt like she was in mourning. Like someone had just died. Or maybe a part of her had died. She didn't know how to describe the feeling. Whatever it was ... it hurt like hell.

When Serenity got in the bathroom, she closed and locked the door behind her. All she wanted was some space. She needed a moment to calm down; however, the longer she sat in the bathroom, the angrier she became. She couldn't believe Yosohn. She'd given her all to him and loved him deeply for the last seven years. Knowing his upbringing of foster homes, caused her to love him that much harder. He had no family so her own family had embraced him and treated him like one of their own. After all that she had given him, cheating on her was basically a smack in the face. It felt like everything she'd done for him, loving him the way that she'd loved him, wasn't enough.

For several minutes, she sat in the bathroom and sobbed, her teary face resting in the palm of her hands. She was furious, and as much as she tried to control her emotions, she couldn't. She felt helpless. With a mixture of hurt, devastation, and rage coursing through her veins, she jumped up and emerged from the bathroom with every bit of her mixed emotions on full display.

Yosohn had been waiting patiently for her to come out. He was hoping she had calmed down; however, when his eyes met hers, he knew she was about to act a fool. He knew the look. Hate danced around wildly in her eyes. Her jaws were tight, and her chest rose and fell angrily.

"Ren, baby please just listen for a minute," he said, easing over towards her, while she stormed around and snatched up more random things she would need for her pending departure.

"I fucked up. I made a mistake, but I don't give a fuck about her. I love you." Yosohn admitted. "Please don't do this," he begged while eyeing the random items she was grabbing. He stared at her and waited for a response. Serenity refused to acknowledge him or even look at him. Yosohn reached down again and tried to take the suitcase out of her hand.

"Don't fucking touch me," she snapped, snatching away her hand and the suitcase from Yosohn. While she trembled in place, she glowered at him. Just the sight of him disgusted her. She now knew what hate felt like. However, at the same time she hated him, she also loved him just as fiercely. She wanted answers.

"That bitch said you fucked her raw! You at her crib playing house the same way you do with me! What the fuck is that Yosohn?" she inquired in disbelief.

"Serenity ... baby, she is lying. You gotta understand that. She knows exactly what she's doing. Look ... I fucked up." Yosohn took a deep breath and forced a swallow. He knew if he wanted to keep Serenity in his life then he was going to need to tell the truth. As much as he hated to, he decided that he was going to keep it as real as he could without hurting her more than he already had.

"Baby ... I fucked up," he repeated, his voice cracking. He cleared his throat the best he could to avoid sounding like a bitch. But the truth was, Serenity was his heart. She was everything to him. He couldn't imagine his life without her, and he didn't want her to leave him.

"I slept with her, but it's over. It's been over. She's just upset because I don't want to be with her. Everything that she's doing right now is out of spite. She's been begging me to leave you for her. She wants you out of the picture. She was just a fuck. I fucked up. Please. She's jealous of you, Serenity, so don't believe shit that bitch says!" he whined.

Yosohn knew the game all too well. He knew how bitches played. He was just surprised that Serenity hadn't caught on. While Serenity was thorough and book smart, she wasn't as street smart as Jocelyn. Early in their relationship, he'd gotten caught up with other females. Up until today, no bitch had ever really gotten the opportunity to get under her skin the way Jocelyn just did. He cursed himself and promised himself he would fix it.

"Please, Ren. I'll do whatever it takes. Let me fix it. Give me a chance to fix it," Yosohn pleaded.

"Fuck you, Yosohn." Serenity grabbed her keys and began dragging her bulging suitcase out of the room and out of the house. She was leaving. She didn't give a damn how much he begged. Before Serenity could get to the door, Yosohn beat her to it and blocked it with his tall body. He was desperate. He didn't care what she said, she wasn't going anywhere.

"You not going no fuckin' where," he argued. He reached down and tried to pry the keys out of her hand, but she refused to let them go. With Yosohn pulling and Serenity pulling, they began to scuffle over them. Yosohn knew it wasn't the right thing to do, but he felt like it was his only option. He would hold her ass hostage in there if he had to, but she wasn't leaving.

"Get the fuck off me, Yosohn! Give me my fucking keys!" she screamed. "Let me fuckin' go!" she wailed as loud as she could. He had her by the waist and was pulling the keys out of her hand while she struggled for dear life to maintain possession of them.

"Fuck no," he growled. "You not leaving!" He was scared that if he let her leave, she would never return. Despite how much Yosohn had done, Serenity was his weakness and he refused to let her leave over a bitch that meant nothing.

"Serenity, please!" Yosohn begged. "Owww, shit! Yo, stopppppp!" he hollered as he yelped in pain. Serenity was now fighting him. She had bit down on his hand as hard as she could and was grabbing his shirt and swinging with all her might to keep her keys so she could leave.

Through all the commotion they hadn't heard Yosohn's friend Mann walk in through the front door. He had been knocking and calling Yosohn's phone when he heard the commotion. The door was unlocked, so he let himself in like he always did. He wasn't prepared for the drama he had stumbled upon.

"Mann! Help me please," Serenity called to him. "I just want to leave," Serenity cried; her pretty, chocolate face streaked with tears. Mann sighed. He hated domestic shit, and he knew this situation was going to eventually happen. He knew all about the bitch Jocelyn, that Yosohn was creeping with. She'd been drama since the day she popped up. It had been a long time coming. He was surprised it hadn't happened sooner.

Yosohn released his grip when Mann came in. He was almost embarrassed. He didn't want to look weak over a female, so as much as he hated to, he knew he would have to fall back for a minute. As he let go, Serenity raced out the door alone, dragging her suitcase behind her. She was thankful that it was the weekend, and her daughter Heaven was at her mother's house. There was no way that she'd want her seven-year-old subjected to the fuckery.

As Serenity drove off, Yosohn stared hopelessly out the door feeling sick to his stomach. In a matter of minutes, his world had begun caving in around him and it was nobody's fault but his own. The overwhelmingly agonizing feeling in his chest convinced him that his heart was breaking. He didn't like the feeling. He closed his eyes briefly and shook his head in frustration. He couldn't even honestly answer why he had even cheated. He loved Serenity with every fiber in his body and didn't want to be without her. He felt like a fool. Everything that he'd ever wanted and ever dreamed of had walked out the door. Yosohn sat down onto the chocolate brown leather sofa and exhaled sharply in defeat.

"Fuck!" he yelled, punching the wall.

"What just happened?" Mann asked, not really wanting to pry but he figured it would be better than just standing there silent. He took a seat in the recliner adjacent to the couch that Yosohn was sitting on.

"Fuckin' Jocelyn called Serenity." All Mann could do was shake his head. "On God — I'm gon' fuck that bitch up," Yosohn vowed. "You got some green?" he asked, his eyes weary. "I need to smoke."

Yosohn dropped his head into his hands unsure of what he would do next. He figured he would give Serenity a few hours and then call her. He was going to pay Jocelyn's ass a nice little visit and find out what the fuck type of shit she was on. She knew what her role was, and she also knew that the role was limited. He didn't understand why she felt the need to cause drama.

While Yosohn sat lost in his own frustrated thoughts, Mann glanced down at him and shook his head. He didn't feel sorry for him. Not even a little bit. He was a grown man. Not some teenage boy running around with nothing to lose. Yosohn knew the game. He also knew females and how unpredictable they could be when they became jealous. He should have been cut the cord on Jocelyn. Yosohn had already expressed how she had pulled a few minor stunts to sabotage his and Serenity's relationship. It was only a matter of time before shit hit the fan.

Mann never understood what Yosohn was thinking. There was no way he would jeopardize a relationship with Serenity for a broad like Jocelyn. He didn't care how good she looked. Serenity had everything a nigga could want: drive, looks, body and brains. Standing around 5'3, Serenity was petite but built thick and solid like a stallion. Beautiful, dark chocolate skin. A pretty face with dark sultry eyes. Mann would kill to have a chick like her. Yosohn was a fool.

"If there's anything I can do to help, hit me up. Serenity a good girl. Fix that shit. I put that bread on the kitchen table. That's yo' cut from the last order. I'm picking up the next order later today, so I'll be ghost for a few hours." He dug in his coat and pulled out a bag of weed, tossing it to Yosohn. "Get some rest my nigga. Call yo' girl … and check that bitch." He gave Yosohn dap and left him sitting on the couch sulking.

CHAPTER 2

Serenity checked into a suite at the Chestnut Hill Hotel, a posh inn on the outskirts of Philadelphia. She chose it because it was close to the home Yosohn and her shared, so it wasn't far from her daughter's school. After checking in, she wiped away her tears and drug her bags inside. She didn't bother to put anything away. She simply crawled into the bed and cried. Despite doing her best to calm down, relax and get some rest, her thoughts landed on Yosohn.

She and him had been together for years. They had their ups and downs, but they always stuck by one another. She remembered when they first met. They were both at a bar in Germantown. She was with her best friend Naomi celebrating their recent graduation from undergrad. Yosohn was there with Hakim and a few others. Although they weren't sitting far from each other, she never really noticed him until he followed her out as she went to leave. Serenity believed that God made masterpieces and that was confirmed when she saw Yosohn because he was nothing short of exquisite. Pecan colored skin, tall and tight with broad shoulders. Hazel eyes that twinkled as he spoke. A strong beautiful face that was half-covered in a rich black beard. She had been drawn to him since that day, and every day for seven whole years. She had been good to him. Never caring about his money and even helping him build a legitimate chain of laundromats through the city. Serenity knew she didn't need him. As he came up, so did she. She had plenty of money in the bank, had a degree in business and was close to finishing up graduate school with an MBA from Temple University. Hell no, she didn't need him. That's what her head told her; however, her heart said otherwise.

After laying in her bed for a few more minutes, Serenity decided that she needed to call her mother. She figured it was best that her daughter Heaven stayed another night. At least until she got her emotions in check and figured out how things were going to play out. She knew Heaven staying longer wouldn't be an issue. She and her mother were close, so Heaven stayed over often. Since she wasn't ready to talk about what had just happened and didn't want her mother Gina all up in her business, she told her that something had come up unexpectedly at one of the laundromats. She hated lying to her mom, but she was in no emotional state to be answering any questions. She would deal with this on her own and talk about it when *she* was ready.

After lying in bed and sulking for another half hour, Serenity decided to take a bath to calm her nerves and get settled in her temporary home. For the first time, she looked around and admired the giant space. The suite was cute and cozy, although overpriced. She had paid for a stay of thirty days upfront, which cost over $3k after using her rewards card. She didn't care though since she charged it to Yosohn's business credit card. His ass was footing the bill for it. She was glad she held onto it after paying their suppliers.

She hated having to pull Heaven out of their home, so she wanted her to be comfortable. The suite had two double-beds, so it would do for now. She noticed there was no stove. She knew she wouldn't be able to stay too long without one. For now, she would just have to work with what she had. Besides, there was a restaurant right on sight. Serenity scanned the bathroom to make sure it was clean and then ran her a bath. While she was in the tub, she checked her phone and saw that she had twenty-one missed calls from Yosohn and nine new voicemails. She wanted to call him back so bad and work things out, but just couldn't bring herself to do it. She was tired of going through shit with Yosohn. Those looking in, saw her life and falsely believed that she had it made and that Yosohn was her knight in shining armor. She wouldn't deny the fact that she believed Yosohn loved her dearly; however, he did a lot of dumb shit, and it mostly involved other females. He had eased up over the past few years and she truly felt that he had changed; unfortunately, she was sadly mistaken.

Over the years, she had threatened to leave on many occasions but never did. But this time was different. This time she wasn't sure if she wanted to go back. She'd been hurt before. But she'd never felt heartbroken *and* disrespected. She'd never forced Yosohn to change. One thing she knew that was true in life: whatever you're not changing, you're choosing.

YOSOHN SAT POSTED UP OUTSIDE OF HIS SEAFOOD TRUCK WITH his best friend Hakim and watched as business progressed smoothly. Yosohn had multiple businesses. He had the laundromats with Serenity and the seafood trucks with Hakim. It wasn't often that he hung out at the laundromats. Although they generated the most money, the business itself was boring to him, so he let Serenity handle everything pertaining to it. On the other hand, Yosohn visited the seafood trucks nearly every day. It was his chance to mingle in the hood and shoot the shit with his right hand, Hakim.

"So, you mean to tell me that bitch called her?" Hakim gasped in surprise and choked on weed smoke simultaneously.

"Yeah." Yosohn glanced at Hakim and saw the comical smirk on his face. "Nigga, that shit ain't funny. It's takin' everything out of me not to kick in her door and break her fuckin' jaw. Ren ain't wit' that shit. She left me behind Jocelyn ass."

"Damn." Hakim paused and realized just how serious things were for his friend. "I ain't mean to laugh my nigga. It's just that, Nikki would never leave me over no shit like that. All I gotta do is beg, tell her I'm sorry, buy her something expensive, and then throw some dick up in her."

Yosohn sighed wearily, before taking the blunt back that Hakim was handing him. "Yeah, well that's Nikki. She a different breed. She strong and she know how bitches play. Serenity, on the other hand, be on some uppity shit. She knows her worth and won't let anyone tell her *or* show her different."

"Facts. Ren not for the bullshit. You try to call her?"

"Yeah. She not answering though. I done left hella messages. Called her mom, her dad, her sisters. Shit … I even blew up Heaven's flip phone," he added. He looked up at Hakim and they both laughed together. They couldn't help it.

"Damn!" Hakim shouted.

"You know me nigga. Ain't no pride with me," Yosohn laughed. "I love her. Heaven too." Yosohn sighed and threw down the blunt remains. "You think you can get Nikki to reach out to her."

Serenity and Hakim's wife Nikki got along very well.

Yosohn knew that she would probably answer her calls. She damn sure wasn't going to answer Hakim's.

"Yeah, she won't mind. She'll hit her up for you. I'll tell her tonight." Yosohn got up from the hood of Hakim's car, where he'd been sitting for the last half hour. "I'm 'bout to jet. Go back to my empty ass crib. Look, don't forget we gotta meet up tomorrow to go over them numbers for the trucks." He and Hakim owned three trucks scattered around North Philly.

"Bet. I'll be there. And I'll let you know what Nikki say after she talk to Ren."

"Thanks, my nigga."

"And there go Mann," Hakim added before walking off to tend to the food truck. While Yosohn was again a silent investor in that business, just like the laundromats, Hakim loved mingling with the people and was way more hands on. He nodded his head and threw his hand up to speak to Mann before disappearing.

While Hakim and Mann were cool, Mann was ultimately Yosohn's friend. The two had met years earlier when Yosohn and Hakim were sent upstate for burglary charges. Back in the day when their sole source of income was jackin', and they didn't know any better, they used to hit up ATM's with crowbars instead of blowtorches. Needless to say: it was time-consuming and they ended up catching prison time while in the process of busting one down. Since they were co-defendants, Yosohn got sent to one prison and Hakim got sent to another one.

He and Mann met in prison, becoming fast friends when Yosohn was involved in a cafeteria brawl that left him outnumbered. While Yosohn was getting beat down, Mann would jump in to assist him. After realizing they were both from Philadelphia, they'd been friend's ever since. To

Yosohn, Mann was rugged and loyal. To Mann, Yosohn was loyal and *rich*.

Mann got out of his car but left it running. He was an average height, stocky, bald-head nigga that drew in his fair attention from the ladies. He was dressed simply in dark blue denim jeans, a pair of wheat Timberlands, and a white t-shirt underneath his bright yellow Helly Hansen jacket.

"Glad I caught you," he said as he approached Yosohn.

"Wassup." Yosohn threw out his hand to embrace Mann's.

"I tried to hit you on the phone, but I didn't get no answer."

Yosohn glanced towards the inside of his car, where his phone was charging.

"Yeah, my jawn had died. My bad. Wassup witchu though?" he asked. Yosohn did his best to stay available, since he and Mann did business together. After coming home several years after Yosohn, Mann went right back into the streets. That was the only thing he knew and the only thing he felt like he was good at. With no money, he would ask Yosohn to loan him some money so he could hit the ground running. Instead of loaning him money, Yosohn offered to match him on whatever number of drugs he was purchasing. If Mann spent $20k for a shipment, so would Yosohn.

In return, Yosohn would get all his money back, in addition to a percentage of the profits. Since he wasn't out there actively moving work, he figured the arrangement was more than fair. Just like a businessman, Yosohn kept his hand in any pot he could.

"We out of that shit already," Mann said proudly. "I'm about to shoot up top to pay the connect. I wanted to see how you felt about doubling up."

Yosohn turned and studied Mann with arched brows. "Double up? We already doing $50k each cop. You know my max is twenty-five," he reminded him.

Mann sighed quietly. He figured Yosohn wasn't going to be with copping more even though things had changed. For the last year, he re-uped every two weeks. However, recently, he'd found some buyers who moved much more product, resulting in his need to re-up every week. Mann wasn't fond of running back and forth to New York with large amounts of cash on him. He needed to start grabbing more product that would hold him over longer. Unfortunately, he needed Yosohn to agree because he needed his monetary match.

"Yeah, but that was before these little young niggas started gettin' rid of that shit way sooner. They're helping us move double the work in the same amount of time. I need to be coppin' larger loads."

"I can't agree to that right now, my nigga," Yosohn responded hesitantly. "The more work, the hotter it gets. The bigger you are, the hotter you get. You can't risk getting jammed up because of some money-hungry, young boys. We got more than enough. We eatin' good. Get greedy and you get caught. What you need to tell them is that they need to make what they got last. If they need to, they up the price. Supply and demand."

"Cool. But can you at least give it some thought?" Mann asked. Yosohn nodded, although his mind was already made up.

CHAPTER 3

J ocelyn smacked her teeth in exasperation as she listened to the voicemail pick up before the phone even rang. It had only been a few days since she'd spoken to Yosohn, but every day felt like torture. She didn't know what it was about him that had her stuck like glue; but whatever it was, it had her. She hated the word obsessed, but at times that's exactly what it felt like: *obsession*. She yearned for him. Feined for him. Needed him. She didn't understand it. Her brain told her that he wasn't shit, but her heart said otherwise.

Jocelyn had met Yosohn seven months ago when she and her homegirl rolled up at their childhood friend, Hakim's birthday party. He was a little older than them, but they'd lived in the same hood and had known each other for a long time. Although Hakim lived in Philly since he was sixteen, he always showed love to the city that had birthed and raised him. Hakim turned thirty in April, so to celebrate, he gathered up his closest friends from Philly to Brooklyn and had a party at a club called Spazum's. It was there that she met Yosohn.

She'd been minding her business when he started kickin' his shit. From the drinks, compliments, and attention, he had her in no time. She should have been able to peep game. She should have handled the nigga accordingly. After all, that's what she did for a living: fucked for money. She should have never gotten attached from the beginning. Unfortunately, she let her guard down with Yosohn. He claimed he was different, and she believed him. Now she was in her feelings and the only bitch that Yosohn seemed to care about was his bitch's. She didn't remember him caring when he was fuckin' on her for months on end. Shit was sweet in the beginning. He was seeing her often, spending time with her, all while whispering sweet nothings in her ear. Getting her hopes up to believe that they would be together. By the time she realized it was nothing but lies, she was in too deep emotionally and Yosohn had done a three-sixty.

Yosohn began treating her like a side bitch without all the pretty perks. All she got was his ass to kiss and his hard dick to hop on or inhale. When she threatened to be done with him, he would act like he didn't care at first. They'd argue. He'd accuse her of causing trouble. Bringing drama. She'd cry and then he'd comfort her. Talk her out of being upset. Saying she had no reason and that she knew the role when she took it. Somehow, someway, he'd end up back in her bed and the cycle would continue.

That's exactly how Jocelyn expected things to play out this round. Only this time, she'd brought Serenity into the mix. She'd never done that before. Maybe if Serenity left him alone then he would see that his rightful place was with her. Jocelyn picked her phone back up from the nightstand and checked to see if she had any texts or missed calls. She put it back down when she realized she had none. She looked around her studio and wasn't happy with what she saw. Jocelyn bounced around from hotel room to hotel room. All her life consisted of was partying and fucking. She didn't even have a place of her own. Not that she was worried about that. She was only twenty-seven years old but after living a fast life for the past four years, she was ready to settle down. Unfortunately, the man that she wanted was taken. She hoped that would soon change though. She didn't see what Yosohn saw in Serenity that made him so head over heels in love with her. In Jocelyn's eyes, she was just as pretty, if not prettier.

Born to Cuban immigrants, she'd been hearing she was beautiful since she was a small child. Warm, honey-almond skin with thick curly locks, Jocelyn was stunning. Although average height and build, she still pulled in men from near and far. Bouncing back and forth between New York and Philadelphia, kept her bills paid and money in her pocket, but the more time went on, the more she found herself unfulfilled. She just wanted to be with Yosohn. She just wanted him to look at her with the same passion and warmth that he looked at Serenity with. She wanted that same love.

A week ago, she'd seen them together. She did some digging and learned that Yosohn was a businessman that had a chain of laundromats. She never would have guessed it since he wasn't generous in any capacity with her. Jocelyn took it upon herself to visit one of his fine establishments. To her surprise, Yosohn would arrive with Serenity in tow. It was the dead of winter and Jocelyn had taken two busses to get to their North Philly location. Seeing Serenity walk in with a thousand-dollar coat on and stepping out of a brand new foreign didn't sit well with her. Jocelyn saw the way he looked at Serenity. Saw the way he doted on her. His smile when she spoke. The attention he gave to her. It made her blood boil. She was tired of playing the background. She wanted Serenity to know exactly who she was.

Yosohn had admitted months ago that he was engaged. He admitted he loved her. Admitted he wasn't leaving. Jocelyn didn't care about any of that. She didn't care about what he wanted at the moment. Eventually, he would want all that in Jocelyn. Until then, her tears would be shared. Her pain would be share.

"Bitch, you didn't hear me knockin?" her best friend Bianca called out, startling her out of her thoughts.

"Girl, you scared the fuck out me!" Jocelyn clutched her chest in surprise.

"I was knockin' for the longest. Didn't even matter though because the door was ajar. I told you about that," she reminded her. Jocelyn had a habit of not making sure her door was closed all the way.

"Where you headed to all dressed up?" she asked. Bianca was picture perfect in a white bodycon dress that gripped her lean frame. She was a beautiful caramel girl with a thirty-inch weave that dangled past her ass.

"Girl, I was supposed to meet Hakim, but that nigga stay flakin' on me. I think he got a brand-new bitch." She rolled her eyes at the thought of Hakim. "The nigga got so many; he probably can't even keep count. Anyway, that's a whole notha story. I'm 'bout to slide out with this trick nigga Phil for a few and then meet Tommy later. He supposed to give me a couple hundred."

Just like Jocelyn, Bianca had a stable of men. If she wasn't going out with them, she was getting them to buy her things. When she wasn't getting them to buy her things, she was simply fuckin' for cash. There was always some type of exchange for her time or her pussy. There was no shame in her game. That was the way things had been since they were eighteen.

Bianca looked at Jocelyn and couldn't help but notice how sad she'd been the last few days. She knew it was about

Yosohn. She felt kind of bad. She was the reason they'd met. Back in April, Bianca had been invited to Hakim's birthday party. She'd been linking up with him for some time, fuckin' him on and off when he came to New York. When he invited her to his party, she couldn't say no. She knew it was going to be hella ballers in there and she had to grab her one or two. Since she didn't want to go alone, she asked Jocelyn to come with her. Bianca didn't know Hakim had a fine, paid ass friend. He stepped to Bianca and the rest was history. She'd warned Jocelyn that Yosohn was in a relationship. After realizing her friend was diggin' him, she asked Hakim about him. Even though she warned Jocelyn, she didn't listen. Now, she was seeing for herself. She knew the cardinal rule: no crying over niggas. To Bianca, the heartache was self-inflicted. She couldn't relate, and she damn sure didn't want to.

"Girl, why don't you get out of this slump and get out? Get some fresh air or something. You been sitting up in this damn room all depressed. Is you even makin' any money?"

Jocelyn smacked her teeth. "Yeah, I still be lining shit up. I just don't want to go out and party right now. My mind on other shit."

"Well, you need to get your mind off that other shit. You in here all sad about Yosohn and he out there living his life. He's unavailable, and you gon' end up getting yaself caught up fuckin' with him. Hakim told me about the shit you pulled."

Jocelyn sighed and didn't respond. "You lucky he didn't fuck you up. Hakim told me that he wanted to. You better stop playing them games girl. You know what we in this for," she reminded her.

"You need anything before I head out?"

"Na, I'm good."

"Well, if you do, I'm right down the hall or a phone call away."

"Okay," Jocelyn said, sighing in relief when Bianca walked out, and the door closed. She wasn't trying to hear the sermon she'd just preached. She wanted what she wanted, and she wasn't going to stop until she got it.

CHAPTER 4

Yosohn sat in his truck with the heat on high. His coat was in the trunk and all he had on was some jeans and a black t-shirt with thermals underneath to keep him warm. He hadn't heard from Serenity in three days and he was feeling a mixture of emotions. He was hurt because she had left him; yet, he was angry at the same time. He couldn't believe she would let a bitch come between them. He blew out a thick stream of weed smoke from his mouth, adding to the lingering fog that saturated the air in his Range Rover.

The night was bitterly cold and even though it was only around eight in the evening, it seemed eerily dark and quiet. The streetlights flickered and cast a glow over Yosohn's truck while he waited for Hakim in front of The Clock Bar. He was running awfully late to their agreed upon meeting to go over financial figures for the seafood truck business that they owned together. He'd just seen him the day before. There was no way he could have forgotten that quickly.

He and Hakim had been best friends since they were teenagers. While Yosohn was the more serious out of the two, Hakim was outgoing and silly. His personality is what won Yosohn over. He was a likeable guy that was fun to be around … and he had the same "get money" mentality that Yosohn had as well.

Eventually they would come together and start jackin' atm's all over. With ski-masks and blowtorches, they'd take their thirst for money and eventually get rich from it. Years later, and they were still as close as ever. Hakim had settled down, got married, and even had children. Yosohn was their godfather, and his wife Nikki was like the sister he never had. Regrettably, just like his best friend Yosohn, Hakim was also a man that couldn't seem to keep it in his pants. Unfortunately for his wife, Nikki, Hakim cheated far more often. He was probably somewhere creeping now, choosing to let his friend and business partner wait around.

Yosohn's thoughts drifted to Jocelyn. Even though she had basically turned his world upside down, he couldn't really blame her. Although he tried to tell himself that he hadn't led her on, in his heart, he knew that he truly had. He may have told her what she wanted to hear at times. Downplayed the importance of his relationship in the beginning. Only when he realized how serious she was becoming did he admit that Serenity was his other half. He didn't love Jocelyn; she knew that. However, he did give her the impression that he could eventually love her. Yosohn couldn't even really explain why he'd done it. He only dealt with Jocelyn for the sex. The thrill. The deviation from the norm. He was wrong and he knew it, but he didn't feel like he deserved to lose the love of his life over it.

When he met her at the party, he was drunk, and she was beautiful. He couldn't help but approach her. Soft long hair. Beautiful skin. Killer curves. He had to have her. In another life, he may have taken her serious; however, it wouldn't be in this life. Despite how beautiful she was, Hakim had briefed him on how she and her best friend were easy. With that knowledge, he treated her accordingly. How was he to know that she was going to fall for him? Act a fool over him? It wasn't worth it. He couldn't lie that he missed the sex they had; however, if he could take their time together back, he would be a man and do so.

A light knock on Yosohn's truck caused him to jump. The weed was making him paranoid. He looked to his window, expecting to see a familiar face. To his surprise, it wasn't Hakim. Instead, it was a beggar asking for loose change. He grabbed some quarters from his cup-holder and handed the change to the disheveled looking man. He had a set of jagged yellow teeth and a dirty, salt and pepper beard. The fiend eyed the change in dissatisfaction and stood there a few more seconds until Yosohn snapped.

"That's all I got nigga — Don't want it? Give it the fuck back!" he grumbled irritably. Considering everything he was going through, he wasn't in the mood. Besides, he hated when motherfuckers had the nerve to be ungrateful. He shook his head as the fiend walked off. Yosohn rolled up another blunt and continued to smoke while he waited.

Thirty more minutes passed, and Hakim still hadn't shown up. He looked down at his phone to see if he had any texts or missed calls. None from Hakim. There were also none from Serenity, who he was praying contacted him since her phone had been going to voicemail every time, he tried to call her. Of course, Jocelyn had called and texted, but he would deal with her later. If he tried to deal with her in his state of mind, he would fuck around and catch an assault charge on her.

Yosohn called Hakim's phone several more times, but there was still no answer. He wondered what the fuck was up. He knew it wasn't about a bitch. The only female that could hold him from money was Nikki. He wasn't sure what was up with Hakim, but one thing he did know: he wasn't sitting there waiting any longer. He would meet up with him on another day. He glanced across the street one last time to see if he spotted him. With no one in sight, he put his truck in drive and drove home to his empty house.

~

HAKIM REACHED OVER TO GRAB HIS RINGING PHONE; HOWEVER, Kiesha grabbed it before his fingers touched them and moved it across the room.

"No interruptions. I'm almost finished," she purred before going back to work on Hakim's pole.

Hakim knew the caller was likely Yosohn. He was supposed to meet him over an hour ago but had gotten side-tracked when he decided to stop by Kiesha's crib. Yosohn had been calling him relentlessly but he ignored him. He figured he would meet up with him soon ... Right after he finished getting ate up by his favorite little hood rat.

At nineteen, Kiesha wasn't the prettiest chick off the block; however, she had a body grown women envied, and some first-class head. Hakim's toes curled as she gobbled up his shaft. He felt like he was about to explode.

"Damn," he groaned. "I'm 'bout to cum," he warned her. Kiesha prepared for his release and swallowed every drop when his body began to quiver, and he proceeded to empty himself down her young, willing throat.

"Damn girl. You ready to have a nigga broke. "Bout to start breakin' you off right to keep getting that," Hakim joked.

Kiesha smiled, knowing full well that Hakim was full of shit. She had been dealing with him for months and he was hardly kicking out any real paper on her. She knew damn well she deserved it since she was blessing him on demand with fire head and grade-a coochie. She wasn't worried about it though, because her payout was coming very soon, and it would be bigger than he knew.

"Go ahead and handle yo' business boo," Kiesha said to Hakim as he lay sprawled out on her bed, his soggy member laying limp.

"The wash rag is in the cabinet in the bathroom. Same as always," she reminded him. As much as he was over there, he figured he'd ought to know where everything was. Kiesha's sex was so good that he was sliding through there several times a week.

After laying still for a few minutes, Hakim got up and walked through the small cluttered room, kicking shit out of his way as he headed to the bathroom. Although Kiesha's kids weren't home, their belongings were all throughout the room.

Bitch need to clean up, he thought. *Nikki would never have the house looking like this.* Once he reached the bathroom down the hall, he proceeded to grab some soap and wash away the residue Kiesha had left behind. Back in the other room, Kiesha quietly grabbed her phone and dialed out. She checked to make sure that Hakim was still in the bathroom before she spoke. When the call connected, she began to talk in a whisper.

"He's here. Come now."

THE TWO MEN WERE SITTING BEHIND AN ABANDONED apartment in the alleyway on some old, plastic crates when the call came through. They were glad. The cold, night air was brutal, and their legs were starting to fall asleep while trying to balance their weight on the crates. Once they hung up the phone, they gave each other the look. It was time.

They made their way up the dusty, side-alley that was

littered with cheap beer cans and all kinds of trash. After a brief walk, the two men arrived at their destination in one-minute flat. The side door was unlocked just like they had planned, so they let themselves in and began to tiptoe their way into the back bedroom. Just before they reached it, they looked at one another. Adrenaline pumped through their bodies as they prepared to perform an act that they'd grown accustomed to.

They held their guns to their side and peeked around the corner. Kiesha's door was ajar. The set-up was too perfect. Kiesha was sitting on the bed and their target had just emerged from the attached bathroom. With nothing but boxers and a wife beater on, he was unprepared and unarmed. That was the way they wanted it. That was the way they'd planned it.

Kiesha had been helping her brothers orchestrate a robbery since the first week she met Hakim. He'd set himself up by making it noticeably clear that he had lots of money. It wasn't unusual to see him with large stacks of money. He practically showed it off. While he wasn't necessarily stingy, he wasn't generous either. That was the main issue for Kiesha. Hakim tossed her tens and twenties like she was a schoolgirl and expected her to be satisfied with that. She didn't understand why a rich nigga driving around in Jaguars and BMW's thought a broke bitch from North Philly would be content with that. A hundred dollars here and a hundred dollars there was all she got. Meanwhile, he slid down Versace boxers before he fucked her.

She had something for his ass though. Kiesha knew that once she put that fire head on him, he would stick around — around long enough for her to sic her brothers on him and take some of those stacks off him.

~

HAKIM WAS COMING OUT THE BATHROOM WHEN TWO MEN stormed into Kiesha's bedroom waving guns. Hakim scanned the area with his eyes very quickly and swiftly determined that there was nowhere to run. They were aggressive and he knew that they meant business.

"Get the fuck on the ground pussy. This is a robbery … Don't turn it into a homicide," the shorter of the two brothers yelled. Kiesha had already dropped to the ground and was playing an Oscar-worthy performance. With her face down on the carpet, she whimpered quietly and even forced out fake tears.

Hakim dropped to the ground carefully, ignoring the toys and clothes that were scattered around him. When he was completely flat, the shorter of the two men came over and stood over top of him. Hakim realized that he would be the more aggressive of the two. He stared at the man, studying his clothed face carefully. Just like his partner, he wore a mask. Hakim didn't recognize either's voice, build, or eyes.

"Where the fuck the money at?" asked Teddy, who, although was the oldest, was the smaller of the two. Nootie, who was the taller, younger brother, stood by Kiesha with his gun aimed on her as planned.

"I don't have any bread on me," Hakim replied nervously.

Teddy cocked his foot back and kicked Hakim in his face. Blood rushed from his mouth. Hakim groaned in pain.

"I'm gon' ask yo' bitch ass again. Where the fuck is the money?" Hakim's mind went into overdrive. He had to give them something, or he wouldn't make it out of the apartment.

"There's no money on me but I got some in the car. It's like twenty racks. I'll take you to it, just let me go. I'll give you niggas all that shit."

As blood trickled from his eye, Hakim thought of his wife Nikki and their two boys. He prayed he made it home to them. If he managed to get out of his current situation, he vowed to be a better man to his family. He also vowed to find the identity of the two men who were robbing him. And when he did, they would pay dearly.

"Now we talking!" Nootie sang after hearing they were about to come up on $20k. Although Hakim wiped his ass with $20k, it was a jackpot to siblings Kiesha, Nootie and Teddy.

"Get dressed pussy. You got two minutes. Then we going to get the money."

Hakim slowly stood up, and through his good eye scanned the floor for his clothes. His face and mouth were bleeding, and his right eyes was quickly swelling shut.

"Act normal nigga. Try some funny shit and I'ma lay you on the concrete," Teddy said coldly when they made their way out the house and began walking through the alley towards Hakim's car.

Hakim cursed himself for parking on a side block. He should have parked further away on a busier street so he could make a public getaway. Unfortunately, the side street they were headed to was dark, quiet, and just as deserted as the alleyway. Hakim wasn't concerned about giving them the money because he knew he would make it back just as quick as he lost it. His concern was the fact that he didn't trust the two men that were close behind him with guns pointed at his back. He also couldn't help but question the motives of Kiesha's ass either. As he walked, all kinds of thoughts ran through his head. *How did they get in? Who was she talking to on the phone when he was in the bathroom?* Although she tried to whisper, he still heard her. Something wasn't right. He slowly realized that Kiesha's dick-suckin' ass had probably set him up. Another problem for him was that his name was well-known in the city of Philadelphia. In his younger years, he and his right-hand Yosohn had been connected to countless homicides. They were not to be fucked with and that was well documented. If Kiesha had participated in getting him robbed, wouldn't she be worried about the repercussions? Something in his gut told him that he wasn't supposed to make it out of the planned robbery alive. If that were the case, then they weren't concerned with the repercussions.

The walk to the car went by fast, leaving Hakim little time to think up a plan to make it home safely. As his mind raced, Teddy's deep voice brought Hakim out of his trance. When he looked up, they were at his car.

"Get the bread," he demanded.

"Okay," Hakim mumbled. "It's in the glove box. I just gotta reach in and grab it." He dug his car key out of his pocket and unlocked the driver's side door of his Jaguar. He leaned down and opened the glove compartment, slowly pulling the money out. As he slid out the rubber-band secured knot, his fingers brushed lightly against his revolver he also kept in there. Out the corner of his eye, he checked to see if the two men would notice if he grabbed it. Noticing their eyes fixed on the street, instead of directly on him, Hakim rushed to grab it so he could turn around and fire. Unfortunately, he was too slow, and his flawed plan unraveled quickly.

"Pussy ass nigga!" Nootie hollered before he dumped two shots into Hakim's back. Although Teddy was more aggressive of the two, he was only known for rumbling. Anyone that knew him, knew that he'd go toe to toe with anyone in the streets. Nootie, on the other hand, was known for squeezing triggers. Hakim was totally unprepared for the pain the hot slugs produced when they penetrated his back. He crumpled face down back into the car.

"Thought we was fuckin' playin nigga," Teddy growled. He reached near Hakim and snatched the money and gun off the floor where it had fallen. They smiled at one another and took off from the scene on foot.

Hakim struggled to get up while he gasped for air. He was rapidly growing weak, and he could barely breathe. The blood was coming out fast. He knew the bullet had hit an artery or a lung. Still struggling for breath, he reached to his pocket to grab his phone. He was going to call 911 or his wife. Before his hand could reach all the way down, he remembered he had left his phone in Kiesha's house. He decided that he would have to make it to the hospital on his own.

Groaning in pain, he pulled his body up and grabbed his keys from under him. He had dropped them and then fell on them after being shot. Hakim staggered to the driver's side door and used all his strength to pull the door open, leaving a trail of blood along the side. He plopped down in the front seat and started the car, heading down the street. His chest felt so heavy, and he was so weak. With little strength to even sit up, he slumped over the wheel, doing his best to drive the car. Temple Hospital was only a short distance. Unfortunately, Hakim was growing weaker by the second and his breathing was becoming more and more shallow. His eyelids grew heavy as he felt the blood and life slowly escape from his body. Five seconds later, he had fallen into an eternal sleep. His car continued to drive until it crashed into a parked car, just two blocks from the hospital.

CHAPTER 5

It was around midnight when Yosohn received the devastating news that his best friend had been murdered. A couple of teens had found Hakim as he lay slumped over in his wrecked car. Yosohn felt as if a piece of him had been taken away. He was crushed. He tried to keep busy so depression wouldn't consume him. Losing his girl and then losing his friend was a lot for him to handle.

Even though their relationship was strained, as soon as Serenity heard the news, she rushed to be by Yosohn's side. It had only been a few days since she'd found out he was cheating on her, but she insisted on being by his side. Their relationship was still very tense, and Serenity still didn't know what their future held. Despite how she felt, she couldn't let Yosohn go through the death of his friend alone. The next few days were a blur as Nikki and Hakim's mother arranged to bury him in Brooklyn. Serenity did her best to be there for them since she knew how close Yosohn and Hakim were. Despite not being particularly fond of Hakim, she knew how important he was to Yosohn. Hakim visited their home often. Her daughter even called him uncle. Serenity also considered Nikki her friend. She could only imagine the pain that she felt.

That Sunday, Hakim was laid to rest in an elaborate candlelit ceremony. White roses adorned the entire front of the church and outer pews, as well as Hakim's casket. Everyone knew that Hakim was flashy and over the top, so it was only right he go out the same way. The church standing room only and was filled with people from his hometown of New York to Philadelphia. Nikki sobbed uncontrollably while her mother struggled to comfort her. She was beautiful in all black, but her face told another story; it told a story of defeat and betrayal. Rumors had been swirling the streets that Hakim had been robbed and set up by a female he had been creeping with.

Although there weren't many details to the story, Nikki knew in her heart they were true. Everyone knew that Hakim stepped out on her constantly and played around in the streets. It was no secret. It pained her that Hakim had sealed his own fate and became a victim at the hands of a bitch. As much dirt as Hakim did, Nikki swore to herself that if she found out who the female was, she would kill her personally for taking away her husband and children's father. She didn't care about his dirt, she loved Hakim like no one ever could. She didn't know how she was going to go on. She didn't know if she even wanted to go on. As she sobbed and wiped away her tears with a Kleenex, the pastor begun his sermon in a loud and powerful tone.

"We are gathered together for the homecoming of our dear brother Hakim … He's been called home by our dear Lord. Although we are sad by his premature departure, we rejoice because we know he is with God. He is in a much better place and will be at peace there, resting eternally in the heavens."

He continued to preach as people in the pews cried. He spoke of Hakim and his silly, colorful personality, causing many to smile at the memories. Most importantly, he left everyone with the message that life was beautiful and was not to be taken for granted. The reality of the situation sunk into Yosohn as the preacher spoke. Life was short. Ironically, Hakim's life had been cut short by betrayal, while he was in the process of betraying his future wife. Even though they were just rumors, Yosohn knew they were true. He remembered their missed meeting and waiting all night for Hakim to contact him. Besides, the streets were already talking, and he knew the type of females Hakim dealt with. Because he and Hakim were so close, he had an idea of who had something to do with his friend's untimely death. He vowed to later settle the score.

As Yosohn thought about Hakim, he forced back his tears. In his legit world, he only had two friends: Hakim and Mann. While Mann was his homie, Hakim was more like his brother. It hurt him so bad that his life was cut so short. He looked to his side and glanced at Serenity. Her eyes were glistening with tears. She was a good woman and she'd always been there for him. Her and her family. To him, she was simple perfection, beautiful in mind and body. With smooth, flawless chocolate skin, her heart was just as stunning as her looks. Serenity was loving, caring, and highly educated. What really made his love run deep for her was that she wasn't like all the other girls that came and went in his life; she genuinely cared for him as a person and never worried about his money or what she could gain from being with him. Her love for him appeared pure. She listened when he talked, gave him sound advice, and was affectionate. He wanted to be the man that he promised. He refused to end up like his best friend. Dead, because he decided to chase a broad that meant him no good.

He took Serenity's hand into his and gave her a sad smile. She looked to him and smiled back. That gave him all the hope that he needed. That everything would be okay.

~

ALTHOUGH MANN AND HAKIM WEREN'T AWFULLY CLOSE, HE still came to the funeral to pay his respect. If not for Hakim, then for Yosohn. The ceremony only lasted an hour and right after, everyone quickly dispersed the church building and proceeded to the burial. Once they laid Hakim to rest, Yosohn began acting anxious to leave, suggesting they skip the repass and head back to Philadelphia. However, before they could leave, all hell would break loose.

Serenity and Mann weren't aware that Yosohn had spotted his mistress Jocelyn with Bianca. Yosohn spotted Bianca first. Being well familiar with Bianca, he knew that Jocelyn wasn't far. After all, they were best friends. When he met Jocelyn, he also met Bianca. He did his best to slip through the dense crowd of attendees undetected without looking suspicious. He'd been ignoring Jocelyn's calls for over a week and he knew that as soon as she spotted him, she was going to act an ass. Her personality wouldn't allow for anything else. His plan was to block and ignore Jocelyn indefinitely. However, if she spotted him, he knew that his plan of ignoring her wasn't happening. She was going to force him to deal with her. If he were alone or with one of his niggas, he wouldn't have a problem doing that. He didn't want her causing a scene in front of Serenity. There was no telling what she would say. Their relationship was already strained. With Yosohn leading the way, the three began exiting the cemetery and heading toward the rental they came in. Unfortunately, before they could even get halfway out, he heard his name being called.

"Yosohn!" Before Yosohn could even turn around, Serenity was already looking back and asking questions.

"Yosohn, who is that?" she quizzed, her eyes narrowing so she could make out the woman calling her man. Serenity began slowing her pace to get a good look at her. The woman looked young. Looked like she was in her early twenties. She was a very pretty girl, dressed in all black with neat Senegalese twists that touched her ass.

"Just keep walking," Yosohn replied, taking quick glances back from the corner of his eye.

"Yosohn!" Jocelyn called again. "I know you hear me calling you! Oh, so now you actin' funny 'cuz you got yo' bitch with you." The comment caused Serenity's slow pace to come to a sudden stop. Now she knew exactly who the bitch was. It all made sense. It was the same broad who had called her phone a week ago. Serenity saw what type of games she was playing. One minute the bitch was pretending to be respectful, and the next minute she was being flat out disrespectful. Apparently, she hadn't been briefed.

"Excuse me?" Serenity asked angrily, staring Jocelyn directly in her eyes. "You got a problem or something?"

"I was talking to Yosohn, not you. So please mind yo' business," Jocelyn replied nastily. Jocelyn was surprised Serenity had even responded. Judging her based off appearance, she seemed like a bitch that thought she was too cute to fight or argue. Jocelyn was glad she did have the balls to speak up. Now she wouldn't feel bad when she slapped the weave off her black ass head.

"Yosohn's my fiancé, so that makes it my business," Serenity responded, matching Jocelyn's icy tone and stare.

Jocelyn smiled. "Ohhhhhh … You must be Serenity," she replied, as if she had no idea. "I keep forgetting he has a bitch, especially since he keeps his dick up in me," she taunted.

Just as Jocelyn went to laugh, Serenity swung, driving her

fist into her mouth, causing her to stumble back into Bianca. With nothing but red in her vision, Serenity continued to swing wildly. She didn't even care that she was outnumbered. She had Yosohn with her. Businessman or not, Yosohn was from Southwest Philly where niggas swung and smacked broads for jumping on the women in their life.

Caught off guard by the fury of punches, Jocelyn struggled briefly to regain her composure. When she did, she quickly overpowered Serenity with one hit. Serenity was no slouch, but she wasn't really a street fighter. Jocelyn, however, was from the streets. She'd been in plenty of fights and had a roughness to her that came straight from the streets of Brooklyn.

Before Jocelyn could grip Serenity's hair and get a second blow in, Yosohn rushed her. With his hand gripping her neck, he forcefully shoved her to the ground where she landed on some leaves. Mann had already snatched up Bianca who was trying to take a swing at Serenity.

"Kick rocks, bitch!" Yosohn screamed. "The fuck you come over here wit' that nut shit for? It ain't shit for us to talk about! We never had shit then and we don't have shit now."

Jocelyn scurried up from the ground, all the while glaring at Yosohn with a deathly gaze. Clearly, he had chosen. Bianca shook loose from Mann and rushed over to her friend. Jocelyn went to say something to Yosohn, but Bianca cut her off.

"Girl, fuck that nigga. He ain't shit. That hoe not winning by being with him. She just a kept bitch that's getting dogged."

Jocelyn continued staring at Yosohn with tears in her eyes. She knew he loved Serenity. He'd told her multiple times when she begged him to leave her. Despite professing his love for his fiancé, Jocelyn didn't care. Yosohn was still a man. A man that would still fuck her. If she could still reel him in with pussy, then she had leverage.

Jocelyn looked at Serenity and saw the look of anguish. The look of hurt and defeat. *That bitch will be leaving real soon*, she thought. That, in itself, was satisfying. She had accomplished exactly what she had set out to accomplish. Funny thing was, she was hurt too. Yosohn would pay for making her feel this way. She would destroy what he cared about the most, his relationship with Serenity. Jocelyn knew Yosohn didn't have much family and to him, Serenity was his family. There was no other way to hurt him; he had money, cars, clothes, and could get any hoe he wanted, but only one woman had his heart.

"Fuck you, Yosohn! You'll be crawlin' yo' ass right back! Believe me, this ain't ova hoe!" she spat towards Serenity.

Yosohn nor Serenity bothered to respond. Walking hastily to the car with Mann close behind, Serenity stood stiff when she got to the truck and waited for Yosohn to unlock the door. She shook her head in disgust at the disgusting excuse of a man in front of her.

"This what we doin' Yosohn?" Her voice cracked, while she wiped the tears from her face with the back of her hand. She was so embarrassed, she wished that she could disappear.

"I'm sorry you had to go through that." He shook his head solemnly. "I'ma make this shit right." Yosohn knew the situation was fucked up and really didn't know what their future held. He was scared and angry at the same time. He fought to conceal his emotions in front of Mann.

"You got that, Yosohn," she said, nodding her head up in down. That's all Serenity said to Yosohn before they got into the Suburban and made their way back to Philadelphia. The feeling in her heart was indescribable. She loved him so much, but he was taking her for granted. Abusing her emotionally. She was tired of giving her love to someone like that.

One day he will see. The tables will turn, Serenity thought, as she fastened her seatbelt and looked away from Yosohn. She wished he could feel what she felt. Wished that he hurt, like she hurt.

Mann watched the whole scene unfold and couldn't help but feel a mixture of irritation and disgust. He knew Yosohn loved Serenity, but the shit that had just happened, was unacceptable. Yosohn already knew there was a possibility that Jocelyn would be at the funeral since she and Hakim grew up together. He should have been prepared for this and never had let it happen because Jocelyn should know her place. He would never entertain irrelevant bitches the way Yosohn did. Pillow-talking and boo-loving with hoes was a no-go. Had he been in that situation, he would've slapped blood out the bitch mouth as soon as she even looked like she was going to get disrespectful. He didn't play that shit, and he didn't give a fuck about no bitch, especially no bird like Jocelyn. He had no patience for hood-rats. His mother was one and he suffered through life because of it. He grew up poor and on welfare relying on his disabled grandmother when his mother should have been there. She was too busy chasing fun, dick, and drugs. Because of his upbringing, he had no tolerance for broads like that.

Mann stared at Serenity out the corner of his eye through the rearview mirror. She had chosen to sit in the back for the ride home. He watched her discreetly. Her eyes shined with tears. She had a look of despair on her dark, pretty face. She looked defeated. Like she wanted to give up.

A part of Mann envied Yosohn. He had a person that was so beautiful—both inside and out, that adored him. Every time he came around, Serenity was so welcoming. So sweet. So nurturing. She was a good mother. Yet, it wasn't enough for Yosohn. Nobody was perfect, but if there were such a thing as perfection, then she would be close to it. Yosohn was hardheaded. It was inevitable that he would learn Serenity's worth the hard way.

CHAPTER 6

With his cousin Zeke trailing closely behind him, Mann led the way through the desolate hallway of the apartment building where he usually met his Jamaican plug, Dodda. Based on their appearance alone, no one would ever be able to tell that they were there to participate in a drug deal. They both wore State Farm hats and polo style button-ups, appearing more like insurance salesmen rather than drug dealers. Mann had taken this walk plenty of times; however, it was the first for Zeke. While they walked, he couldn't help but detect the familiar stench of urine, while he noticed that the concrete flooring was coated with layers of dirt that probably came from years of dirty shoeprints and trash. Mann and Zeke walked through the first floor and at the end, entered the last door on the left. He always took the stairs. Mann hated elevators and avoided them if he could.

After a short, two flights up, Mann walked down the hall and eventually reached the door where he proceeded to knock five times, pausing after knock number three. This was a custom knock that Dodda requested so he knew who was at the door. No one ever came by unannounced. You called first, and you knocked accordingly. Even though Dodda wasn't the smartest man, he wasn't a dumb one either. He always tried to move cautiously and limit his circle.

The door opened slowly, and Mann was greeted by Dodda's cousin Ty. Ty was tall, lanky, and wore short, wild-looking dreads on his head. He was what many would consider unattractive. Mann glanced around. The scene in the apartment was usually the same every time. When he came to pick up his drugs, Ty would open the door, Dodda's other cousin Garlan would be in the hall of the apartment by the window, and Dodda would be in the back room. Mann figured they never changed positions because if anything out of the ordinary ever occurred, they would peep it because they were so familiar with the normality of their position and its surroundings. Problem for them was that Mann came so often, he too knew the scene and setup. He intentionally and discreetly watched their movement. From observation, he could tell that Ty was the flunky of the group and Garlan was the muscle. In his opinion, that was the reason why Dodda kept him in the hallway closer to him. He knew that if anyone ever attempted to rob them it would typically start at the door. It made sense to keep the weakest man by the door. The weak were always sacrificed. The idea was that if someone were to rob the place, the person at the door would likely be overpowered because of the element of surprise. Dodda certainly didn't want his strongest man overpowered.

Mann observed all these things because he planned to be the one to rob the place. Mann had no intention of barging the front door, kicking it in, or being loud. He planned to take them down nice and quietly. He had it all figured out and his cousin Zeke was going to help him. Mann wasn't exactly sure when it was going to happen, he just knew that it was *going* to happen.

They would come quietly, let Dodda leave, and then

quickly ambush their targets while they were relaxed and unaware. It wouldn't take long. The silencers would already be in place and one shot to the head would have them out in ten seconds. Once his security was down, they would follow Dodda and let him take them directly to the drugs and money. Since he had known Dodda for so long, he no longer felt the need to check him for weapons before letting him in. He considered Mann a friend as well as a customer. That would soon cost him his life.

Ty allowed Mann and Zeke to enter the small, dimly lit apartment. He secured the doors and ushered them to the back where Dodda usually sat. The apartment was completely empty except for a few plastic chairs, empty food containers, and a small trash can. They trekked their way over the dirty, mustard-colored carpet and entered the room Dodda was in. Dodda stood up as Mann greeted him with a warm smile and a hood handshake. Dodda was a thin man with skin as black as midnight. He had large poppy eyes and shoulder-length dreads. He was what some would consider a dull-looking man, a far cry from the Marijuana King Pin he really was.

"Wassup, big homie," Mann greeted Dodda.

"Wassup, boi. Glad you see me again so soon." Dodda spoke with a heavy Jamaican accent, but Mann understood him very clearly. He'd met Dodda several years back when they were upstate together. Being the opportunist that he was, he befriended the older man with dark plans formulating from the very beginning.

He handed Dodda $13k for the twenty-five pounds of weed he was picking up. Mann was able to get the weed from Dodda cheap compared to what his competitors were paying elsewhere. Dodda was connected enough to get it straight from Jamaica. Knowing several growers there personally, he was able to get it at the best price. Because of this, Mann was able to sell each pound at $900. A little less than the competition. He was also able to get rid of it much quicker because it was a better grade. It was a win-win situation for him that brought him in around $10k a week in profit. Of course, that was before he paid Yosohn his thirty-five percent he invested. It wasn't a lot to some, but the hustle was a gold mine for people like Mann who grew up poor. $7k a week had him feeling rich. The way the work was moving, they could double those numbers. That of course was only if Yosohn was on board with it.

Dodda counted the money like he usually did, and then headed out the door to grab the product from wherever it was stashed. Mann made himself comfortable while he waited with Zeke. They didn't speak even though they were alone. Ty and Garlan paced through the house on point, just like they were trained and paid to be. After about thirty-five minutes, Mann's phone rang indicating Dodda was downstairs with the product. It was too risky and too obvious transporting the packaged weed up and down the stairs in that neighborhood.

Mann and Zeke made their way down the steps, so they could retrieve the package out of Dodda's trunk and head back to Philly. As they approached Dodda's silver Toyota Sienna van, the trunk popped open and they quickly scooped up the duffel bag and moved it to the rented Ford Windstar Mann was driving. So that they wouldn't draw suspicion, they always used vans when making the transactions. They wore professional clothing such as slacks and button-ups, with the intention of looking like working family men. This helped them avoid being pulled over by the cops and going to jail. Mann didn't bother to count the bundles since Dodda was always accurate. After loading up all the drugs, Mann said goodbye to Dodda and began the drive back to Philadelphia.

CHAPTER 7

Jocelyn pulled from her blunt and inhaled deeply to allow the thick smoke to absorb in her lungs. She had a date in a couple of hours and smoking weed was one of the ways she prepared mentally. She picked up her cell phone and dialed Yosohn's number for the hundredth time, hoping he would answer. It went straight to voicemail. It had been a few weeks since the funeral incident and Yosohn still wasn't picking up. Jocelyn looked over at Bianca who was on the bed sprawled out sleep on a faded outdated comforter.

"Bianca … Wake up hoe, I got a date." Jocelyn shook Bianca, causing her to stir. She needed Bianca to go back to her own room so she could meet her date there in a few minutes.

"Aight, I'm up." Bianca smoothed back her fresh, long braids, wiped her eyes, and headed out to her own room, which was only a few doors down. "Come over when you done."

"Alright," Jocelyn replied. Jocelyn went to the bathroom to put on her lime-green, hip-hugging lace chemise. It was her favorite piece of lingerie because it made her look exotic when she had it on. The color looked stunning in contrast to her smooth tan skin. She stared in the bathroom mirror and smiled in satisfaction. Her twists had only been in a few weeks and they still looked good. The guy coming was a new client and she wanted to impress him. Just as she finished applying several heavy coats of Lancôme ultra-shiny lip gloss, her phone rang. She ran over to it, assuming it was her date calling back. She was right.

"Hey, boo," she purred, recognizing the number. She told him which room she was in and went to the door to wait for him. Her new client was older and went by Ace. She didn't know much about him because he didn't talk much. She assumed he had his shit together because he dressed professionally and drove a nice car. She'd met him on her Only Fans account. Most of the men she dealt with courted her, but some preferred to get straight to the sexual part. She didn't mind. If the price was right, she had no problem with it. When Ace finally came up, he greeted her with a smile and a light hello. As he entered the room, a breeze of alcohol and cologne trailed behind him. Jocelyn hoped that him indulging in alcohol wouldn't prolong his stay.

When Ace slid into her messages, he advised her that he only wanted head. However, he didn't want any ordinary head. Ace liked everything rough, included his fellatio. Jocelyn didn't mind. She charged him double and was more than happy to give him what he came for. Jocelyn was high as a kite from the Marijuana she had just smoked. She led the way to the bed and motioned for Ace to follow. When he reached her, he stood at the foot of the bed while Jocelyn took a seat on the edge. Without a word, she slowly began caressing his chest and unbuttoning his shirt.

"Come here, baby; let Jocelyn take care of you."

Once she got his shirt open, she began to lick and suck. Ace tilted his head back in satisfaction. Jocelyn reached down and rubbed the bulge in his pants. When his manhood felt as stiff as it could get, she began unfastening his belt buckle and loosening his pants. Once they slid to the ground, his full length and girth stood in front of her. Jocelyn began stroking his shaft, causing Ace to pant in ecstasy. As Ace's breathing deepened, Jocelyn backed away and laid on the bed, turning her body so that she was upside down facing him from the opposite direction. Ace got completely naked, and grabbed the thin, cherry-flavored condom Jocelyn had grabbed from off the dresser and slid to him. Jocelyn had a safe sex policy. She regularly turned down offers for double and triple to go bareback. It was never worth it. She was a hoe, but she wasn't a dumb one.

After putting on the condom, Ace straddled Jocelyn's face backward. With his full length in and his balls near her chin, he began easing in and out of her mouth. Jocelyn took his thighs and assisted him. She figured, the quicker they came, the better. Jocelyn licked, sucked, and rolled his balls around her mouth until they were soaked with her saliva. In ecstasy and with excitement mounting, Ace held the sheets as he pounded away at her face. Jocelyn sucked, slurped, and choked with every thrust. Being inside of Jocelyn's mouth was heaven to Ace and it was worth every penny he had just paid. Sometimes he just wanted freaky sex and a quick nut with no strings attached.

A few minutes later and they were done. Jocelyn got up to wash her face and wash her mouth out. Ace sat naked in the room recliner until she came out, and then he proceeded to go and clean himself up as well. Ace didn't talk much after the engagement. Jocelyn always collected her money up front so there wasn't much for him to say. Once washed up, he gave her a light hug and told her he would hit her up soon to see her again. That was it.

Jocelyn enjoyed the money that being wild provided;

however, it was times like this that made her unhappy. She didn't want some random, emotionless nigga fucking her face. She wanted her own man. She wanted Yosohn. Someone she could cuddle with after sex. Who she could cum together with; who would kiss and hold her after? Yosohn had never done much with her, but he would hold her a little in the bed, make her feel loved. Even if he didn't say it, she felt it. She felt special when they were together. Even if was only for a few hours. She had never had that type of intimacy with anyone. No one had ever made her feel that way. She'd never had those warm and fuzzy feelings with anyone.

Growing up, Jocelyn never knew much about her father. All she knew was that he went to prison when she was about two years old. Since she was a little girl, all she remembered was her mother struggling. She didn't speak much English and she had no education so she couldn't get a job. Jocelyn was the youngest of four. She had two brothers and an older sister that she didn't see much of. She barely knew them. They were a lot older than her and they often ripped and ran the streets, doing as they pleased.

To make ends meet, Jocelyn's mother kept multiple boyfriends. A revolving door of men was her life. It was their normal. To cope with her way of life, her mother often drank. When she drank, she was mean, uncaring, and unloving. That was all Jocelyn knew. At eighteen she left, never knowing the feeling of love. The closest thing she had to it was her best friend. Bianca could lead her off a cliff, but Jocelyn would still follow … because she loved her. She knew it didn't make any sense. It was toxic. Unfortunately, Jocelyn didn't use her head. She wasn't led by her brain. She was led by her heart. Her head could tell her that she was being rejected; however, her heart would hang on to hope. Hang on to dysfunctional relationships just so she could get the feeling back that she longed for.

Shaking her thoughts, Jocelyn went over to the dresser and dialed Yosohn's number again. Once again, the phone went to voicemail. She yelled out in frustration. For a second, she hated Yosohn. *Why didn't he just leave me the fuck alone*, she thought. She couldn't stand nigga's at times. A bitch could be minding her business and one would come along ... beg for their time ... promising to treat them right. The whole time he wasn't shit. Now she was just like the next regular bitch. Feelings all involved.

Jocelyn paused for a minute and then dialed Serenity's number. This was something she had been doing for the past couple of days. If she had to be miserable, she wanted to make Serenity miserable too. Maybe, in turn, she would make Yosohn miserable and that would lead him back to her. Serenity, unfortunately, would never stay on the phone long. She would say hello a couple of times and then hang up. Jocelyn knew that Serenity already knew who was calling. She wanted her to get mad. Yell at her. Curse at her. Argue. But Serenity never engaged.

It was getting late so Jocelyn laid down. Every night she prayed for her heart to be whole again. Prayed that her feelings for Yosohn would magically disappear. How she wished it were that simple.

CHAPTER 8

S erenity usually didn't work past five. She preferred to spend the evenings at home with her daughter Heaven and or studying. Unfortunately, her assistant Susan, wasn't feeling well and she had to step in. It was Monday and supplies usually came in around four. Today, the truck was significantly late, not showing up until well after midnight. With four locations, Serenity knew that it would be after midnight before she got in.

Luckily, her sisters Shyanne and Shanita didn't live too far from her last stop, so they offered to bring her some food by and make sure she locked up safely. Serenity also had another sister Shameka who was a year younger than her. She lived on the other side of Philadelphia and had went out to party with her girlfriends. Out of everyone, she was the party animal. Heaven was with her mother Gina, while her sister's children were tucked in bed, at home with their fathers.

"Damn, this chicken is hitting. Who made it, Mommy?" Serenity asked, while digging into a foam plate piled high with crunchy, moist chicken wings. She shoved her fork into a side of sautéed spinach and followed up with some buttered rice. She knew her mother's cooking anywhere, and she had no doubt that she was the one who had made the bangin' plate that she was tearing into.

"Yeah, she let them marinate overnight. Heaven fucked it up, with her lil' fat self," Shanita joked. Heaven was indeed chubby; however, her baby was a beautiful, well-mannered child.

"Hey, lay off my baby. You know she love her food, especially mommy's cooking. I am going to have to put her on a diet though. She is getting a little big."

"A little?" Shyanne joked.

"Fuck y'all bitches," Serenity countered. She knew they meant well. They loved Heaven damn near like she was their own, and Serenity loved their children just the same. The four of them were close. Their mother Gina had raised them to be. She'd raised them to always stand by one another; right or wrong.

"So wassup with you and Yosohn?" Shanita asked. "He still keeps calling everybody, especially Mommy. Getting on her damn nerves. She told him … when you ready to talk to his ass you'll call or come around."

"Girl, fuck Yosohn," Serenity responded half-heartedly, her face frowned. "He still calling me too of course. I ain't answering. He been leaving voicemails and shit. Same old apologies and excuses."

"Yo' ass gon' be right back over there," Shanita said, talking shit. She was always the one that spoke the truth. She was the smallest one of the bunch, standing a mere 5'2; however, she was also the one who talked the most shit. Long hair with glasses, she looked just like their father.

"Bitch … I don't know. I told you the hoe called me and then a few weeks later she was at the funeral talking shit. Out of all places to act a fool. Her and her home-girl. That situation didn't help *at all*. It put us in an even worse place. Honestly, I haven't talked to him much since then. If I do, I keep it short and sweet."

"Damn, I wish we were there, so we could've fucked them bitches up. Straight out of line. Acting a fool at a nigga funeral like that," Shanita said in disgust.

"Yeah I wish y'all could have come. I didn't even bother to ask since nobody really knew Hakim that well. I ended up apologizing to Nikki though. It's just mad disrespectful to be fightin' at someone's funeral. She's mourning, and we acting like fools. I didn't care much for him—God rest his soul, but I still have respect for the dead."

"Girl, that wasn't yo' fault. Ain't nobody 'bout to be disrespected. I don't care where you at," Shyanne added. Even though she was the quieter sister, Shyanne didn't take any shit from anyone. "I just hope you and Yosohn get back together," she added. Serenity shook her head. She wasn't so sure.

"Despite the fucked-up shit he's done, you know Yosohn loves you. He takes care of y'all. He probably going crazy right now."

"Yeah *probably*, but that's what his ass gets. He can't be cheating on her and thinkin' motherfuckers gon' feel sorry for him," Shanita added.

"Y'all hear that?" Serenity asked her sisters, shooting them an awkward look. She frowned and then turned her ear to the door where she suspected the noise was coming from.

"Na," they both responded. They didn't hear anything. They looked at Serenity like she had lost it.

"You don't hear yelling? Hold up," Serenity paused. She put down her chicken and wiped her hands on a nearby napkin, before exiting the office and heading into the main part of the laundromat.

"Bitch come out of that office, I know you in there," someone yelled.

The voice was unmistakable, and Serenity knew exactly who it was.

Serenity's heart pounded in her chest when she looked out of her office and saw Jocelyn, along with the bitch from the funeral. She couldn't believe their nerve. She wondered what they wanted. She also wondered how the hell she knew about the business. The drama never seemed to end. Walking back into her office, she stood in front of her sisters with a strange look.

"What's the matter?" Shanita asked.

"This Spanish-looking bitch in here," she whispered.

"Spanish bitch? What Spanish bitch?" Shanita asked, staring at Serenity wide-eyed like she had lost her mind.

"The bitch that Yosohn was fuckin'. Jocelyn."

"What? That bitch is here!" Shanita asked in disbelief. "And why the fuck is you whispering? This ya shit! These bitches got shit fucked all the way up!" Shanita snapped with fire now flowing through her veins.

Shanita jumped up and quickly walked out the door. Shyanne and Serenity followed behind her.

"Wassup?" Shanita asked Jocelyn when she got out the door. Shanita studied the two women. The fairer skinned one must have been Jocelyn. The other one was clearly African American, so Shanita assumed that was the friend she brought along. She truly didn't care who was who. They were tripping if they thought they could walk up in her sister's business and run up on her. She was with the shits and she certainly didn't have a problem enforcing respect.

"You looking for my sister, right? Wassup?"

Jocelyn and Bianca had both been drinking when they got the sudden idea to go to the laundromat and confront both Yosohn and Serenity. They didn't like the way shit had went down at the funeral and they wanted to settle the score. Jocelyn had been calling Yosohn all day, but of course, he wasn't answering. Eventually, she would call, and the automated system would politely inform her that the number she had dialed was unreachable. Jocelyn knew that she had been blocked. With a battered heart and liquid courage running through her, she and Bianca hopped on the bus and headed over to the place where her jealous heart had been pierced for the first time. The laundromat where she saw first-hand, Yosohn's relationship.

"This ain't got shit to do with you. I came to talk to Serenity," she lied, pointing around Shanita, where Serenity was standing. They hadn't come to talk. They had come hoping that Serenity was there alone so they could beat her.

"Okay, so there she is." Shanita said, glancing at her sister. She noticed that Serenity looked hesitant. Her baby-sister was no punk; however, she didn't like drama. Nevertheless, Shanita knew that it had to be dealt with. The hoes had shown up at her business, so today was going to be the day.

"If you want to address some shit, then please do so. If not, then you and that raggedy bitch you got with you, can get the fuck out."

Finally chiming in, Serenity turned to Jocelyn. "What the fuck do you want? We already talked and you told me what it was. There's nothing else you need to say to me. Real funny though … you were at a nigga's funeral … out of all places, talking shit like you were so sure of yourself. Yosohn been blowing up my phone all day. I guess you tryin' to reach him. But of course, he not picking up. He too busy callin' me. Ya plan didn't go how you wanted?"

Although she wasn't as street savvy as Jocelyn, she still was able to eventually realize what she was trying to accomplish. It was unbelievable what lengths some women would go to get a man. Another chick's man at that. Serenity didn't really want to argue or fight. She just wanted to cut Jocelyn where it hurt: her heart. Serenity knew that Yosohn wasn't picking up Jocelyn's phone calls; he was too busy blowing her cell phone up.

"Yeah whatever bitch. I'm still fuckin ya man. He loves all of this," Jocelyn taunted, rubbing her body with her hands.

"Girl, bye. You makin' a fool of yaself over his ass anywhere you can. Yo' issues aren't with me. If you want Yosohn, call him. Otherwise, leave me the fuck alone," Serenity said harshly. "Matter of fact, I'll call him for you."

She dug in the back pocket of the jeans she was wearing and pulled out her phone. She dialed Yosohn's phone and put it on speaker. She wanted everyone to hear how much Yosohn didn't give a fuck about her. Serenity was angry and she was tired. Tired of Yosohn cheating. Tired of him calling. And tired of the stupid bitch who couldn't seem to get the fact that Yosohn didn't want her, through her head.

"Hello?" Yosohn answered on the second ring. "Hello!" he said louder this time. He hadn't talked to Serenity in a while and it was damn near a miracle that she had even called him back. He prayed that the call hadn't dropped. "Serenity baby? Can you hear me?" he called out.

"Yosohn, yo' sidepiece is in our fuckin' laundromat. I suggest you bring yo' ass down here and check this hoe," Serenity barked into the phone enraged.

"What? How the fuck?" He had never told her he owned any business. Let alone what kind or where at. "Which one you at? I'll come down there and handle that shit."

"I'm at Broad and Girard. You wanna talk to ya hoe?" she asked, knowing what his response would be. She wanted to thoroughly rub it in Jocelyn's face.

"Fuck her. I'm on my way," he said, hanging up.

Looking up at Jocelyn, Serenity smiled devilishly. "Oh, I'm sorry. He didn't wanna talk to you." Feeling the sharp sting of rejection, Jocelyn suddenly charged at Serenity. Before she could connect her fist with her face, Shyanne drew back and hit her with a right hook, sending her crumbling into a dryer. Bianca instantly rushed in and the brawl began.

Shyanne, Shanita, and Serenity pounced on the two and quickly overpowered them in their drunken state. Serenity didn't want to really hurt them but Shanita and Shyanne showed no mercy for the two. With little effort, Shyanne slung Bianca to the ground by her hair and began punching her repeatedly, while Serenity and Jocelyn threw blows close by. Shanita dashed over and knocked Jocelyn to the ground and then proceeded to connect kick her. Seizing complete control, the three women beat the other two until they were tired. By the time they were finished, weave pieces, bus tokens and loose coins were strewn all over the floor.

Five minutes later, Yosohn showed up. He hadn't been far when Serenity called him, so he sped to the laundromat under the impression that she was alone. He had come prepared to smack Jocelyn and anyone she had with her. His life was unraveling, and he was getting fed up and desperate. He wanted to put a stop to the madness.

Damn, was all he could think when he entered the laundromat. He saw Jocelyn and Bianca getting up off the floor and scrounging for their belonging. They looked raggedy, beat and worn. Intoxicated and too busy getting themselves together, neither of the women noticed Yosohn come inside. He shook his head in disgust and proceeded to the office where he saw Serenity and her two sisters worked up and angry. He was relieved that they were there, but he knew that he was about to become public enemy number one.

"Yosohn you might as well carry yo' ass back to wherever the fuck you came from," Serenity argued, grabbing her keys to leave. He was the last face she wanted to see. She was still breathing heavily and was furious from the fight. She didn't want to talk.

"Serenity baby, please just talk to me," Yosohn pleaded, following behind her after she stormed out towards her car.

"Didn't she say she don't want to talk to you. Damn. Let it go and leave her alone," Shanita snapped, following behind Yosohn as he followed Serenity.

"Shanita, please," Serenity turned around and replied, still agitated. She did her best to smooth her hair down, before continuing her walk to her car.

"No, fuck that Serenity. He got you in here looking like a cold nut. Bitches running down on you at yo' job. Straight out of line. No fuckin' respect. He came in and didn't even say shit to the bitch. If he not addressing it, he's condoning that shit!"

"Yo, why don't you mind yo' fuckin' business," Yosohn said, whipping his head around to face Shanita. The situation was bad enough already, and her ranting wasn't making it any better.

"I didn't say shit to the bitch because she's irrelevant. Y'all done already beat the fuck out them, so my focus is not on them. My focus is on Serenity."

Shanita smacked her teeth and rolled her eyes. "Whatever nigga," she replied sharply. She knew Yosohn would be as respectful as possible, but he would draw the line after a while. She wasn't trying to go back and forth with him, especially since she knew Serenity would eventually end up right back with him. Even though Yosohn said it was none of their business, to her it was. If a bitch tried to run down on her little sister, it became her business. Anytime she had to lay hands on a bitch, it became her business. If they hadn't been there, they would have jumped her sister. She glared at Yosohn. She wanted to lay into him some more but to keep the peace, she held her tongue.

"We get what you're saying Yosohn, but this isn't the right time to try to talk to her —" Shyanne tried to add as she walked up.

Cutting her off, Yosohn replied, "Don't tell me when the right time is. I need to talk to my girl!"

Even though Yosohn was upset, Shanita knew that someone had to be rational. She continued what she was saying. "Yosohn, now you know I fuck with you the long way. I watched you support my sister and her dreams. You've helped me plenty of times. All of us." She glared at Shanita just in case she got amnesia. While her sister was correct with her statement, they both knew that Yosohn wasn't all bad.

"I know you a good dude deep down despite your short-comings. But do you really think that running her down and forcing her to talk, is going to help the situation?"

Yosohn sighed heavily, running his fingers over his thick beard. He didn't want to hear it. He was tired of Serenity running off. They needed to talk about things like adults.

"Hear me out, Yosohn … A bitch you were *fucking*, just came up to her. At *her* business. How the fuck would you feel? You're her fiancée Yosohn. The man that gave her a ring. The man that she's supposed to marry. Start a family with. Serenity doesn't want to talk. She's pissed, she's hurt, and that hoe keep dragging the situation on to hurt her more. The early morning phone call was to say, I'm fuckin' yo' man. The funeral was a reminder that I'm fuckin' yo' man. Her visit just now, was another reminder that I'm fuckin' yo' man. Whatever the bitch is trying to do, is working. *That's* what you need to fix first. Then, you can fix it with Serenity. As much as you want to think you done with that hoe, you aren't. Because the reality is … she's not done with you."

After Shyanne finished speaking, Yosohn paused for a

moment. He had to admit that she was right. He did need to give her some space to digest things. Even though he didn't want to, he decided to leave and let Serenity be. He gave Shyanne a brief hug and needlessly thanked the two of them for riding for her. He knew that was a given. They were raised with loyalty and would literally catch a charge for one another. Shanita rolled her eyes at Yosohn in return. She wasn't impressed the least bit with Yosohn.

Although he caught her facial expression, Yosohn didn't get offended. He didn't care if Shanita liked him or not. He also knew her personality. Shanita was fiercely loyal to her sisters, but she was also stubborn as hell and could hold a grudge for a little while. She would come around eventually.

After locking up the laundromat, the three women headed out for a drink. Serenity would finish putting up materials tomorrow. The whole way to the lounge, Shanita expressed her concern over the situation. She felt like Yosohn controlled Serenity with money and materials. Shyanne, on the other hand, knew the love they had. The whole time Shanita expressed her concern, Serenity didn't even bother to respond. She didn't have to explain shit to anyone. She *was* in control and resented the fact of being told she wasn't. She'd left him; wasn't that enough? Besides, she took care of herself and had her own damn money. She didn't need anyone telling her what they thought. She knew Shanita wanted what was best for her, but she drew the line when it came to people giving her advice on her relationship and personal life. For now, she would continue to stay at her hotel suite and wait for shit to play out, however it played out.

~

December had rolled around before anyone had knew it. It had been a month since her and Yosohn had separated and frankly, Serenity was tired of wallowing in self-pity. She thought that she would feel better by now, but that wasn't the case. She missed Yosohn more than ever, and she was tired of being cooped up in her hotel suite. She decided she would call her best friend Naomi and see what she was getting into. She had to get out.

After hanging up with Naomi, Serenity agreed to drive over to her place so they could have a girl's night out. Naomi wanted her to get out and have fun instead of moping around. Since she hadn't been out in months, Serenity was excited and wasted no time getting up to look for something fly to wear. She wanted to look good. Maybe she would find a new man.

After getting ready and driving over to Naomi's, she found herself waiting restlessly, parallel parked against the curb. Serenity glanced at the dashboard clock and then honked her horn. Since she'd known her, Naomi had always operated on her own time. Serenity had been waiting outside her apartment for over five minutes. After another couple of minutes, Naomi finally came out in a black, wrap around dress and thigh boots. She knew how to dress her plus-size frame and Serenity had to admit, she was killing it.

Naomi and Serenity had met in undergrad. Both majoring in business, they had a bunch of classes together. With both eager to meet new people, they became fast friends. Naomi was a beautiful girl with chestnut brown skin and slanted eyes. Even though she was overweight, Serenity found her drop-dead gorgeous. Unfortunately, Serenity had to constantly remind her. Insecure and lacking confidence because of her weight, she'd often struggle in relationships, falling for men that used and abused her.

"Ok. I see you boo. You look good girl," Serenity squealed,

hyping her friend up as she sashayed her voluptuous body to the car.

"Thanks boo. Always do," Naomi joked. Serenity noticed that she often did her best to fake confidence. Despite her words, her actions told another story.

"What you got on?" she asked. Serenity had on her coat, so her outfit wasn't visible. Dying to show Naomi her newest ensemble, Serenity hopped out the car.

"Remember that gold bodysuit I was telling you about that I wanted. Well, I found it online in my size," Serenity said with a cheesy ass grin. Taking off her jacket, she briefly stepped out of the car in the cold to show off the fit. The gold stretchy fabric looked like it was painted onto Serenity's voluptuous frame. She didn't even bother to add any accessories since the bodysuit spoke for itself.

"Wow," was all Naomi could say in response. "That jawn is crazy. You definitely turnin' heads tonight," she said almost jealously.

"Shidd … bitch we both are. I'm excited. I haven't been out in God knows how long and I'm tryin' turn up."

"Girl, bye," Naomi laughed, knowing full well that Serenity didn't turn up.

"Real shit," Serenity confessed. She really did want to enjoy herself. It had been a long time since she felt good and alive. "And what you been drinking on anyway? You over there looking faded. I'm trying to get like that."

"I got some Goose in my bag, and you can definitely get some … after you park this damn car. Yo' ass ain't gon' kill me up in here drunk driving."

"Whatever hoe," Serenity responded, smacking her teeth. "If you don't give me that damn bottle, so I can get a few swigs of that shit. I won't even feel it until we get to the lounge." Naomi reluctantly agreed and then handed over the small bottle.

The ladies had decided to go to a nice lounge on South Street for the grown and sexy. While they headed to the lounge, they passed the bottle back and forth, laughing and talking about the latest events happening in their life. Instead of taking the expressway, Serenity took the long drive up Roosevelt Boulevard just for the scene. Besides, she hadn't kicked it with her girl in a long time and wanted to enjoy her company for as long as she could. By the time they got to Broad Street, Naomi found herself hungry and begging for Serenity to make a pit stop in North Philly for some food. She had a taste for crab cakes.

"Come on bitch, go to that seafood truck Yosohn has with Hakim. It's on the way, right near Allegheny."

"Girl, I know where it is, but I ain't feeling that, Naomi," Serenity responded hesitantly. "What if Yosohn out there? I ain't trying to hear that shit he spitting tonight. And why the fuck you trying to be chomping down on some damn crab cakes before you go to a damn lounge? Yo' ass gon' smell just like fuckin' crabs," Serenity frowned.

"I don't give a damn; I'm hungry. And anyway, I have some gum with me … Just stop over there so I can get my damn food," she argued.

"Yo' ass gon' eat it with the window rolled down. I ain't going up in no lounge smelling like crab meat," Serenity countered. As much as she loved her friend, she was growing irritated. Naomi could be so demanding and difficult when she was drunk. However, to avoid an argument, Serenity bent the block and just like she expected, there he was.

CHAPTER 9

Yosohn had mixed emotions the moment his eyes landed on Serenity. He didn't know whether to jump for joy or snatch her up and proceed to knock her head off. He hadn't seen her in a month. The most communication she would allow was through text messages. Yosohn stared at Serenity and admired her beauty. The gold bodysuit she had on looked stunning against her chocolate skin, but it also caused every nigga within eyesight of her to stop and stare. She commanded attention with her thick body owning the fabric. Her weave was bone straight and flowed down to her ass. She literally stopped movement when she stepped out of the car. Becoming instantly jealous, Yosohn did his best to hide it. Unfortunately, his best wasn't good enough. Mann immediately noticed Yosohn's discomfort and growing jealousy.

Exiting the car, Naomi walked up to the window of the truck and ordered her food. Serenity came and stood beside her, not bothering to speak to anyone. She simply flashed a large smile at the two men. Yosohn walked over to greet her. He did his best to maintain his composure with a smile.

"Hey bae, wassup?" he asked, leaning in to hug her.

"Hey. Wassup with you? Hey Mann," she waved.

"Wassup. Y'all look nice," Mann added, while walking up.

"Yeah. Where you going?" Yosohn asked, not beating around the bush.

"Out," Serenity replied coolly, matching Yosohn's gaze.

"Yeah? Out where?" he asked again.

"Not sure yet. Naomi wanted to stop and get some food though so that's how we ended up here," she said, smiling again. She knew she was taunting Yosohn. The alcohol had started to set in, and she was getting in her feelings. She knew she looked damn good. The stares around her confirmed it. She was all his, but he fucked that up. Now he was worried about the next nigga chopping her down. Serenity snickered to herself while she thought.

"What's funny Serenity?" Yosohn asked irritably. He knew she was playing games and it was starting to make him angry.

"*Everything* is funny." She put her hands on her wide hips and shifted her weight from one Louboutin to the other.

"Ok. Enlighten me? As a matter of fact, come over here and talk to me," Yosohn insisted, reaching out and grabbing Serenity's hand.

"I don't wanna talk right now," she replied sharply, snatching her hand back. She looked to Naomi who was now standing beside her and asked, "How long they say yo' food gon' be? I'm ready to go."

"Five minutes. You okay?" Naomi asked, sensing Serenity's uneasiness.

"Yeah I'm going back to the car," she said walking off. Yosohn followed. He was tired of her walking off.

"Serenity hold up." They were now at the car and Serenity had opened the door and was ready to get in.

"Yeah wassup?" she asked, rolling her eyes, uninterested in whatever he had to say.

"Why you doing this? You been gone for over two months. I learned my lesson. When you gon' come home?" he asked, getting straight to the point.

Smacking her teeth, Serenity responded, "Yosohn I heard this same shit before. I'm good."

"You good? What that mean?" Yosohn narrowed. She was really starting to push his buttons.

"I'm good. I don't know what else you want me to say. I'm not ready to go back into that bullshit, and frankly, I don't know if I ever will."

"What? Where the fuck this shit coming from Serenity?"

"I'm not doing this with you right now Yosohn" She couldn't believe some of the shit he said sometime.

"You been drinking?" he asked curiously.

"What does it matter?" Serenity responded, confirming his suspicions.

"So, you been drinking, and you think you supposed to run out with that shit on?" he asked, looking her up and down.

Serenity ignored him and got in her Camaro. Yosohn stood in the doorway preventing her from closing it.

"Move Yosohn. We're leaving." Naomi walked up to the car and got in, leaving Yosohn no choice but to move or look like a nut.

"Well, can we meet up later? You can come to the house or I can come to where you stayin'."

"Aight Yosohn. I'll think about it. I'll call you." She wasn't really going to call him. She didn't want to hear shit he had to say. He had already said everything possible. She was going to do things on her own time.

"Okay, don't forget?" He knew that was as good as it was going to get. It would do him no good to lose his patience, so he did his best to remain calm. The time apart was getting under his skin and he was starting to think she was seeing someone else. The outfit she was wearing didn't make it any better. The reality was that she was a good woman. If he lost her to someone else, he wouldn't know what do; he wouldn't be able to handle it.

CHAPTER 10

The girls ended up at a packed lounge and just as expected, all eyes were on Serenity. Ignoring all the attention, Serenity did her best to enjoy herself, but her thoughts were still on Yosohn. She needed to figure out what she was going to do soon. She couldn't keep staying at the hotel. Not only was it expensive, but it was becoming cramped. Heaven was calling her grandmother Gina to pick her up every day. When Gina couldn't come, Heaven would go down the line calling her aunts. Her baby was growing tired of being cooped up in the cramped suite. She needed to figure out if she was going to return to the home that she and Yosohn shared, or if she was going to get a new place. She couldn't continue to let her love life affect her daughter's life.

Partying hard, Serenity and Naomi hit the dance floor while taking turns hitting the bar. After two Long Island Iced Teas and a shot, Serenity was drunk. She could still function, but she was becoming hot and bothered and any nigga in the club was looking appealing. She figured that was her cue to leave. After searching around the lounge for Naomi she finally found her at the bar. Surprisingly, she was seated right beside Mann.

"Hey hoe, what you doin' over here," Serenity said, smiling curiously before taking a seat.

"Hey, Mann. You look nice." Still seated, he had on a black Polo button up, khakis and black Timberland boots. He looked hood, but nevertheless, he did look good.

"Thanks. You look like you havin' a nice time," he laughed.

Serenity smiled. "Yeah. I am," she said taking a seat beside Mann. Naomi glanced over at her since there was a seat next to her, further from Mann. Serenity had tried and failed to hook Naomi and Mann up in the past. They'd kicked it a few times, but Naomi found him to be distant and uninterested. She thought it was because of her weight, but Mann would later admit that he was simply too busy. Focused on other things, he wasn't really interested in a love life. He was more focused on stackin' paper. Naomi still reached out to him from time to time since she really liked him; however, he just wasn't interested.

"So how you end up here on girl's night?" She glared at Naomi, knowing exactly how.

"I invited him back at the truck. I figured you wouldn't mind," Naomi answered.

"It's cool. So wassup? What we bout to do?" Serenity glanced at her watch and saw that it was nearly one in the morning.

What the fuck you mean we? were the thoughts that were going through Naomi's head. "I don't know about you, but I'm ready to go. My head is spinning a little and Mann and I were thinking 'bout getting some food," Naomi replied.

"Girl, you 'bout to eat—" Serenity caught herself. She was about to ask her why the hell she was about to eat again;

however, she didn't want to embarrass her friend. She knew that Naomi's weight was a sensitive subject.

"Well listen, y'all have fun. I'm out. Bye, boo," Serenity said to Naomi. She knew the little early morning meal was her cue to leave. Naomi was trying to shoot her shot with Mann and she was no cock-blocker. She reached over and gave Naomi a hug. She also gave Mann a hug. She couldn't help but notice how good he smelled. How strong his body felt when she embraced him. She wondered what they were going to be doing. She quickly shook the thoughts. Mann was like family, and she knew she shouldn't have been thinking that way about him; however, she couldn't help it.

Mann was low-key fine as hell. She'd never paid him too much attention because he was Yosohn's friend. But dude looked good. With his clean bald head, broad shoulders, and gangster swag, she couldn't help but appreciate all of him in her drunken state. She couldn't lie, the alcohol had her panties wet and her thoughts racing. How she wished she had a man to go home to. If she weren't so stubborn, she would call Yosohn over to her suite, but she wasn't ready just yet. Shaking her thoughts, Serenity grabbed her Chanel clutch and headed out.

Deciding they were also ready to go, Mann and Naomi followed behind her. As they walked outside, Naomi suddenly jerked her way to the side of the street and threw up all over the sidewalk. Serenity heard the sounds and ran over to her. Naomi began to gag and cry as she emptied the contents of her stomach on the ground. Serenity rubbed her back and held her weave to keep her from making a mess. When she finished, Naomi had tears in her eyes. She was more embarrassed than anything. Even though she hadn't drunk as much as Serenity, all the extra food she had eaten caused turmoil in her stomach. She didn't even want to look up at Mann who was now standing close by.

"Listen, I'm gon' take both y'all home," he said, looking towards Serenity. "You're drunk, and she's throwing up and shit. I'd hate for anything to happen to y'all. Where yo' keys," Mann demanded to know. "I'll park yo' car in the garage up the street. You can come back for it tomorrow."

Serenity reached into her bag and retrieved her keys. Handing them to Mann she asked, "You not gon tell Yosohn about this are you? Not that I care, but I don't want him thinking we some sloppy drunk bitches." Her eyes shifted to Naomi. Yosohn had expressed several times that she didn't know how to conduct herself. Needless to say, he wasn't her biggest fan.

"And I'm not quite ready for him to know where I'm staying," she added.

"I got you. You have my word I won't tell him anything," Mann promised.

ALTHOUGH INTOXICATED, NAOMI COULDN'T HELP BUT NOTICE that Mann had decided to drop her off first. She figured it was because she had become sick. She guessed their late-night meal wasn't going to happen. Before exiting Mann's Charger, she gave Serenity a quick hug and told her to text her when she got in. Still a little embarrassed, she thanked Mann and scurried into her home to clean herself up and get some rest.

"So how you feelin'?" Mann asked Serenity on the drive back to her suite on the other side of the city. For some reason, she was so easy to talk to. He felt comfortable making small talk while they rode from Northeast Philly back to Chestnut Hill.

"I'm okay, just a little fucked up," she said smiling. "How

come you didn't chill with Naomi? You know she would've loved the company." Mann laughed before responding.

"She was drunk as fuck. Throwing up and shit. That ain't classy," he said with a light-hearted frown.

"So, what you trying to say? I ain't classy either?" Serenity asked, faking an attitude.

"That's not what I'm saying. I'm just saying that's not the way a lady should conduct herself. At least you know ya limit."

"Yeah, well it's kind of my fault. I asked her to come."

"Na," he shook his head. "That ain't ya fault. That big ass platter she had was the problem," he laughed. "I seen all the food she ordered back at the truck. You can't eat that heavy when you been drinking. She's grown. She knows that."

"True," Serenity agreed.

"So wassup with you and Yosohn?" Mann asked, turning the conversation more serious. Serenity sighed. She figured the question was coming. Since he was around so much, the question seemed normal.

"I don't know," she shrugged. "I love him. I tell myself that he loves me. I just don't know why he keeps fuckin' up," she slurred. "A lot of people see us and automatically assume that we got this bomb ass relationship, but they have no idea what I deal with now, or in the past. The cheating, the lies—I'm tired. Yeah, he buys me hella shit. And for the most part, he's good to me. But being good isn't just about buying someone nice shit, being nice, and being affectionate. It's also about being loyal. About being selfless. I'm a good woman and I know a lot of niggas would love to come home to a bitch like me. He just makes me feel like I'm not good enough." She looked out the window into the sky.

"Sometimes I just wish he could feel what I feel. I love him, but I wish I could just hurt him the way he hurts me sometimes. Maybe if he knew the feeling, he would be hesitant to keep inflicting that shit on me."

"Whatchu mean?" Mann asked, already knowing exactly what she meant.

"Just what I meant. He needs a taste of his own medicine." Serenity paused for a moment. "He just lucky that I'm not that type of bitch." She sighed. "But trust me … You don't know how bad I wish I were like that sometime." She stared at Mann, waiting for his response.

"I get whatchu sayin'." He turned away from her lingering gaze. She was starting to make him feel a little uncomfortable. For some reason, he felt like it was intentional.

"Make that right," she pointed as they neared her hotel. "You can pull right over there. I'll go in through the side door," Serenity said. Mann had just pulled up to her hotel. Even though it was two in the morning, she wasn't ready for bed just yet. She didn't get tired when she drank. She just kept going and going. She figured she would watch some T.V for a little while.

"You good?" Mann asked, noticing that she was a little wobbly. He also couldn't help but notice the way the fabric of her dress was gripping her ass. He quickly looked away. He knew he shouldn't be having thoughts like that about his man girl, but he couldn't lie; she was finer than a motherfucker. It wasn't like he had a crush on her. He was just attracted to her. He couldn't think of any nigga that wouldn't be.

"Yeah, I'm fine. Thanks, Mann." She shot him a charming smile.

"No problem. Had to make sure y'all got in safe. You go and get some rest. I'm 'bout to hop out and take a piss on the side of this building," he admitted, feeling mounting pressure in his bladder from the couple drinks he had.

"Boy, no you are not. All these damn white people that be

coming in and out on a Saturday. They be done called the police on you. You can come up and use the bathroom." She waved for him to follow her up.

"You sure?" he asked.

"Of course," she insisted, happily.

CHAPTER 11

Once inside her cozy little suite, Serenity kicked off her Louboutin's and plopped down on one of the accent chairs to get comfortable. Mann was in the bathroom. She walked up to her little kitchenette and pulled herself another shot. She knew she should have called it quits but with everything going on in her life, she didn't want the euphoric, carefree feeling to end.

"Mann, you want something to drink?" she called out. Even though she knew Yosohn would flip if he found out Mann was over there without him, she didn't care. She was simply happy to have some company, even if it was for only just five minutes.

"Just a little," he replied, emerging from the bathroom.

"Good. Hang out and chat with me for a few. It's still kind of early." Reluctantly, Mann agreed and took a seat at one of the stools.

"So, how's everything going at the businesses?" he asked, making small talk before quickly throwing back his shot of Tito's.

"They're going ok. I'm bored honestly," she admitted. "I

need a new project. Yosohn and I were just talking about that before shit went left." She shook her head and quickly rolled her eyes. "I wanted to open up some new spots and maybe look into some low-cost investment properties."

"That's definitely wassup. So, you gon' still do it?" he asked.

"I don't know. I have some money, but not enough. I don't think it's enough anyway."

"So, if you and Yosohn really do call it quits you gon' definitely need a nigga with a coupla dollas," he joked.

"Damn right. You know any?" she countered with a laugh.

"Yeah … I do actually," he said quietly. Serenity glanced at Mann. It was his tone when he said it. She figured she'd better change the subject.

"Well look, I'm 'bout to change. This tight ass suit is killing me," she laughed.

Serenity walked off to the bathroom and peeled off her bodysuit. She hopped in the shower so she could freshen up before bed. With the alcohol coursing through her system, she quickly lost track of time. By the time she got out, she figured Mann was long gone.

Serenity emerged from the bathroom thirty-minutes later feeling relaxed and refreshed. She picked up her phone from the bed and saw that she had ten missed calls from Yosohn. She didn't bother to check them since she knew what he wanted. She also saw that she had a few text messages from Jocelyn. The bitch was still playing on her phone. She should have blocked her a long time ago, but for some reason she had not.

She scrolled through her phone and read the comments. Within a few seconds, her blood began to boil. It was hard getting over Yosohn's deceit when she had a hoe throwing it in her face every day. Reading the messages instantly put her in a slump.

"You still here?" she asked after walking further into the room and noticing Mann sitting at the small eating area.

"Yeah, I'm about to go through. I don't drink much. I sat here and dozed off," he admitted, yawning lightly.

Mann couldn't help but admire Serenity. Her long hair flowed loosely around her face while she wore an oversized t-shirt. She looked simply beautiful.

"You're fine," she said plopping down beside him on the couch.

What better way, Serenity thought, looking at Mann. He damn sure was easy on the eyes. In another life, he could get it. She took a deep breath and shook the wicked thoughts. She knew the thoughts shouldn't had even entered her mind. She couldn't help it though; she had no control over her thoughts.

"Have you ever met Jocelyn before?" she asked Mann unexpectedly.

"Whatchu mean?" Mann asked uncomfortably. He wasn't sure where the conversation was going, and he didn't want to accidentally say something that would get his boy into more trouble.

"I mean, have you ever met her? Y'all know how y'all do."

"Naaa, I never met her," he admitted. He'd heard Yosohn on the phone with her plenty of times. Seen her on Face Time. But he'd never actually met her.

"You think Yosohn crazy?" she asked. Mann knew what she meant. She was referring to Yosohn's cheating.

"Yeah … I think so," he replied honestly.

"And why do you think?" she quizzed.

Mann shifted in his seat nervously but decided to answer the question honestly. "In my opinion, yeah. To keep it a buck, we getting older. Finding a solid broad out here is hard. Most of 'em don't even care about you. They care about what you can do for them. They aren't loyal, and will leave you at the drop of a dime. So, if a nigga found someone who is smart, beautiful *and* loyal … why risk it for some little wack bitch who ain't about shit? It wouldn't have been a risk that I would have taken. A real nigga that isn't already in a situation would love to have a chick like you by their side."

"Including you?" she asked boldly.

"Yeah, including me," he said, meeting her gaze from across the room. Serenity smiled, turned her head, and then outright laughed.

"What's funny?" Mann asked curiously.

"Nothing … It's just that … For some reason, I always felt like you had a little crush on me." She stared intently at Mann. Her narrow gaze matching his.

"Something like that," he replied, uncomfortably. "I would say, more of an attraction. But as my man's girl … you know… That made you off limits."

Serenity stood up from the bed and headed to the kitchenette to pour herself another drink. Mann admired her once again. Her exposed chocolate legs. Her bare feet polished perfectly in a snow-white color. She was perfect. She was beautiful. He felt his manhood stiffen.

"Can I ask you a question?" Mann asked, figuring he might as well go for it.

"What's that?" She turned around and smiled while lightly fingering back a few loose strands of hair that lie in her face.

"If you and Yosohn over for real, am I someone that you would have … or even would consider?"

Serenity stopped, turned to face him and then gave him a flirty smile. "Yeah … definitely would consider it," she admitted.

"So, what do you plan to do? After everything that's

happened, do you plan to go back to him?" he asked. They'd been separated for well over a month. To him, that looked like a woman that was ready to move on with her life.

Serenity smiled and sauntered over to where he was sitting him. Standing in front of him, she replied, "Fuck Yosohn. Even if I did decide to go back to him ... I'll do what the hell I want. He does all the time, right? I'm not worried about him. Why do you seem to be?" she questioned. The statement came out bold. Like she was challenging him. Mann knew it was the liquor talking. But he was always told that a drunk tongue was an honest one.

Without thinking, Mann reached out and gripped Serenity's waist, pulling her into him. "Why you playin' games, Serenity?" he asked her firmly.

"I—I—I'm not playing games, Mann," she said uncomfortably, stunned by his bold move. "Can you let me go," she panted. It came out in nearly a whisper. She shouldn't have been excited by his touch, but she was. He needed to get off her, but her tongue felt heavy and she couldn't find the strength to demand he let her go.

"I think you are playing games. You trying to make Yosohn jealous?" he asked, staring into her pretty face. "Because if that's the case ... then you may not want to play that game with me," he stated boldly. He released his grip and watched as she exhaled a deep breath.

"I'm not trying to do anything," she said drunkenly. "And as you can see, I'm a big girl, and I can handle whatever consequences come with what I do."

Her intention was to say that and walk away, but for some reason, her body wouldn't budge from the spot she was in. Mann stood up and put his arms around her waist. He buried his head into the nook of her neck and inhaled. She was sweet. Like berries and cream. Still holding her, he leaned in and kissed her gently. She knew they were out of line. They were going too far, but she couldn't find the strength to turn away.

This is wrong. What am I doing? she thought to herself. She turned her head and broke free from Mann's kiss and tried to speak. "Mann — this isn't right. We can't do this," Serenity pleaded.

"Yeah we can," he hissed.

He knew it was wrong, but she had started. Now, he wanted what he wanted. This was his opportunity. His heart pounded in his chest with anticipation. He leaned in and kissed her again, backing her into the bed nearby. Serenity moaned. He was aggressive. Lust had overpowered them both, and with Mann seizing control, she knew there was no turning back. A part of her was terrified. Another part of her couldn't wait to enjoy every minute of him. With her back on the bed, he gripped her legs and pulled her closer to him.

"No Mann ... I'm sorry we can't." Once again, it came out in a near whisper. Her brain said stop; her body had other plans.

Mann didn't respond. He climbed on top of her with his chiseled body and began to kiss her all over. At that moment Serenity's body took over completely and the only thing functioning in her brain was her pleasure senses. Mann was so strong. So warm. Felt so good.

Her anxiety soon faded ... along with the feelings of guilt and betrayal. Mann pulled up her t-shirt and began to plant kisses all over her. Using his tongue, he made a wet trail up her belly that sent her body into a frenzy. Mann glanced down at her jewels. She didn't have any panties on. Pushing her back lightly onto the bed, he dropped to his knees and began to feast on her core while cupping her soft breast. With her head tilt back, Serenity moaned in pleasure while gripping and guiding his slick, bald head as he went to work. Her chest rose and fell while her hips rotated with the movement of his tongue. Her pleasure mounting, she groaned loudly as she finally reached her peak. Mann didn't stop. He kept kissing, sucking, and tonguing away, catching every drop of juice she released. Serenity's head rotated from side to side in satisfaction. Before she could tap out, Mann rose and quickly undressed. Still immersed in a world of pleasure, Serenity didn't protest when he gently eased himself inside of her. Mann groaned in pleasure as he slipped in and out of her wetness.

"Sssssssssss," he hissed in ecstasy. She felt so good, he never wanted to come out. Serenity dug her fingers into his strong back, guiding his body and thrusting her hips back against his.

"Fuckkkkkk," he shuddered, doing his best to hold on to the moment. "I'm 'bout to come," he confessed. He couldn't contain himself any longer. Mann lowered his head into Serenity's chest and began sucking on her breast until he finally let go and exploded inside of her. Serenity moaned and locked her legs around his body so she could suck up every inch of him into her thirsty canal.

"Shittttt," she moaned when his dick hit her g-spot, causing her to cum for the second time. Even in her drunken state, the sex felt too good to be right. As soon as the euphoric feeling from her orgasm passed and she looked into Mann's handsome face, she instantly remembered why the hell it felt so good … because it was *so* wrong.

CHAPTER 12

Sitting idly at home, Yosohn couldn't help but continuously check his phone to see if he had any missed calls or text messages from Serenity. She still wasn't picking up or responding. He did his best to be patient with her, although the entire situation was worrying.

He pulled from his Backwoods and absorbed the thick smoke into his lungs. That would calm him for now. Yosohn got up from the couch and walked into the kitchen. He grabbed a bottle of Hennessey from off the counter and twisted the cap back, drinking it right from the top. This was the worst his life had been in a long time. He prided himself on creating a stable home for himself. Well ... Serenity made it stable. Now that she was gone, it no longer felt that way. As much as he hated to, he decided that he would have to accept the idea that she may not come back. He didn't want that to be the case, but deep down he knew it was a possibility. So much had happened over the last month and he couldn't dispute her feelings of being fed up. He didn't want to let her go. As a man, he knew that he should be selfless enough to do so. However, as a heavily flawed human being, he didn't want to. He simply didn't want to accept a life without Serenity.

Yosohn took another sip from his bottle, closed the top and went and sat back down in the living room. He checked his phone again. Still no missed calls from Serenity. Of course, he had a million from Jocelyn. Even though she was part of the reason why Serenity had been gone so long, she still managed to break get through to him. He knew he should have blocked her, but he didn't. For some reason, he wanted to hear her out. Hear what she had to say. As miserable as he was, it gave him a sick sense of satisfaction to see her just as, if not more miserable.

She had been texting him for weeks. At first, he was afraid of what he might do to her if he did, but as time went on, he had to admit that he wasn't even as mad anymore. He was most afraid of word getting back to Serenity. He didn't want to take the chance of allowing Jocelyn to make the situation even worse. She was far too unpredictable. Nevertheless, he hadn't had sex since Serenity had left him. Since she'd been gone, he had been focusing solely on money. He couldn't lie though, he yearned for a body beside him. He wanted Serenity back, but it had been so long, a hook up would do. He was doing his best to stay focused. Lord knows he didn't need to get caught up in anything else.

Since Hakim's death, he had been more hands on with the trucks, even showing Nikki the ropes. The seafood trucks were Hakim's idea, so it was only right that Nikki continued to receive his portion of the money. Besides, she was his wife, so she automatically became co-owner. She didn't really need it since Hakim had left her a life insurance policy for a half a million dollars. Nikki however was like his sister, so he was glad that she agreed to step in. With her and the boys around, he still got a sense of family.

~

GOING AGAINST HIS BETTER JUDGMENT, YOSOHN WALKED INTO the Roosevelt Inn to meet Jocelyn. Loneliness, drugs, and alcohol played a role in Yosohn going against his better judgment and meeting her. He needed a sexual release and a random bitch just wouldn't do.

"Hey, boo," Jocelyn purred, as Yosohn entered her room.

"Wassup?" Yosohn said dryly before sitting down in the chair by the bed. He looked at Jocelyn and couldn't help feeling a bit of resentment. As beautiful as she was, she really was no good for him. She was like sweet poison. He knew if he took it, he would harm himself. He couldn't stand the sight of Jocelyn, but he was more focused on his own selfish needs.

"You said you wanted to talk to me, right?" he asked.

"Yeah ... You wanna hit this first?" she asked, passing him a lit blunt. Yosohn declined.

"I'll take something to drink if you have it though."

Jocelyn grabbed a clean Styrofoam cup off her dresser and poured him some Pepsi. Yosohn took it and quickly threw it back on his parched throat.

"So wassup with you and ya bullshit?" he frowned, sitting his cup down on a nearby nightstand. "Why the fuck would you call her and blow my shit up like that?"

"I couldn't reach you."

"Okay? And? So, fucking what? That's some corny shit you did. You got me going through a bunch of bullshit. My household turned all upside down. Why would I even want to fuck with you after all that?" he questioned while eying her angrily. Jocelyn looked at Yosohn and couldn't answer the question, so he continued.

"Look, Jocelyn, the situation could've worked out for you, but you fucked it up 'cuz you got out of line. That's my situation. That's my wife. That's me. You should've played yo' position."

"My position Yosohn? My position? What position is that?" she scoffed. "If you haven't noticed, I live in a fuckin motel," she argued, throwing her hands up for emphasis. "I ride around on the fuckin' bus while you and ya bitch ride in foreign's. I suck ya dick and you fuck me whenever it's good for you. When you call, I'm supposed to answer, but when I call you, I don't get an answer. One minute you fuck with me and don't want to lose me, but I don't see you rushing to put me in a new car or put me in an apartment. Did you ever ask if I needed anything? I struggle every day," she admitted. "On top of that, I was feeling you. How was I supposed to feel?" Jocelyn explained, laying the truth out on the table.

For a few seconds, Yosohn was at a loss for words, more so because everything she was saying was true.

"I would've helped you," Yosohn lied. He would've thrown her a little something but setting her up like a kept bitch wasn't happening.

"Whatever," Jocelyn replied, rolling her eyes.

"Look, I ain't come here to argue. Come here," Yosohn motioned for her to come closer. That's all it took. Yosohn's wish was her command. She got up and sat down on his lap.

"Why don't we forget about what we were just arguing about and just enjoy the night?" he slurred. The Henny had him buzzed and carefree. He just wanted to enjoy his time while he was there. He used his hand to turn Jocelyn's chin so she could face him.

"You gon' give me what I've been missing?" Yosohn asked.

Jocelyn forced back her tears. He was doing it again. Making her feel wanted and needed. But all he was going to do is make her feel it … and then take it away. She knew she should have said no. She knew she should have asked him to leave but she didn't. Instead, she nodded in agreement and then got off his lap. She was going to please her man; however, she was going to start making plans to get something out of it.

Jocelyn rose from Yosohn's lap and dropped to her knees. As she began unbuckling his pants, she noticed that Yosohn's head was slightly tilt and was swaying side to side. He rubbed his forehead, then the side of his face, and then his beard. Jocelyn stopped for a moment and observed him. A light film of perspiration coated his forehead. His pupils looked dilated. Yosohn was high as a kite ... and that's exactly how she wanted him.

CHAPTER 13

"*I*'m *not trying to do anything. And as you can see, I'm a big girl, and I can handle whatever consequences that come from what I do.*" Serenity remembered saying the words but now she wished she could take them back. She had screwed up... *big time.* She felt Mann's naked, muscular body pressed against her own. Her head throbbed and her weave lay wild and untamed against the white hotel pillowcase. Somehow, they had ended up in the bed. She didn't remember the whole night, only vague parts. She honestly didn't want to remember. Mann being in her bed was bad news for the both. Serenity slowly and quietly crawled out of the bed so she wouldn't wake Mann.

"Hey, where you going?" he asked. She froze. She had hoped he remained asleep; the situation was already awkward enough.

"I'm just going to get myself together," she replied stiffly. She didn't turn around to face him. He reached and gently grabbed her arm, stopping her from getting up.

"You okay?" he asked.

"Yeah, I'm fine," she replied. She already knew what he

meant. He wanted to know how she was feeling about what had just happened.

"We need to talk … I was thinking we could go to breakfast," he suggested, sitting up.

"I don't know about that —" she started, but Mann quickly cut her off.

"I mean, I know we can't go anywhere around here, but we can drive out somewhere and talk there. Listen, I don't want you to worry about anything ok," he stated. "I know this situation is kind of crazy, but at the same time it was I don' regret it. And we need to talk about it."

"Yeah but Yosohn is going to fucking go ballistic if he finds out —"

Feeling his jaw tightening, Mann paused and took a deep breath. "Listen, we'll deal with Yosohn when the time comes. But right now, we need to talk about things."

Serenity stared ahead. There was no way she was letting Yosohn find out about what they had done.

"Okay," she reluctantly agreed.

YOSOHN ROSE FROM THE HOTEL BED FEELING A BIT disoriented. His head pounded against his skull. He wiped at his eyes and blinked a few times as they adjusted to the light. Yosohn looked back and saw Jocelyn sleeping peacefully. He drew in a deep breath and sighed. A sick feeling lingered in the pit of his stomach at the sight of her. Yosohn knew that to get his life on track, he had to rid his life of her completely. *Fuck is wrong with you?* he thought to himself. *You risking your entire relationship and life over a fuck?*

Yosohn knew that he needed to grow up and start making better choices. He needed to stop hurting Serenity. He glanced back down at Jocelyn. He knew he was about to hurt her even more. He couldn't keep seeing her on the side. He wanted his life back and he knew he was never going to get it if he kept seeing Jocelyn.

Yosohn threw on his clothes and boots and left Jocelyn sleeping. As he walked to his truck he reached into his pocket and pulled out his phone to call Serenity. Of course, she didn't answer. He figured he would ride by her mother's house to see if she was there. It had been long enough. He wanted her back and he was going to do whatever it took. Yosohn knew he did a lot of wrong, but he loved Serenity. He was about to start showing it.

MANN ALREADY KNEW THAT YOSOHN WAS GOING TO SOON BE A major issue if he found out about what happened between him and Serenity. He knew that he had crossed the line by sleeping with her. But the problem was the line had already been crossed. He really liked Serenity. He didn't want her to go back to Yosohn. He didn't deserve a woman like her. Serenity didn't deserve a man like Yosohn. She deserved a man like him. A man that would love her and take care of her. A man that would help her achieve her goals. Lastly, a man that would put his own needs and wants aside to make sure she was happy. He would never cheat on a woman like Serenity. He wouldn't ever inflict that kind of pain on her.

"Whatchu thinkin' about over there?" he asked Serenity, coming out of his own thoughts. She was being extremely quiet, and it was making him nervous. They had been at the quaint diner for quite some time and she had barely said a word.

"What we did was fucked up Mann," she blurted out. She stared at him with a worried look on her face. "I was drinking, and I let my emotions cloud my judgment. What I did was out of spite and I don't want to come between you and Yosohn. Y'all been friends for a long time," she admitted.

Tears welled up in her dark eyes as she sat and analyzed the damage that she had done. She felt so guilty. She wanted to take what happened to the grave. She just hoped that he was willing to do the same. Serenity used her fork to continue to pick at her uneaten breakfast.

"I know it's a lot to absorb but everything does happen for a reason. I mean you two are separated, and you have been living apart for months."

"True," she said, lowering her eyes back down to her plate.

"I'm not trying to step on Yosohn's toes, 'cuz he is my nigga ... but I think this could be something bigger. Now I know you're used to Yosohn taking care of you but he not the only one that can do that," he said.

He had money but not the kind of money Yosohn did. He would real soon though after putting in a little work. He just needed a little time. She looked up at Mann and gave a half-smile. She was flattered that he liked her, but they could never be. Besides, it wasn't about the money with her. She loved Yosohn. If he changed and stopped cheating, then he was the man that she wanted to be with. What worried her was the fact that Mann even wanted to pursue a relationship with her when Yosohn was his friend. He knew just as well as she did that Yosohn wasn't going for that. It would destroy their friendship... maybe even lead to something more. It didn't seem like Mann was concerned one bit about any of that.

About a half hour after leaving the restaurant, Mann pulled up to his new home and turned off his Dodge Charger. He looked over at Serenity and smiled. He hoped she liked it.

"This the new house ya real estate friend hooked me up with. Remember you referred me to him. I've been in it for a few weeks now," he smiled. When he took her to breakfast, he purposely drove thirty minutes outside the city to the small town of Blue Bell, Pennsylvania where he had just bought a house for him and his grandmother. He wanted her to see it so she could get an idea of what he could give her.

"I do," she grinned. "Steve." Serenity carefully admired the house. It was beautiful. It was a single-story home, but it had a beautiful wrap around porch and gorgeous, colorful land-scaping. "This is beautiful. Steve really hooked you up," she gushed, while continuing to marvel at the home and neigh-borhood. It made her miss her own home more.

"You wanna see inside?" he asked. He didn't wait for an answer. He opened the door and hopped out.

"Yeah sure," she mumbled and exited out of the car. They walked into the home and Serenity found it was just as lovely inside as it was out, with up-to-date fixtures throughout.

"I wanted it to be two-story, but my grandma can't walk up the steps that good. I want her to be comfortable and able to enjoy it all without getting too tired," he explained.

"Well, that was thoughtful of you," she said, still admiring the details of Mann's new home. After looking around the house, Serenity asked Mann to take her to pick up her car. She had to pick up Heaven and check on the laundromats to ensure everything was running smoothly. Mann agreed since he too had some business to handle. He enjoyed the short time he spent with Serenity but also had to go since Yosohn had been calling and texting him non-stop most of the morning. He wasn't sure exactly what he wanted but he figured he needed to hit him back and see. Mann pulled up to the parking lot near the club where they had left Serenity's car. Without thinking, Mann got out with Serenity and walked her the short distance to where her car was parked.

"So, am I gon' see you again?" he asked, getting straight to the point. Hesitating, Serenity responded.

"I don't know if that's a good idea Mann." I want things to go back to normal and for us to remain friends," she said as sweetly as possible.

"So, you're going back to Yosohn?" he asked almost jealously. Serenity exhaled, slightly frustrated.

"Mann, look. You a cool ass dude. You are. But me and you can't be. It would be bad. You know that. Our circumstances won't allow us to be. I mean — I love Yosohn and I can't say what I'm honestly going to do. I may or I may not. I don't know. But whatever choice I make, I can't be with you. "

"But you could fuck me tho?" he asked snidely.

Serenity smacked her teeth. "You know what we did was a mistake. What's with all the extra shit. I mean … Let's be logical. Y'all friends. You been to our house. You and him have business together. All that's dead if we were to even try to be together."

"I know that," he said blankly.

"Mann … Look, I gotta go. What we did was wrong, and I'd like to keep it between us."

"I respect it," Mann said before saying goodbye and seeing her off.

Mann sighed and walked back to his vehicle. The truth was, he didn't respect it. He believed that if you wanted something, you should do whatever it was to get it.

CHAPTER 14

"What's up bull. Where you been at? I been calling you all morning nigga?" Yosohn waited for a response through his car speakers. He actually was a little irritated that he had to call and text Mann several times before he finally called back. He wasn't used to being on hold for anyone and that included Mann.

Fucking ya wifey, is what Mann really wanted to say in response to Yosohn's question, but he figured that wouldn't be the best response. After sleeping with Serenity, Mann's feelings for his friend Yosohn changed instantly. He really liked Serenity and he felt that she deserved better. Most of all, he wanted her for himself. Some niggas had it all and didn't deserve it; Yosohn was one of them.

"My bad. My phone had died. I hit you back as soon as I got home and put it on the charger," he answered.

"Oh. You must have been creeping last night. Let me find out you was laid up all night with' a hoe." Yosohn laughed jokingly.

"Na my nigga. I don't do hoes," Mann replied.

"I hear that." Yosohn responded. "But look, I hit you up because I wanted you to run down the numbers for what you talked about the other day."

Mann thought for a second and then remembered what Yosohn spoke of.

"Cool. Just let me know when you want to meet up and I'll let you know what I had in mind."

The two men made plans to meet later, but first Yosohn had to handle a few important things.

YOSOHN ROCKED HIS HEAD TO KEVIN GATE'S LATEST SONG AND waited for Serenity to pull up to her mother's house. It was Soul Food Sunday, and he knew she would be showing up to eat with her family. She never missed it.

After about another thirty minutes of smoking and waiting, she finally pulled up. He mashed his blunt out into the ashtray and watched at her as she walked up. She had on a pink Victoria's Secret sweat suit and wore her hair up in a messy bun. Before she could walk up the steps to Gina's home, he started up the car and drove closer to the house, honking twice so she would notice it was him. Serenity stopped to look and quickly recognized a waving Yosohn; however, she didn't recognize the vehicle he was in. After allowing the temp tags to register in her brain, she immediately knew what he was up to. She rolled her eyes.

"Hey babe," he called out to her with a smile, his head hanging out the window. He hopped out of the car and quickly approached her. He looked at her and then pointed to the brand new 2020, egg white Audi Q56.

"That's yours. An early Christmas gift," he said, hoping she liked it. He wanted to make the conversation quick since it was cold out.

"Thanks, but no thanks," she replied sharply, before continuing to walk up the steps. She wasn't impressed. Before she could make it to the top Yosohn gently grabbed her arm.

"Yo come here. Come here," he motioned quickly, turning her to face him. Serenity huffed and waited for him to talk.

"Look, I know that I haven't been the best. I fucked up, but I promise to change. I want you to take the truck and I want you to come home," he said with sincerity.

Serenity let out another huff and turned around to face him. Despite how angry she was, she undoubtedly loved him. She looked into his eyes for some sign of sincerity. She saw a glimmer of hope.

"Yosohn, you always say you gon' change but I don't see you doing anything but making me look like a fool. You think I care about a truck?" she scoffed. "I don't care about that. I already have a car and you already know that I was never with you for what you could do for me. So, don't come over here thinking you can buy your way back into my life. I want a man, not gifts!" she said sternly before walking off up the steps and into the house.

Seeing the door slam in his face, Yosohn felt defeated. He wanted to grab Serenity by her bun and throw her ass in the truck; however, he didn't want to cause a scene in front of Gina's house. He wasn't sure what else to do. He'd been begging and apologizing for months. Serenity was being very stubborn and truthfully, she had every right to be. The average man would have given up. Yosohn refused to do that.

LATER THAT DAY, YOSOHN PULLED UP TO THE BEAUTIFUL, colonial stone home of his former friend Hakim. He made it a priority to stop by and check on Nikki and the kids to make sure they were doing okay and didn't need anything.

"Uncle Yosohnnnn," Hakim's youngest child Xavier called to him in a melodic manner. Xavier was five years old and was cute as a button with a chocolatey complexion like his dad. He had on an Iron Man shirt and his black Jordan's were on the wrong feet. Yosohn laughed at the adorable sight in front of him and got out of the car. He scooped his nephew up and hugged him tightly. When Hakim passed, Yosohn vowed to remain a permanent fixture and positive male figure in the boy's lives.

"Hey little man! How you been?" Yosohn asked, swinging him around before putting him down.

"I'm good Uncle Yosohn. Where've you been? And I thought you said you were going to take me to see the mouse man." Yosohn had told the boys he was going to take them to Chuckie Cheese, but it had innocently slipped his mind.

"Awww, my fault buddy, I forgot. How about ... you go get your brother and if it's okay with your mom, I'll take you both now." Yosohn didn't mind. It was Sunday and it wasn't like he had anything else to do.

"But Xavier, you gotta do one thing for me before we leave," Yosohn stopped his nephew and looked at him with a serious face. He dropped to a squat, lowering himself to the child's level.

"What?" he asked with his eyes wide, excited to tell his brother that they were headed to the arcade."

"You gotta put them shoes on the right feet. Swag 101. Girl don't like boys with mismatch, clumsy feet," he whispered before laughing. Xavier giggled and ran back into the house to get his older brother Hakim Jr., who was busy playing on his Xbox.

"Nikki!" Yosohn yelled, walking into the house. As usual,

the place was impeccably clean and warm, while a pleasant aroma emanated from the kitchen.

"Hey, Yosohn," Nikki emerged smiling. She wiped her wet hands on a towel to dry them. She looked very pretty with her hair up in a knotted bun and a Chinese bang covering her eyes. With her light skin and thick frame, she resembled the model Blac Chyna. "I just finished making the boys some lasagna. You want some?"

"Hell, yeah. I ain't had a home-cooked meal since—" He stopped himself. Nikki looked at him and felt a bit sorry for him. She knew he loved Serenity, and she knew that she still hadn't gone back to him. She and Serenity had become a bit closer after Hakim passed since Serenity consistently reached out to check on her and the kids.

"How are you?" she asked with concern. "I know you come by here to check and make sure I'm good, but how are you holding up?" she asked. He knew what she was asking, and it wasn't regarding Hakim.

"I've been better," he admitted. "I'm just empty you know," he said before taking a seat at the built-in kitchen bar. "From everything. Losing Hakim. Losing Serenity … I try to fill my life with people I love. You… the kids. But I'm missing her and Heaven. She doesn't see it, but I love her a lot. She's my world. I don't want to lose her. I don't want to lose anyone else," he said with sincerity. If he were a bitch nigga he would have cried. But he was a G and he refused to let tears escape his eyes.

"I'll talk to her," Nikki said. "I know we aren't the closest, but she'll value a female opinion. You just gotta wake up. You say she's your world … well treat her like it. Look what Hakim lost. You may not lose in the same way, but ultimately you will still lose. Is she worth losing?" she questioned.

"Not at all," he answered.

"Well show her," Nikki said, ending the conversation by

sliding Yosohn a plate of lasagna with some garlic bread and a glass of tea.

"Eat up. You gon' need your energy to keep up with them bad ass boys. They told me you are taking them to Chuckie Cheese."

"Yeah. As soon as I finish eating and Xavier figure out which shoe go on which foot," he laughed.

CHAPTER 15

With her knee-length pea coat wrapped around her body tightly for added warmth, the crisp air felt refreshing against Serenity's face as she made her way up the manicured walkway of her home. It had been several months since she had been to the home her and Yosohn once shared, and the warm feeling it brought to her reinforced that she deeply missed being there. After speaking with Nikki the night before, she decided to go and talk with Yosohn. Keeping her word, Nikki reached out to Serenity after Yosohn had taken the boys to Chuckie Cheese. Although she knew Nikki's opinion about cheating would be different from hers because Nikki had willingly endured it so long, she decided to listen to someone who knew and loved Yosohn like she did.

Serenity didn't know how her conversation with Yosohn was going to go, but she did know that eventually, a decision would need to be made. She knew she needed to decide on whether she was going to move forward with Yosohn or make peace with the life they had and move on. She knew no one was perfect. She had to live with mistakes of her own. If the shoe were on the other foot, she'd want a second chance. However, she hated to compare her wrongs to Yosohn'. To her, sleeping with Mann was a mistake, while Yosohn's constant cheating was a choice.

Serenity used her key to let herself in and was shocked at what she saw. Empty bottles of Hennessey were scattered throughout the living room floor, while empty pizza boxes lay strewn around. The house was downright filthy. She walked into the kitchen and saw dishes filling the sink and nets quietly buzzing around them. Serenity made her way to the bedroom and prayed Yosohn was alone. She hoped he hadn't stooped to the ultimate level of disrespect by bringing another bitch into the home that carried both their names on the deed.

"Yosohn," she called after pushing the door open.

She breathed a sigh of relief once she saw he was alone. However, her heart instantly ached when she saw him passed out sleep on the floor. He hadn't even made it to the bed. A small trashcan that contained vomit stood beside him. She knew he had at some point been in a drunken stupor. Serenity got out her phone and called Merry Maids, a cleaning franchise that she used several times a year for her heavy-duty cleaning. She had quickly decided that several months of filth was not going to be cleaned up by her. After arranging for them to come out in the morning, Serenity once again tried to wake up Yosohn.

"Yosohn," she called again. This time he opened his eyes and abruptly turned over. He was happy to see her but knew he looked like shit. He felt like it.

"Hey, babe," he looked up and whispered hoarsely, before gently lying his head back down on the floor.

"Yosohn, you gotta get up and get yourself together. I have the cleaning company on the way. And we need to talk."

Yosohn slowly pushed himself up to his feet and sat on the bed. He had been waiting months to sit down with her and he felt a glimmer of hope fill his chest. If he could get Serenity back, he vowed he wouldn't lose her again. He would make her happy. He'd do whatever he needed to do.

CHAPTER 16

J ocelyn dialed Yosohn's number again and listened to the message that was playing. She wanted to make sure she had heard it correctly. *"The number you have called is not in service. Please check the number and try your call again."* She slammed her phone down in anger before lying back on the faded hotel comforter. It had been over a month since she'd seen or spoken to Yosohn. At first, she thought it may have been a mistake until time passed. He'd changed his number.

Jocelyn knew she would find him eventually. Yosohn's laundromat addresses were public, and she would eventually run into him sooner or later. Truthfully, she didn't have the energy to chase Yosohn down. Literally. Just like most mornings, she'd been throwing up and hadn't been able to keep much down except some ginger ale and crackers. She knew her pregnancy wasn't going to be an easy one. She couldn't wait to share the news with Yosohn. She already knew how he was going to take it. *He'll hate me for a while, but eventually, he'll learn to love me*, she thought. The baby would bring them together, just like she had planned.

~

SERENITY WALKED INTO THE SMALL, SOUL-FOOD CAFÉ ON Cheltenham Avenue and peered around. She smiled when she saw her sister Shameka sitting at a small table in a corner by the window.

"Hey, Meek," she said, as she approached the table and sat down.

"Hey, girl. 'Bout time you got here, I'm hungry as shit and you were taking forever," she complained.

"Whatever. Ain't nobody tell you to bring yo' ass early," Serenity responded. "I told you 12 o'clock, and it's 12:05," she stated, placing emphasis on the times. "We're waiting on Naomi anyway. She'll be here shortly."

"I'm not waiting on her ass. You are. I'm about to order something to eat," Shameka countered bluntly before picking her menu back up off the table.

Serenity couldn't help but laugh at her sister. Shameka was very forward and outspoken just like her other sister Shanita. The only thing was Shameka had even less patience and was quick to — as she liked to put it, *put paws on a bitch*.

Shameka was a short and cute curvy chick. She always had a head full of wavy curls and kept a pair of four-inch heels on. However, she was quick to kick them off and go in the trunk of her Dodge Durango and pull out her Air Force One's if she had to. She was spicy like that.

"There Naomi go now," Serenity said, looking over to the door. She was glad that she showed up when she did. She was hungry as lawd knows what. Shameka didn't even bother to look up. Instead, she continued to focus on her menu.

Shameka didn't particularly care much for Naomi since she found her bourgeois and unauthentic. She still did her best to be as polite as she could without being fake

"Hey, boo!" Naomi said, greeting Serenity. "Hey, Shameka!"

"Hey, girl," Serenity responded to her friend while quietly shaking her head at her sister who hadn't bothered to respond. Naomi took off her pea-coat and took a seat.

"So how you been? I haven't seen you in forever." Naomi didn't seem to mind the blatant disregard from Shameka. She was used to it.

"I been busy with home and class. The laundromats have been hectic also. A pipe burst a week ago and it was water everywhere. We had to close for a few days. It cost a grip to fix."

"Damnnn. That's crazy. It has been cold as fuck though'. I can only imagine how that went."

"Definitely. Yosohn cried like a baby when they told him how much it was going to be to fix it," Serenity laughed.

"Yosohn so gotdamn cheap," Shameka chimed in. She liked Yosohn and knew of his notorious penny-pinching ways.

"Yesssss, honey. But will spend hundreds of dollars per month on his smoke. He kills me with that shit. But that's my boo though'."

"Yeah now he is ... He wasn't a month ago," Shameka laughed.

"Whatever hoe, mind ya business," Serenity laughed. It had only been a month since her and Yosohn had gotten back together, but for the most part, she was happy.

"So, what's up with ya boy Mann? I tried to call him, but he stopped responding completely," Naomi said.

Serenity grew uncomfortable at the mere mention of Mann. She hadn't seen Mann in almost a month. She didn't want to flat out tell Yosohn that she didn't want him at the house since he would question her about why. They conducted business, and Mann was his friend, so Yosohn wouldn't understand her reasoning if she stated such. Instead, she told him she wanted them to work on getting their house back to a home and preferred to stay private for a while. Yosohn still allowed him to come by but not as often. When he did show up, Serenity would scurry to her room and pretend to be sleep.

"Girl, that's Yosohn's boy, not mine. I was just trying to be a matchmaker," Serenity replied "And I don't know what's up with him ... The nigga just weird sometimes." She knew why he wasn't answering his phone; he was too busy calling her instead. He made it noticeably clear with his voicemails and text messages that he was very interested in Serenity. It was hard for her to even address his disrespectful behavior since she didn't want to be at odds with him. And she couldn't tell Yosohn because then she would be basically throwing herself under the bus.

"Yeah, he does act odd," Naomi agreed. "I think he likes you," she said bluntly, surprising Serenity. She looked to Serenity and waited for a response to her random statement.

"*What?*" Serenity said with a cough. "Na. I don't think so ... What happened to the dude you were talking to that you told me you met in Jollies?" Serenity asked, referring to a popular bar in North Philly. She wanted to change the subject.

"Girl, nothing. He was mess, a user ... A lot of these dudes are. Times have changed, and a lot of these niggas be trying to live off females. The shit is sad."

"They definitely do, but it depends on how you carry yaself that determines what type of men you attract," Shameka said, butting in rudely.

Serenity decided to get off the subject of men completely. She didn't want her ignorant ass sister saying something else dumb. Shameka always thought Naomi was a weak broad that faked her confidence. She always expressed how Naomi seemed thirsty, desperate, and shady. Shameka agreed that she was indeed a beautiful girl, albeit overweight. Although she carried her weight well, she still detected insecurity. Shameka couldn't understand why Serenity couldn't pick up on it.

"There's our food," Serenity stated. She was glad they could eat and put an end to the conversation.

~

AFTER LUNCH, SERENITY AND SHAMEKA WALKED THROUGH Michael's Arts and Craft Store looking for decorations for Gina's upcoming birthday party. It was the middle of January and her birthday was in a few weeks.

"These are cute. We can make some nice glass center-pieces," Shameka said, picking up a nice but affordable "do it yourself" set.

"Yeah, they are nice. Get nine of them. The room we're renting has ten tables. The main table, the one Mommy's going to be at is going to be set up differently."

"Ok ... Let me ask you a question, Ren." Shameka said curiously.

"Why you look like that when Naomi started talking about Yosohn's friend?"

"Who Mann?" Serenity asked, playing dumb.

"Bitch you know who I'm talking about?" she laughed.

"I ain't look no type of way ... Naomi likes him but honestly, he's not interested in her like that. Naomi is kind of aggressive with guys though, and I don't want to hurt her feelings by telling her she needs to tone it down a little," Serenity confessed.

"Which one is Mann anyway? I remember Hakim, the one that died but I don't think I ever met Mann."

"Umm, he got a bald head—kind of dark skinned. Hood ass nigga that got a black Dodge Charger."

"Ohhhh ok. I met him at the house. He was outside talking to Yosohn when I dropped off Heaven … He fine as hell."

"Yeah, he okay," Serenity said, desperate to end the conversation. She wasn't sure why Shameka nosy ass brought him up.

"Does he really like you like Naomi said?"

Serenity laughed. Her sister was so persistent. "Yeah, he does … but—" she began, before Shameka cut her off.

"Un huh. I knew you looked like that for a reason. He is fine though … I'd piss all on that bald head if he asked," she laughed.

"Would you shut the fuck up!" Serenity laughed hysterically. "You say anything out yo' ratchet ass mouth."

"I say what a bitch wants to say but won't. Let me find out you want to give Mann some of yo' milk and cookies," Shameka teased in her best Bernie Mac imitation. "Or maybe yo' little sneaky ass has already," she suggested.

"Girl, bye! I'm going to the car. You're paying."

"Yeah alright bitch. Those tables will be as bald as Mann's head," she joked, before the two walked up to the sales counter to pay for their items.

CHAPTER 17

Yosohn fumbled with his keys as he struggled to get his front door open. It was bitterly cold, and Mann was standing behind him blowing onto his hands, while rubbing them together vigorously for warmth. Once entering the house, they hung up their coats and took a seat in the den. Serenity suddenly appeared from the back room and was ready to greet Yosohn but stopped abruptly when she saw he wasn't alone.

"Shit," she said aloud when she saw Mann's beady eyes staring at her. She hated when Yosohn just popped up at the house with company. And she had already told him she preferred some alone time around the house.

"Yoooo, go put some fuckin clothes on, we got company," Yosohn said once Serenity came out.

He walked out of the room to follow her, attempting to block all the ass she had on display. Mann had already saw her and made no attempt to redirect his gaze when she came out. Yosohn didn't notice his roaming eyes, but Serenity noticed.

"I don't know what you snappin' for. I told yo' ass I didn't want a whole bunch of company. I can't walk around my own damn house 'cuz you got his baldheaded ass here," she argued.

Yosohn laughed lightly. "We got some business to handle, and besides, it's three in the afternoon and you got ya whole fuckin' big, black ass hanging out. I thought you was cool with Mann though?" he asked jokingly.

Serenity had on some boy shorts that clung to the middle of her ass. The rest of her backside was exposed. She dug quickly dug through her dresser and threw some sweatpants over the shorts. She didn't bother to change her half-shirt.

"How long y'all gon' be?" she asked, irritated and ignoring the question he asked. She didn't want Mann's wierdo ass hanging around all day. The whole situation was already awkward enough and he wasn't making it any better staring at her when he came around.

"I don't know," he shrugged. "We got some important shit to handle."

"Well, wrap it up, Yosohn, I want it to just be us, and I want to be able to walk around, — with my ass hanging out, especially since my name is on the damn deed," she reminded him.

"Yeah, well pay the mortgage then," he said sarcastically.

"Yeah. Ok smart ass. You do payroll, use QuickBooks, and write a business plan. When you learn to do that, then I'll be happy to switch places with you and *just* pay the mortgage," she said with a satisfied smile.

"You stay talking shit," he laughed. "You got me though, I'll take care of the mortgage … and I got something for that smart mouth later," he added, before walking out.

Serenity laughed to herself and shook her head while Yosohn headed back out to do business with his friend.

∽

THE FOLLOWING DAY, SERENITY SAT ON THE FLOOR OF HER spacious bathroom and read the plastic stick she was holding for the second time. She had taken two tests and this one said the same thing: POSITIVE. She was pregnant. After eating her normal light breakfast, Serenity didn't feel so well. Nausea and dizziness invaded her body shortly after consuming the small meal. She hadn't missed a period, but she had been experiencing bouts of tiredness over the past week. Today she decided to confirm her suspicions. Serenity was happy that the fertility treatments she had months back had been successful, but she was now faced with a new problem: she wasn't sure if the baby was Yosohn's. She didn't remember a whole lot from the night she slept with Mann. What she did remember was that Mann didn't use protection and she cursed herself for not being smart enough, or responsible enough to get emergency contraception after the encounter.

She didn't plan to say anything about the pregnancy until after she met with Dr. Davis. She had already called him, and he had told her to come in that week. He would confirm the pregnancy and then perform an intravaginal ultrasound to determine how far along she was. She prayed she wasn't too far in the pregnancy. She and Yosohn had recently become intimate again and if it were his, she wouldn't be any more than around six weeks pregnant. Anything past that would make the baby Mann's. Serenity took a deep breath and hoped for the best.

∽

SERENITY TURNED OFF THE ENGINE AND TOOK OUT THE KEYS of the new truck Yosohn had purchased her. Even though she wasn't initially impressed with the gift, she still happily accepted it once she moved back in. She couldn't lie, it was dope. The Audi was gorgeous inside and out, and she had to admit she loved every bit of it.

After moving back into their home, life went back to normal for the three and Serenity had been busier than ever. She was almost to the end of her master's degree program and was about to begin her practicum, which was basically several semesters of her applying all that she had learned from graduate school in a practical business setting. She was having trouble coming up with ideas about ways to apply what she had learned to her business. Since she knew she wouldn't be able to fully juggle her coursework and conduct business, she and Yosohn decided that they would promote her assistant Susan, who helped her with the laundromats, as well as hire another full-time attendant. Serenity wanted to focus on finishing her degree.

Yosohn had been unusually sweet to her since she had moved back in. Serenity figured it was because of her absence. She knew he loved her, but she sometimes didn't know if that love alone was enough to keep him on the right track. He did make some changes, starting with changing his phone number and committing to being home every night by nine for dinner. She prayed they made it. Lord knows she loved him.

"Hey, Susie Q," Serenity said to her top employee when she walked into the office of Squeaky Clean 4, which was located at 21st and Lehigh. It was their largest laundromat and it also was also the location of their main office.

"Hey, Serenity, how are you?" Susan asked.

Susan was an older, short, and plump Puerto Rican lady who she had known for many years. She met Susan when she opened her very first laundromat. She knew she would need help when she first started and decided to reach out into the poor community to give someone a job. To find help, she walked into the welfare office workforce center off Lehigh and saw Susan diligently searching for jobs. She hired her on the spot. She was an awesome employee and was an incredible asset to Squeaky Clean. She and Yosohn both adored her.

"How's it going?" she asked.

"Laid back really. I had to put a few people out who were loitering and stealing muffins and coffee," Susan replied.

"Oh, you mean the homeless guys?" Serenity asked, her brows raised.

"Yeah, unfortunately."

"Ok. Well, we can't have them standing around, but next time, go ahead and let them grab whatever's up there. I don't want to turn them away if they're hungry. After that, they do have to move out the front," Serenity instructed, while going over an inventory sheet.

"Okey dokey, boss lady ... Oh! I forgot to tell you someone came by here for you today." She snapped her finger profusely trying to remember what he said his name was.

"What did he look like?" Serenity asked, after Susan failed to remember after a few seconds.

"Oh, umm, he was kind of tall ... Well, taller than me ... Dark-skinned, bald head — drove a black sporty looking car. "

"Oh ok, Susan. I know who it is ... Thanks," she grumbled.

She knew it was only Mann's ass. She hadn't seen him in over a month before yesterday, and he still was tripping over what happened.

"Oh yeah, he left his number. I put it on your desk."

"Ok, I'll grab it. Thanks, Susan."

She was going to rip the number up as soon as she got the

opportunity. Besides, she already knew Mann's number. She had called him and Hakim both on multiple occasions when she couldn't reach Yosohn. She wondered why he felt the need to show up at her place of business looking for her when Yosohn could have been present. He was up to something. She just didn't know what.

CHAPTER 18

Mann walked into his home carrying a noisy, plastic bag that held soup and tea. He had drove all the way into Philadelphia to get the items and hoped his grandmother would be able to hold it down on her weak stomach. Mann closed his door but didn't bother to lock it since the neighborhood was extremely safe. He didn't even own a security system yet. He planned to get one as soon as he returned from New York in a few days.

"Hey, Grandma," he said with a bright smile.

Mann's grandmother Darlene was laying in her queen-sized bed watching Good Times. It was one of her favorite shows, so Mann went and found her several seasons on Blue Ray.

"Hey, baby," Darlene responded with a profound cough. The cough sounded like it came from the deep pits of her soul. Her chest heaved and her body shook as she let it out.

"You okay?" he asked with concern.

Darlene had been sick for several weeks and her health was deteriorating because of her age. In just a couple of weeks she had been to the hospital several times. It pained him to see her in the condition she was in. Lately, he had begun thinking about how he would carry on his life without her when the time came.

She and his cousin Ezekiel or Zeke were pretty much the closest things he had to him. Zeke's mom had died from drug abuse just like his own mother. While Zeke was primarily in and out, Mann took care of his grandmother Darlene. Their living family members were so selfish that they didn't even bother to reach out or check on her. For that reason, Mann didn't acknowledge them. It was as if they never existed.

"I'm okay, Manny; just a little under the weather, baby," she replied hoarsely, calling him what she had called him for years. Everyone else called him Mann, which was a nickname derived from his given name Damon, but Darlene called him Manny.

"Well, I got you some soup and the tea you like from 4th street … Where's Sonya?" he asked. Sonya was the caregiver he hired to take care of her while he was out. She didn't need around the clock care, so he paid Sonya to be there full time in the morning.

She would help Darlene bathe, get dressed, take her medications, and would also prepare all her meals for the day. The remainder of the day, Darlene would watch T.V and sometimes Mann would drive her into Philadelphia to see some of her elderly friends or play bingo. At one point she had been fond of the slot machines at the Sugar House Casino, but once her health began to fail her, she stopped going. Mann was secretly happy since she could easily go in there and waste hundreds of dollars. He wasn't into squandering his money, but he wouldn't dare tell her no since she had provided and cared for him since he was a baby.

Both he and Zeke's moms were fast girls living in a big city. They partied, had loads of fun and tried different drugs. When crack hit the scene in the 80's, their young lives were cheated the chance to blossom properly because the drug ravaged through the community and devastated families. Mann's mother was killed when he was twelve. She had been found alongside the Schuylkill River in West Philadelphia. The cops ruled it most likely drug-related. To them, she was just another dead crackhead.

Zeke's mother would eventually end up in a dangerous love affair with Heroin when crack was no longer good enough for her. She too would eventually succumb to an overdose.

Darlene raised the two side by side the best she could and loved them as well as she knew how. His grandmother was his life and his hero.

"I told Sonya she could go get some lunch. She took care of everything for me and I could tell she was hungry," she said, responding to Mann's earlier question. She was smiling. For as long as he could remember, she always had a smile on her face, even when things were bad.

"Oh, that's cool. Well, look, Grandma, I have some business to handle. I'm gon' leave your soup by your bed in case you want some before Sonya gets back. There's a spoon and straw in the bag."

He walked over and gave her a kiss on her thin brown cheek and left for his own room. He had to call Zeke. The "come up" day as Mann liked to call it, was swiftly approaching and he wanted to make sure he and Zeke were on the same page since the plans had changed up a little. There was no room for error.

After speaking with Zeke, Mann went to the bathroom and rummaged around his medicine cabinet. He was looking for the Tylenol 3's he had grabbed off someone. For as long as he could remember, he dealt with migraines. Lately, they had been exceptionally brutal, and he needed something a little stronger to alleviate the pain.

As a child he was diagnosed with depression and anxiety that stemmed from him feeling abandoned by his mother. He remembered having the same terrible headaches then. When his mother died it was a traumatic experience for him, especially because of his young and fragile mental state. He was too young to understand that she was sick and because of this he always felt like he was an inadequate child, incapable of being able to get something that should be a given in life: the love of one's mother. In his mind, she had already chosen drugs over him, so when she died that simply solidified that her love for drugs surpassed her love for him. The few people he had left, he loved them fiercely and wanted to hold onto them for dear life. It was one way with Mann. He either cared for you intensely or you were in his way and he would run you over. It was that simple.

With his grandmother becoming sick, his deepest fears resurfaced. What would he do if she left him? He knew it was inevitable; she was old. He knew when the day came, he would have trouble coping, so he focused on the positive. He planned to fill the void he knew would exist in his heart. Although Darlene was irreplaceable, he knew Serenity was the perfect woman to continue life with. Filling the soon to be hole in his heart. He just had to figure out a way to get through to her.

MANN SAT AT YOSOHN'S KITCHEN TABLE AND TOGETHER THEY counted out $25k for the weed they were about to cop from Dodda. Mann had finally convinced Yosohn to double their purchase from their normal weekly twenty-five pounds. They now were going to be buying fifty. Mann knew Dodda's shipments came in monthly and he wanted to make sure he had more than what he normally would coming in.

The extra hundred pounds of weed he ordered for them would be an extra hundred pounds of weed he would jack from his Jamaican mentor.

"How long you think it's gon' take to move that shit?" Yosohn asked eagerly with an unlit Swisher dangling from his mouth.

"Well, I got my team ready for it, and they usually run out completely before I pick up ... so maybe a few extra days. The couple days they usually sitting with nothing, they'll be moving the extra work."

"Cool. That extra bread will come in handy. Ren done planned this big ass party for her mom and of course I gotta foot the bill. Her ass done went and rented a big ass hall, hired a fucking comedian and gon' have lions and tigers and shit roaming around," he laughed.

"Now you know you exaggerating," Serenity smiled, coming out unexpectedly. She had overheard Yosohn running off at the mouth but didn't know anyone was out there with him. She thought he was on the phone.

"Whatever," Yosohn laughed, before pushing the money over to Mann so he could bag it up.

"Wassup, Serenity?" Mann greeted her, staring at her.

"Hey, Mann," she responded dryly, rolling her eyes at him.

For some reason, she was still attracted to Mann, so she preferred he not be around. She really wanted to still like him as Yosohn's friend, but it was becoming increasingly hard for her to do so. He seemed like a good guy, but he was acting in poor taste by pursuing her. As intense as their shared night was, she put it to rest in her thoughts because she loved Yosohn. She felt like he should do the same, but he wasn't. He continued to call her, and he continued to send countless text messages to her phone. Additionally, he had stopped by the laundromat. She was beginning to think she had a fatal attraction on her hands or to put it plainly — the nigga wasn't wrapped too tight.

Her and Yosohn's relationship was far more important than the night she shared with Mann. In her opinion, Mann should have felt the same way about their friendship. That didn't seem to be the case. He instead put his energy into telling her he missed her and wanted to see her again.

"Well this is the first party I threw for my mom and I want to make sure she enjoys herself. It is a little pricey, but nothing that's going to cripple us," she added.

"You keep saying *us*. Why don't you just pay for it?" he asked sarcastically.

"Yosohn, you have plenty of money and it's not like I buy silly things. This party is for my mom. The person that feeds us on Sundays, takes care of Heaven, *and* will be providing care to your child as well. It's my *mom*. Family is everything. We're paying, and you will be happy about it," she smiled.

She didn't see why he was complaining; ultimately, he was going to give her what she wanted.

"She right, Yosohn. Give her what she wants," Mann butted in jokingly.

Yosohn stopped and grilled Mann playfully

"Shut up nigga," he laughed. "As a matter fact, babe, get the money from Mann since his ass agree with you," he suggested.

Mann smiled at Yosohn and then directed his gaze towards Serenity, "Not a problem," he laughed.

Yeah, I bet, Serenity thought, as she walked off and rolled her eyes again. From the corner of his eye, Mann watched her walk off, admiring how her form-fitting sweats gripped her ass.

After loading up the cash by thousands in the duffel bag, Mann left. He was leaving for New York first thing in the morning. He hated driving through rush hour traffic but that made the transport easier. He would be able to blend right in with the average Joe. Besides, tomorrow would be his final drive to the city. He had a new connect lined up in Philly, and he knew that by tomorrow he would have officially worn out his welcome in the city that never sleeps.

∾

THE NEXT MORNING AT 7 A.M. SHARP, MANN AND ZEKE pulled up to the apartment building they usually met Dodda at. It was cold and large snowflakes had begun to trickle from the sky. The forecast called for six inches, so they had to complete their task quickly so they could head out of the city and avoid the soon to be hazardous roadways. Zeke slowly sipped his Arizona iced tea as he sat beside his older cousin Mann. He listened to him repeat the same instructions for the fifth time. Zeke had heard him the first four times and wished his big cousin would have more confidence in him. He knew he had screwed up in the past, but this time would be different. There was a lot of money involved and he wouldn't let his cousin down. He hadn't smoked weed in two days and had made sure he was well rested so he would be fully focused.

Zeke scratched in his scruffy braids and continued to listen to his elder cousin preach. Although twenty-five years old, Zeke didn't look a day over nineteen. Browned skinned with a babyface, he was the opposite of his cousin Mann, who was a dark-skinned, bearded thug.

"As soon as Dodda walks out and closes the door to head to the car, we count to five and we press on 'em. They won't know what hit them. Silencer in place. Head shot. We leave gun still smoking. In and out so we can catch and follow the nigga to the crib. Snatch the nigga at the door, get the bread," he instructed. "We kill everybody in the house. I don't care

COLD LOVE FROM A THUG

who it is. Got it nigga?" Mann asked, running down the game plan for the final time.

"I got it, cuzzo," he responded.

"Good," he said, and then patted him on the back the way a proud father would his son before his first game.

Mann was excited but nervous. However, he displayed a level of calm that was almost scary. Despite the image he projected, he had a lot on his mind. Their grandmother was still sick, and Serenity wasn't returning his calls. Not that he expected her to. But nevertheless, it was still unsettling.

"Good, let's roll," he said, before putting his thoughts aside and hopping out of the car. The two proceeded to make their way into the Brooklyn hi-rise that was a staple in the slums. As they made their way into the dark, piss smelling halls, a mangy gray cat scurried over Mann's feet, further rattling his nerves.

"Fuck," he murmured, before sending the cat sailing from the swift kick of his foot. Mann's actions caused Zeke to chuckle. *It was only a cat.* He figured that Mann just had a lot on his mind. When they reached the door, Mann proceeded to perform the custom knock Dodda requested. Three seconds later, Ty pulled the door open and allowed the two cousins to enter. He didn't bother to greet the two since he didn't care much for the young man Dodda liked so much.

Mann quickly observed his surroundings. Everything and everyone still looked the same, although Ty's dry dreads stood taller than before and appeared to be matted in the back. Mann noticed he still carried the same 9mm in his waist. Garlan was in his assigned spot by the door near the room Dodda sat in. However, instead of a nine, he was heavily armed with an AR 15 assault rifle. They walked to the back where Dodda was talking on the phone. He quickly ended his conversation when he saw Mann.

"Ok boi, I gotta go. I be there soon to grab it," he said,

before using his black hand to push the end button on his phone.

"Hey, Mann. My boy," he smiled cheerfully. He considered Mann a friend and one of his most loyal customers.

"Wassup, big homie. Everything good? Trying to grab and get on the road," Mann said casually. He didn't have an ounce of guilt for what he was about to do.

"Yeah, everyting's good. I just gotta make a run and I be back soon ... Business good eh?" he asked, his dry, shoulder-length dreads dangling at the sides. "You back soon and you buy more," he smiled, his heavy Jamaican accent still prevalent.

"Yeah, business is good. Me and my patna been making some moves."

"Good. Good. Well sit down and get comfortable Mann. I be back soon," he stated before walking off.

As he walked to the door Mann's heart began to race and he felt adrenaline rush through his body. Zeke looked at him for confirmation. As soon as the door slammed, Mann reached in his waist and withdrew his sound suppressed Glock 9. One, two, three, four, five, he counted the seconds before they both emerged from the room they were supposed to be waiting in.

"Swoop-Swoop!"

The silenced gun sounded like a basketball sailing perfectly through the hoop. The bullet ripped through the barrel and pierced Garlan's skull. His big, black body crumpled to the dirty floor. A mist of blood coated the wall along with brain matter.

As soon as Ty heard the sound he swung around wildly and hit the floor, reaching for his gun. He was too late; Zeke already had his drawn. He quickly released two shots into Ty's chest. With big, wide eyes, he struggled for breath while making eye contact with Mann. He should have checked him at the door. It was Dodda's fault. Dodda viewed Mann as family ... but he wasn't. He had warned Dodda about "snake eyes." That is what he called him because he could see through the smooth talk and lies. He knew Mann was a snake; he could see it in his eyes They revealed the darkness of his soul. Now they would pay the price for Dodda's ignorance. Ty went to speak but was silenced by the bullet Mann put through his cheek.

"I told you ... aim for his fuckin head," Mann snapped. "The goal is to kill."

The two bodies lying in the living room floor didn't bother him one bit. He had killed before, and he had no problem killing again.

The two quickly exited the apartment and took the steps to catch Dodda. As they fled the building, they saw Dodda getting in the driver's side of his vehicle. Scared he would drive off, Mann called out to him. Mann could have waited for Dodda to return with the specified number of drugs, but Mann wanted everything Dodda had at his home. It was all part of the plan.

"Dodda," Mann called out a second time, slightly out of breath from running down the stairs.

Dodda peered back at the building and saw Mann approaching his van with Zeke. He gazed at them with confusion, but still waited. He became more puzzled when Mann bypassed his window and hopped in the front passenger seat of the van. Zeke was right behind him.

"What's goin on?" he asked.

Mann pulled his gun back out and aimed it at Dodda's midsection.

"Drive the fucking car to the crib. I want everything. You already know what it is," he calmly stated to his mentor.

"Mann?" he asked as if he was shocked. His large poppy eyes searched Mann's for answers. Dodda was at a loss for words. He continued to search Mann's eyes for truth and found all that he needed. He found deceit and years full of lies. He had grown to care for Mann. Almost like a son. He should have never trusted him enough to let him enter the side house without being searched. He glanced up to the apartment and knew his cousins were dead. Mann wiped the sweat away from his bald head while he kept his other gloved hand tightly gripped around his Glock. Zeke said nothing. He was merely a sidekick, there for added muscle.

"Dere's nothing at da house but my family. I was on my way to pick it up," he stated. There was no way in hell he was taking them to his house with his wife and son. He would die first.

Mann grinned and looked back at Zeke. The words Dodda had just spoken were music to his ears. He had hit the fucking jackpot. Instead of weed, Dodda had cold hard cash. He hadn't even copped his shipment yet. He was heading there with the money. Christmas had come early.

"Where is it?" Mann asked, with the gun still pointed, and a cold smile stretching across his face.

"It's in da side panel attached to da door."

Dodda didn't bother to question Mann about why he was doing what he was doing. He was disappointed since he had shown nothing but love to the young nigga since he met him in the penitentiary. What attracted him to Mann was the hunger in his eyes. His passion. Ironically, that is what would also motivate him to betray him. Mann was hungry for money and Dodda had plenty. He knew better than to put so much trust into Mann. He had nothing when he met him, not even the necessities such as commissary. He remembered feeding the youngster on numerous occasions. Although saddened by his betrayal, Dodda too, had his own reasons for keeping the much younger Mann around.

While locked away, age eventually began to overcome him. While the time on Earth made him wiser, it was like his kryptonite, also making him weaker. He was no longer able to physically defend himself the way he used to. Mann served as his protector. He had a violent reputation in the prison and that alone was enough to keep Dodda from the deadly grasp of the wolves behind the prison walls. Dodda should have known the day was inevitable. He had led himself to foolishly believe something other. There was no such thing as loyalty anymore in these cold streets. As Zeke ripped off the side paneling of the back door of Dodda's Toyota Sienna, Mann's eyes lit up like the lights on a Christmas tree. The bundles of cash were neatly counted and taped to the inside of the door.

"Check the other one," he instructed Zeke.

He knew there was more. Once Zeke ripped open the other side, he saw more neatly stacked bundles. It was $600k in all. Enough for 2k pounds of weed: his monthly shipment. Dodda's eyes frantically darted around the parking lot, searching for a way to escape. Bullets were the norm in that section of Brownsville. He wasn't worried about the money, he had plenty at his home. What worried him was that Mann's eyes displayed a bitter coldness. He knew he planned to kill him. Besides, he knew the old saying well, *"If they're masked up, they're coming for your ice. If they're bare faced, they're coming for your life."* Neither of the two attempted to conceal their faces. He regretted having the dark tint applied to the windows of the van. Mann laughed hysterically at the sight of all the money.

"What you want me to put it in?" Zeke asked Mann. They had come thinking they would be snatching duffel bags of weed. They had nowhere to put the money. Mann thought for a second and then began pulling off his jacket to load the cash. While he did that, he foolishly placed the gun in the center of his lap. Seizing the opportunity, Dodda grabbed for the gun, cocked it, and fired.

The bullet from the Glock shattered the window and missed Mann's head by a mere inch. Dodda continued to fire the powerful gun wildly in the car as Mann fought for dear life to get the gun out of his hands, eventually overpowering the older man. As soon as Mann got ahold of the weapon, he fired three shots into Dodda's chest, killing him.

"Fuck ass nigga," he yelled, shaken by the fact that Dodda had almost bodied him.

"Zeke, get the money," he firmly stated, while wiping Dodda's splattered blood away from his face. They had to get the fuck outta dodge. It was broad daylight, and the cops would eventually show up.

"Zeke, you hear me?" he asked again, as he continued to wipe at his eyes.

Zeke didn't respond. Mann turned around to speak to his cousin but lost his breath when he saw Zeke was slumped over the seat with a hole through his forehead.

"Fuck, fuck, fuck!" Mann shouted hysterically in the van, violently punching the dashboard. The sight of his dead cousin was enough to bring him to his knees.

"Fuck," he continued to cry out. Mann's body rocked as he sobbed deeply. His chest heaving up and down. However, no tears fell. The pain was deeper than that. It was all his fault. He got Zeke killed.

Mann looked back at his cousin and knew what he would have to do. He would have to leave him. Mann threw his hoodie over his head and hopped out of the car. The snow was coming down much heavier and was turning the area into what appeared to be a winter wonderland. However, he knew that it was no wonderland. It was nothing more than a white, snow-covered jungle.

After he retrieved all the money from the door panels, he

quickly walked to where his rented van was parked and loaded up the cash. He opened the trunk and searched for the spare gas container the rental company provided. He was happy to see there was still gas in it. He felt in his pocket for his lighter and carefully headed back to the car, looking around to make sure no one saw him.

After opening the door, Mann quickly doused Dodda with the gas. He snatched a loose bill from his pocket and lit it, before throwing it on Dodda's dead body and running back to his van. The fire ripped through the van, burning every piece of evidence and fingerprint in it. It also destroyed what was left of his cousin Zeke.

CHAPTER 19

S erenity walked out of Dr. Davis's office around 10 a.m. with a smile stretched across her face. She was excited. Her doctor had confirmed she was indeed pregnant and estimated her to be around five weeks. She now knew for a fact that it was Yosohn's baby and she couldn't wait to tell him.

She already knew exactly how she would tell him and Heaven. This was a big moment and she planned to tell them together. She didn't care if it was a boy or a girl; she was just thankful. Life was almost perfect

JOCELYN LOOKED OUT THE WINDOW OF THE CITY BUS AND took in the beauty outside of it. The earth in front of her was covered in a thick blanket of snow at least five inches high. Although the weather made traveling difficult, Jocelyn still faced it in search of her baby's father. For the past several months, a few times a week, she would spend half the day traveling to each of Yosohn's laundromats in search of him. So far, she hadn't run into him, but she knew eventually she would. Jocelyn looked down at her stomach. She was now three months pregnant. Even though she wasn't extremely far, she was already starting to show. This was becoming a problem since her body was her bread and butter. The further along she advanced in her pregnancy, the more she realized how important it was for her to find Yosohn. As she looked in the lightly occupied, snow-covered parking lot, she smiled. Today was her lucky day.

YOSOHN SPOTTED JOCELYN AS SHE SPEED-WALKED TO HIS CAR. He also noticed she had a pocketknife in her hand as he quickly raced to her with his fist balled up at his sides. He already knew what she was about to try to do.

"Yo, what the fuck are you doing up here?" he asked frantically.

He couldn't yell like he wanted since Serenity was nearby inside the back office talking to Susan and reviewing some paperwork. They were planning to leave so Serenity was going to be walking out very soon. He had to get Jocelyn out of sight fast.

"You've been ignoring my calls and trying to flee me like I'm a bum bitch. All you care about is that hoe in there," she said, pointing to the building. She knew Serenity was inside because she spotted her car in the parking lot.

"How she gon' feel when I tell her I'm three months pregnant with your child?" she asked. "You would have known that if you hadn't changed your number."

She folded her knife and safely placed it back in her pocket. She was glad she was able to quietly get his attention. Yosohn stood outside at a loss for words.

Fuck! he yelled internally.

The last thing he needed was for Jocelyn to go to Serenity

and lie about being pregnant by him. Things were going good between them and there was no way on God's green earth that he would let Jocelyn ruin that. Grabbing her by her arm, Yosohn pulled her closely to him. They were now nose to nose.

"Bitch if you are pregnant, it's not mine. And don't you even think of stepping to my girl with that nut shit. I promise you won't get the results you're looking for," he snarled threateningly. He no longer had a use for Jocelyn, and he had no time to play games with her. She had caused enough problems.

"Don't flatter yourself nigga. I don't have to lie on you. The last time we met up in December you were drunk. You fucked me raw, dumb ass. Multiple times that night. Trust me ... it's yo' baby ... I'm having it and you gon' take care of both of us or you can kiss your relationship with that black bitch goodbye," she threatened, while making a bye gesture with her fingers. Just as he was about to respond Susan walked out of the laundromat.

"He's outside Serenity," she said by the door, after seeing Yosohn standing at the car.

Serenity wasn't too far behind, following Susan out. She had been looking for him so they could leave. In a panic, Yosohn reached in his pocket and hit the unlock button on his key fob.

"Get the fuck in the truck before she sees you," he whispered.

Rolling her eyes, Jocelyn slowly got inside Yosohn's Range Rover. The windows were darkly tinted so Serenity couldn't see inside.

"Hey, babe, watchu doin' outside in the cold?" she asked, before leaning in to give him a kiss.

Seeing the two of them made Jocelyn want to cry. She

wished Yosohn would love her like he loved Serenity. Unfortunately, he made it crystal clear that he didn't.

"I had to make a phone call … Listen, I need to handle some shit at one of the trucks. One of the manager's just called and said it's two employees over there 'bout to get it on. I'm gon' run over and talk to them really quick. I'll be home right after. Okay? You want me to bring you anything?" he asked, hoping she would hurry up so he could dump Jocelyn off somewhere.

"No, I'm okay. But what time are you going to be back in? Heaven is having her chorus concert tonight at six. That's just a few hours. Everyone is going to be there to see her sing and she's expecting you there as well."

"I'm just gonna handle this really quick, and I'll meet you at the house. Tell Heaven don't worry. I'll be there," he smiled.

"Okay," she agreed, before giving him a kiss and walking off to her own car. He was happy they had driven separate cars that day.

Still watching the two, the sight in front of her made Jocelyn sick. She was tempted to hop out and cause a scene. Slapping the hell out of both of them would make her feel better.

Once Serenity walked off, Yosohn quickly got in the car and prepared to deal with Jocelyn's ass. After turning on the car, Yosohn quickly pulled off out of the parking lot. He didn't feel secure knowing Serenity was so close by. After driving for a few minutes and making sure Serenity didn't follow him, he let his fury spill out.

"Yo, what the fuck is wrong with you!" he yelled, looking at Jocelyn like she had lost her mind. His anger caused lines to appear on his forehead and sweat to form on his nose.

"I already told you why I had to show up. I'm pregnant, and I've been looking for you. I'm already starting to show, and I can't make any money dancing," she argued back. When she first met Yosohn, she told him she was a dancer. He had no idea that she fucked around with trick nigga's to make ends meet.

"I need security Yosohn ... A house. A car. Stuff for the baby. I need you," she admitted.

"Are you stupid or something?" he asked her. "Can you not hear? You can't keep that baby. If what you say is true and it is mine, you can't keep it. I have my own situation. I have a family ... I already have a kid on the way by my girl," he revealed.

After Serenity came from the doctor's office she went to Hallmark and got a gift box to wrap up her pregnancy test and sonogram. She presented it to Yosohn and Heaven as soon as Heaven got out of school. Yosohn was more than excited. He was thrilled.

"So, I'm good enough to fuck, but I ain't good enough to have your baby?" Jocelyn questioned, growing upset. "You want me to kill my baby, but that bitch can keep hers?" she asked. "You have more than enough money to take care of our baby too!" This was not how the situation was supposed to go.

"Jocelyn, I love her. You know that. I have a family. Whatever we had is over. I'm gon' try to do right by her ... them. As fucked up as it sounds, you can't have that baby. You gotta get rid of it. I'll give you whatever you need to make that happen, and I'll throw in some extra to help you get on yo' feet after ... but you can't keep it," he stated firmly, ignoring the tears welling up in her eyes.

"For what it's worth, I'm sorry for what I put you through, but I gotta do what's right from this point on," he revealed sincerely.

He knew what role he played in the months' worth of drama, but in his opinion, Jocelyn had brought it on herself when she played like a child in a grown-up game. Although what Yosohn was saying made sense to him, to Jocelyn, what he was saying was nothing more than selfish inaudible words that she couldn't make out.

They sat in silence the remainder of the ride, except for Jocelyn telling him where to drop her off. When she finally exited the car, Yosohn gave her his number and told her to contact him when she set up the appointment. He wanted to be with her when it all happened. Even though he wasn't sure if the baby were his or not, he couldn't risk taking the chance and not handling the problem.

She took the number and walked off, crying silent tears. Her pain would soon be shared. She had no intention of calling him. She was having their baby. She had just been struck with an ugly dose of reality. Yosohn didn't care about her and he never ever would. Even though he had shown that numerous times before, today it been signed, sealed, and delivered.

Jocelyn took the torn piece of paper with the number and ripped it to pieces before tossing it to the ground. She reached in her coat and pulled out another piece of paper. This one was more important. It was Yosohn's registration to his truck. She had taken it out of his glove box when he was standing outside talking to Serenity. She had learned three things that day: one, Yosohn didn't care about her; two, Yosohn's new phone number; three, his permanent address that was listed on the registration. That was all she needed.

CHAPTER 20

Yosohn sat on the king-size bed curled up next to Serenity and Heaven. It was Saturday and they were all sitting around watching some old episodes of Serenity's favorite zombie show. He reached over to Serenity and rubbed her belly. He had been spending a lot more time at home since finding out she was pregnant. He was so excited he was about to become a dad. Although he loved Heaven like she was his own, he knew nothing would compare to watching his own child come into the world. It would be epic.

While he continued to watch the show, he heard his phone chirp. He figured it was Mann responding from his earlier text to see how he was doing. Lately, he had been acting very strange and distant. After a little probing, Mann confessed that his grandmother had fallen ill over the course of several days and was in the hospital. Yosohn even went to visit her to support his friend. He was shocked to see her gravely skinny and hooked to oxygen.

After looking down at his chirping phone, he realized it

wasn't Mann. It was Jocelyn texting him. His heart skipped a beat in his chest when he read the message. *Come outside.*

"Who's that?" Serenity asked from the bed. She was perched up on one arm, curled against Heaven still watching TV.

"It's Mann. He still stressing about his grandmother. I'm gonna go and call him back in the living room," he lied.

He hopped up and walked out. Once he closed the door to the bedroom, he raced to the front of their home to see if Jocelyn really had the balls to show up to his house. After peering out the window, he realized she had balls the size of Texas.

Jocelyn and Bianca stood stone-faced in the front of his home like they lived there. Luckily for him, the alarm wasn't set, and he quietly opened the door to see what the two of them wanted. His hands twitched at his sides. It was taking everything in him to suppress his urge to knock the both of them unconscious.

"Yo, are you fucking crazy," he whispered angrily. "Get the fuck away from my house."

"I'm not going anywhere Yosohn. And I suggest you show me and my friend some respect before I cause a scene up in dis funky ass neighborhood of yours," Jocelyn said while swinging her curly hair.

"I just come to tell you I ain't getting an abortion. I want $5,000. Per month. Every month. From this point on."

She knew he had it since he was out in his wealthy neighborhood pretending to be the Huxtables. Jocelyn was tired of playing games with Yosohn. If she couldn't have his heart, she would get the next best thing: some of his money. She was tired of living in a dingy hotel room, catching the bus, while he went home every night to what looked like a half-million-dollar townhouse.

"Bitch, I'm not giving you no fuckin' $5,000 every month!" he argued, ready to pounce on the two. He advanced towards them, causing them to jump back. He was losing his patience. They wanted to act like niggas by approaching him, so he was about to treat them like niggas. He thought about just telling Serenity the truth, but he didn't know how she would react. Knowing Serenity, she would force him to take a paternity test. He couldn't risk it. If the baby ended up being his, he knew it would be over for good.

"You better back the fuck up," Jocelyn threatened, gripping her mace tightly.

"Look, get away from my fucking house. I'll have the money tomorrow," he agreed with an angry sigh. He knew his hands were tied, and he didn't have much of a choice. She had the upper hand. Serenity could walk out any minute.

Jocelyn looked to Bianca and smiled in satisfaction. It had been Bianca's idea to pop up demanding money. Yosohn was selfish and it was her turn to be the asshole. She was far from finished; she was just getting started.

Yosohn watched the pair walk off to the Germantown Cab that was parked quietly up the street.

Fuckin birds, he silently thought.

Closing the door, he walked back into the house. Once he got back in the room, he was happy to see that Serenity and Heaven had fallen asleep. He didn't feel like making up any more lies; he was tired of lying. Yosohn pulled out his iPhone to dial Mann again. After seven rings the voicemail picked up. He wanted to see how he was doing but he too also needed someone to confide in. It was hard being there for Mann when he just closed himself off out of the blue. He wasn't returning calls or text messages and he hadn't even been conducting business either. It was almost like he fell off the face of the earth. That didn't make sense to Yosohn since he had to hustle to survive.

Yosohn decided he would go check on Mann tomorrow. His new house wasn't too far away, and he wanted to make sure he was holding up okay. That was the least he could do. Besides, the fresh air and drive would give him some time to figure out what to do about Jocelyn.

CHAPTER 21

Mann blinked his eyes several times and realized he had nodded off. He had been at the hospital all morning and not much had changed. He took his grandmother's hand and rubbed it in his. She was lying peacefully in the small bed. He prayed she would be okay. He leaned back in the multicolored hospital chair and sighed. His head was pounding from stress. He hadn't even eaten since the day before.

His grandmother Darlene had been asking about Zeke all morning and he was distraught with guilt. She couldn't understand why Zeke hadn't been there to see her when she had been in the hospital for a week. There wasn't a day that passed that she didn't ask Mann to go search for him. She expressed her concern and although Mann knew the truth, he pretended to worry along with her. His heart was heavy with grief.

"Manny, baby, why don't you go on home and get some rest," she suggested, her voice hoarse. It was after nine at night and Mann had been there since visiting hours began.

"I'm okay, Grandma. Just get some rest," he replied as he scratched in his beard.

"Manny, I'm not asking you. I'm telling you. Go home, wash up and get some rest baby. You been up here all day," she said with a cough.

"I'll be fine. Besides I'm a little tired and I'm going to rest my eyes."

After some hesitation, Mann finally agreed. He went home, took a shower, and did his best to get some rest. Unfortunately, the severe headaches he suffered from, as well as grief from Zeke and worry over his grandmother caused him to lie wide awake. He refused to smoke since the THC in the marijuana put him in deep, trance like thoughts. He eventually pulled out an old bottle of E&J from the fridge and threw the whole thing back. Liquor couldn't take away the pain, but it damn sure could suppress it.

That night would be the last night Darlene spent in the hospital. In the early morning hours, she would die in her sleep.

The pain Mann felt was unspeakable. He had no one and he was empty. His mental state was extremely fragile, and the headaches became unbearable. To function he kept alcohol and pain killers in his system. Unfortunately, it wasn't enough to stop the storm brewing inside his head.

YOSOHN MADE HIMSELF COMFORTABLE IN THE LIVING ROOM OF Mann's home the following day. He had stopped by to check on him and was saddened by what he saw. Mann was sitting by the window drinking, his eyes red from crying from the loss of his grandmother. As tough as Mann appeared to be on the exterior, Yosohn knew that he was hurting inside.

"I know that shit hurts my nigga, but you will get through

it," Yosohn said, attempting to offer Mann some kind words. He figured he wouldn't stay long since he knew Mann probably wanted to be alone. "If you need anything, say the word and I got you," Yosohn offered.

"Nah I'm good, I got bread," Mann countered, almost defensively.

He didn't want anything from Yosohn, nor did he need anything from Yosohn. Once he came up on the $600k, Mann no longer wanted to be bothered with him. He had one final use for Yosohn and then he would be done with him completely.

"Oh, I got that bread for you too," he stated, before getting up off the leather recliner and heading to his master suite to retrieve Yosohn's cut of their usual profit. Although Mann had barely sold any of the weed, he wanted to pay Yosohn off. Their business dealings were over.

"I'm gonna fall completely off the weed shit. I'm gon' focus on burying my Grandma and getting myself together," Mann lied, before sitting back down in the recliner.

Yosohn took the money and didn't bother to count it. Something was off about Mann, but Yosohn dismissed it since he was grieving. He didn't care about the dissolution of the business endeavor since he was good one way or the other. The weed investment was more of a favor to Mann. He still had income coming in from the laundromats as well as the two seafood trucks he owned with Nikki.

"That's cool. You just focus on getting yaself together," Yosohn stated, genuinely sincere.

"Hit me up or come through the crib. Anytime you need," Yosohn offered, while Mann stood up to shake his hand before he left.

"Oh, and I almost forgot to tell you, Ren's pregnant.

"Word?" Mann asked surprised. That had garnered his attention. "It's yours?"

"Of course," he laughed at the insinuation. He wasn't sure where that comment stemmed from.

"I mean… y'all did have that lil brief period of separation," he slyly suggested, discreetly trying to put a bug in Yosohn's ear. "But damn … congratulations my nigga."

"Thanks Mann. Listen, take care my nigga. Get some rest and you gon' be alright Bull. Don't drink too much," he added, before walking out the door.

Mann watched Yosohn walk off and went back in his master suite to nurse his bottle. He now had a new task. He needed to contact Serenity's ass and find out who the fuck really was about to be a father. Him or Yosohn?

CHAPTER 22

S erenity sat at her desk and ordered inventory for the upcoming week. She took a deep breath and rubbed her belly. Pregnancy was such an unforgettable time, but she would be glad when it was over. She was tired all the time, felt fat, and although unnoticeable to others, she could detect the presence of ugly stretch marks creeping up on her belly and thighs.

Several months had passed and she was close to five months. Lately, Yosohn had been pressing her about them buying a larger house since he said they needed more space before the arrival of the baby. She thought their townhouse was fine for the three of them. Nevertheless, they had just closed on a large brick house in the same development Nikki and Hakim lived. They were supposed to get the keys tomorrow.

Serenity continued to look through the catalog, selecting products to order until the sound of knocking at her office door stopped her. She got up to open the door assuming it was Susan since Yosohn was watching a boxing match at a bar in North Philly.

"Hey." She went to greet Susan but stopped short when she saw it was Mann.

"Wassup?" he asked with a slight slur. He reached his large hand out for hers, but she quickly pulled it back. His eyes were red, and the profound smell of Cognac filled her nose.

"Yosohn's not here," she replied sharply.

"I ain't looking for Yosohn. I came here to see you," he stated, shutting the office door.

He had waited several months to approach Serenity about her being pregnant because he had been too busy running his growing Marijuana empire. Since he had returned from New York and cut business ties with Yosohn, he had been getting a lot of money. This was because he was able to buy much more from his new connect and keep all the profits for himself. Yosohn had no idea Mann was still selling weight; instead, he was under the impression that his friend had taken a hiatus because of his grandmother's death. No longer focused on longevity and a future, Mann was letting the large cash go to his head. The weed, alcohol, and pills he kept in his system didn't help him either.

"Well, what do you want? I was just about to leave." She walked over to her desk and grabbed her Chanel purse.

"Really?" he asked. "Well it's Monday and I know that's the day you come in and do paperwork. You're usually here 'til around ten." He looked down at his wrist, checking the time on his iced-out watch. "It's 9:03."

Serenity briefly stared at Mann. He had been following her. She was in fact usually there on Mondays until ten, and the only way Mann could have known that is if he had been watching her.

"I ain't gon' take up much of your time though. I only want a few minutes. I heard you were pregnant, and I just wanted to see for myself, as well as determine if that's my baby you're carrying," he stated calmly, while admiring her pregnant state. She was still gorgeous. Not that he expected anything else. Her dark chocolate skin glowed while she carried the extra weight very well.

"I'm not sure why you would think that since we only fucked once. While we were *drunk*," she reminded him. "Besides, I had a very accurate sonogram from a very excellent doctor who confirmed I conceived in January, not in December," she explained. The revelation was an immediate disappointment to Mann since he was hoping there was a possibility the baby was his.

"Does Yosohn know about us?" he asked, almost in a threatening manner.

"He doesn't need to know and why would he know? I'm damn sure not telling him and neither are you," she said, glaring at him intensely. She was trying to figure out what the hell was wrong with him.

Throwing her bag over her arm, she prepared to walk out the door.

"Look I gotta go, is that all you wanted?" she said, not really asking. Mann stopped her. Grabbing her by the arm he forced her into the wall and began to kiss on her neck. Serenity's body couldn't help but respond. Chills swept through her body as she became instantly aroused. She pushed him off her.

"Are you fucking crazy? I'm pregnant, and Yosohn is still your friend," she firmly stated. "Why are you doing this? Look, what happened between us in the past, and I prefer to leave it there."

"What if I don't want to?" he asked. "I want you, Serenity. I don't care about Yosohn," he admitted drunkenly. "I want you ... I care about you," he said with a wild drunken look in his eyes.

The sight of him scared Serenity. She stood quietly, not sure how to respond. Seeing her hesitate, Mann pushed himself back onto Serenity and rubbed his hand between her thighs while he tried to kiss her neck again.

"Mann get off me," she demanded. He continued, so she asked again. When there was no response, she used all her strength to push his stocky body from up against hers. She then drew her hand back and slapped him across the face.

"Get out!" she stated, pointing to the door. He just looked at her and smiled, unfazed by her hit.

"What if I don't?" he asked. "You gon' *call Yosohn*," he asked sarcastically. "Keep playing with me and I'll fuck his ass up, just 'cuz," he spat. "Remember you started this shit back at the hotel. Besides the nigga you love is playing yo' ass anyway. Why don't you ask him about that situation he got?"

"What are you talking about?" she asked, puzzled.

Although Mann and Yosohn were no longer doing business together, they still spoke periodically. Yosohn had met up with him and told him about what was going on with Jocelyn. He hadn't decided what to do about her, but for the last few months, he had been religiously sending her the money she demanded. Of course, Serenity had no idea.

"I ain't telling you anything. You too blind to see who really fuck with you. I could do everything Yosohn can do. I could treat you better. You don't even see how you're really being treated," he added to get her to think. "Once you figure it out, call me."

Mann walked out, leaving Serenity in thought about what he was talking about. Yosohn was hiding something. What? She watched Mann pull away from the laundromat in a 2020 BMW 650i. Serenity admired the car as he drove away. It was a big change from his former Dodge Charger. Mann had come up on some money, and he was letting it go too far to his head. Mann had turned into an entirely different person and she wished she could tell Yosohn how his supposed friend really felt about him. One thing for sure is that he would no longer step foot in her house again. She didn't care how Yosohn felt about it. Mann was a ticking time bomb ready to go off. She believed the loss of his grandmother really sent him over the edge. The problem for her was that it seemed like he wanted to take her along with him.

~

"SERENITY, YOU'RE GONNA HAVE TO TELL YOSOHN THE TRUTH," Shanita said over the phone. Serenity had called her as soon as Mann left. She was now on her way home.

"I don't know about that. How do I go to him and tell him I slept with his best friend?" she asked sarcastically.

"You sit him down and just tell him. You're gonna have to. It happened during a bad time for y'all. One thing led to another ... That crazy ass nigga is gon' keep fucking with you. The crazy part is you just admitted you sexually attracted to him even after the weird shit he been doing. Why I don't know, but y'all gon end up fucking again or shit is just gon' get worse 'cuz he obviously can't take rejection," she added. "And besides, they're clearly not friends anymore. Yosohn told you Mann had been acting weird. Now you know why. The nigga is like a bomb ready to go off at any time. And yo' simple ass don't know when that's going to be."

"True ... I wonder what Yosohn is hiding?" she said aloud, ignoring the fact that her rude ass sister just called her simple.

"Girl, I wouldn't even worry about it. You gotta deal with that nut Mann. Besides, he probably throwing shade and talking about a bitch Yosohn fuckin' ... Some shit that ain't even serious. You can't be stressing, Ren. At the end of the day, you own businesses, have lots of money in the bank, are having a baby and just got a brand-new house in a gated community. Yosohn's heart is yours."

"I hear ya," she said, unimpressed. "Thanks for listening though. I just pulled up and I'm about to head in and get some rest. I have an appointment at eight to go see what I'm having," she said, focusing on something more positive.

"Aight, boo, just text me tomorrow and let me know. Be safe."

"Aight," she stated, before disconnecting the call. She looked up at her soon to be former home and sighed. What the hell had she gotten herself into?

CHAPTER 23

Jocelyn left TD Bank fuming. She had her phone to her ear and was now calling Yosohn for the fifth time. This was her second time coming to the bank and her money wasn't there. He was supposed to have deposited the money several days ago. She stood in front of the bank and waited for the cab she called that would take her to Chestnut Hill. She wasn't playing games with Yosohn. She was going to his house. He wasn't playing fair so neither was she. As she waited, her phone rang. She saw it was Yosohn calling back.

"Hello?" she answered on the first ring.

"Yo, you called me, wassup?" he asked. He already knew what she wanted.

"Yosohn, where's my money?" she calmly asked.

"About that … I ain't giving you another dime. I done already gave you $5k a month for the last three months. That should've covered your rent for months plus brought more than enough stuff for that baby of yours," he stated.

Yosohn felt confident the baby wasn't his and he didn't plan to give Jocelyn another cent. As soon as she had it, he was demanding a blood test and once it came back negative, he was completely done with her.

Jocelyn immediately lost her patience. "Nigga, I want my fuckin' money or I'm going to yo' bitch!" she yelled. She didn't care about the people around her that could overhear her ghetto tirade.

"Yeah, do that and see what happens. And don't even bother showing up to my house … well, my old house anyway. I upgraded!" he laughed. "We in a gated community now so I can rid myself of peasant bitches like you who want to get out of line and pop-up at a nigga house and shit!"

As soon as Jocelyn showed up at his house, he convinced Serenity to start looking for another one. He used the fact that the baby was coming as an excuse for needing more space. The movers had just moved the last of the things out several days ago. Instead of the three-bedroom townhouse, they now lived in a five-bedroom, three-story brick home.

Jocelyn hung up the phone while Yosohn continued to talk shit. She was pregnant and didn't have time to get herself worked up. She wasn't stressing. The baby was Yosohn's. As soon as she gave birth, she was going to give him that blood test he had requested several times. She would let the white man at the courts force him to pay child support.

Although he had sent her $15k, she hadn't saved a penny of it. She still needed to live day to day and was still staying in a room. She had been trying to save up and buy a car. Instead of being modest, Jocelyn had been looking at a small, but brand-new C-class Mercedes. It was just like her to have champagne taste on a beer budget. Jocelyn had something for Yosohn's ass though. She could play with the best of them.

YOSOHN RELAXED ON THE PLUSH FLOOR OF HIS NEW HOME. He was tired from having unpacked all day. It was a fresh start for them, and he was excited. Now all he had to do was convince Serenity to change her number. He had asked her to change it once she moved back in, but she refused since she had the number for years. He had been playing her phone super close since his encounter with Jocelyn earlier that day. What surprised him is that she peeped it since she appeared to be watching him watch her phone.

Ironically, she had been recently secretly wishing she had changed the number as well. She was praying Mann didn't text or call her, while Yosohn prayed Jocelyn didn't text or call her. They both prayed internally that the phone stayed silent the remainder of the evening.

"Bae, where ya phone? I'm gon' order us something to eat," he stated. He really was hungry after unpacking all day.

"What's wrong with ya phone?" she asked, making sure she didn't sound defensive.

"It's dead. I gotta put it on the charger. It's been acting funny. Won't hold a charge long. I think I'm gon' upgrade tomorrow. I can upgrade yours too if you want," he offered, hoping she took the bait so he could convince her in the store to keep the new number they gave her.

"That's cool. I did want to get that new iPhone," she stated. Serenity tossed him her phone and told him what she wanted.

"Get me Shrimp Lo Mein and some fried chicken wings... Make sure you ask Heaven what she wants. She's probably not gonna want what I'm getting," she added.

"Okay," Yosohn replied, before taking the phone and walking up the steps.

As he made his way to Heaven's room on the opposite side of the house, Serenity's phone dinged. She had a new text message. He breathed a sigh of relief knowing it was probably Jocelyn. He was glad he got the phone when he did.

Yosohn navigated to the text messages and saw that it wasn't Jocelyn. It was a text message from Mann. His forehead crinkled as he grew suspicious. He was curious as to why Mann would be contacting Serenity. He opened and read the message.

I apologize for coming at you the way I did. I just wished you would give me chance. I really care about you. That night we spent together got me in my feelings. I really dig u.

Yosohn couldn't believe what he had just read. He read it again to make sure he wasn't seeing things. After re-reading the message, he instantly saw red and felt like a current of emotions was traveling through him. Text messages were always open to be interpreted in many ways. However, if he was interpreting it correctly, then someone had hell to pay.

Yosohn turned and stormed back to the room Serenity was in. His heart banged in his chest and he felt his body fill with adrenaline. Once he reappeared in the room Serenity knew something was wrong. He had an angry scowl smeared on his normally handsome face.

"What the fuck is this, Ren?" he asked rapidly approaching her and jamming the phone in front of her face.

"What is what?" she asked alarmed. His demeanor frightened her. She quickly read the text message and felt all the breath leave her body.

Fuck, she thought.

She wasn't ready to tell Yosohn. She wasn't even sure how to respond. No words came from her mouth when she went to speak.

"What the fuck is you deaf or something?" he asked, growing angrier by the second.

"What the fuck is he talking about — No let me rephrase that! Why the fuck is Mann texting you about a night y'all spent together! What the fuck is he talking about!" he yelled, grabbing her arm. He snatched the phone back and read it back, "*I really dig you.* What the fuck is this!" he screamed.

"Yosohn, calm down, babe … I need to talk to you." She began to cry. The tables had turned, and she didn't know how he was going to act when he heard the news.

"Serenity, please tell me you not about to tell me some bullshit," he pleaded, before releasing her with a push. Her being pregnant was at the rear of his mind.

"Yosohn baby, just calm down please," she pleaded.

"Talk!" he yelled, causing her to jump and stumble back into some boxes. Serenity took a deep breath and then tried to explain.

"Back in December, the night Naomi and I saw you at the crab truck … well she invited Mann. We all were drunk … At the end of the night, she started throwing up. He took her home and then he was going to drop me off at my hotel … He came in to use the bathroom. One thing led to another." She cried with her head down. "I'm so sorry, Yosohn. I was so fucked up, and so was he."

"Is that my baby?" he asked with his jaws clenched. His heart ached. He wanted to kill them both.

"Yes. This is your son," she told him. She had just found out they were having a baby boy.

Yosohn shook his head and looked at Serenity in disgust. Since he met her, he did nothing but place her on a pedestal. She was so special to him and her betrayal was like a knife through his heart. He had never felt the way he was feeling before. Her leaving him was one thing … but this feeling was something else. His girl, his future wife, his child's mother … had slept with one of his closest friends.

"So, this has been going on behind my back the whole time. You two motherfuckers sat in front of me knowing y'all had fucked behind my back! That's why he stopped doing business with me and started acting funny. Over ya fucking ass! I should fuck both y'all up!" he screamed. "I'ma kill this nigga!" he roared, feeling breathless. He realized that everything finally made sense.

"It was a mistake, Yosohn. It only happened once ... Mann is just ..."

"He's just what? He can't get over the fact it was just a fuck! Now he wants to fuck with you right? He not used to an uppity bitch like you!" he added disrespectfully. Serenity was taken back by the way he spoke to her, but she understood he was angry.

Feeling enraged, Yosohn cocked back and kicked over a random lamp that lay on the floor. The broken pieces flew in the wall. He snatched his keys off the nightstand and made his way to the front door. He had to get out of there before he did something he would regret.

"Yosohn, please ... Where are you going?" Serenity asked. "Yosohn, we can work through this. I'm pregnant, please don't leave me," she cried while wiping the tears away from her wet face and staring at his back. For the first time, the tables were turned, and she was the one begging.

Ignoring her pleas, Yosohn walked out of the house and didn't look back. He was going to go deal with Mann's snake ass personally.

YOSOHN SAT IN HIS CAR AND SLOWLY BROUGHT HIS BLUNT TO his mouth. He pulled from it and inhaled, holding the smoke in his lungs extra-long for maximum effect. After putting the blunt out, Yosohn sat back in his seat and peered out his window. He was posted in front of Big Faces Bar and was hoping he spotted his ex-friend Mann. He knew there was only a handful of bars Mann frequented. This was the one he was most likely to show up to. The area was where he sold most of his weed. He had already driven by Mann's home, but he wasn't there.

After sitting in the same spot for over an hour, Yosohn decided to leave. Before he departed, he tried to call Mann one last time. The phone went straight to voicemail. Yosohn decided to leave a message.

"You already know who it is. I found out how you movin' and wanted to address you on some man to man shit. Since I can't do that, I just wanted to let you know that when I see you, we clutchin'. I never been a bitch nigga, so you already know what it is. On sight nigga!"

Yosohn hung up the phone and made his way back to his new home. There was no way in hell he was leaving Serenity. He loved her more than anything in the world. Besides, he knew he had put her through Hell and back; it was only right that he eventually came face to face with karma. What she did still didn't compare to all the years of bullshit he put her through. For every action, there was a reaction. Her reaction had been long overdue.

Yosohn couldn't help but think about negative shit as he journeyed home. He thought about how he called Serenity numerous times the night she was with Mann. He also thought about how Mann made jokes about meeting a chick he wanted to wife. The whole time it had been Serenity. Mann was oh so disrespectful and Yosohn had every intention of punching him in his mouth on sight. Win or lose, it was going down.

CHAPTER 24

Mann listened to the voicemail that Yosohn had left him twice. He had to be sure that he heard what he thought he heard. Yosohn wanted to go to war with him.

Fuck clutchin', he thought.

Those penitentiary days of fighting were over. If Yosohn came to him, he'd better have his gun because he always kept his on him, and he wouldn't hesitate to let that bitch go. In his mind state, any nigga that came incorrectly could get it. Yosohn was no exception.

Mann was getting money and had just recruited a whole new team. Fifty pounds a week with his new connect was bringing him in $40k a week. He felt like a boss. Bosses could have what they wanted and wouldn't tolerate any form of disrespect. That voicemail Yosohn left was pure disrespect and had to be dealt with. Mann leaned over the side of his bed and dialed in the ten digits of a goon he knew in North Philly. Stick-up kid turned robber, Mann knew he would knock Yosohn off for the right price.

"Wassup, Bull," Mann asked Nootie.

"What's good, my nigga?" he asked Mann, who was

always looking for a come up. He had known Nootie since they were kids riding bicycles on littered North Philly streets. Mann wasn't especially fond of Nootie's older brother Teddy since he was essentially a bully in the streets, always fighting somebody, more so because he was smaller and had that "little man" complex. Plus, Teddy talked too much. He wanted Nootie to handle things solo.

"I got a nice little lick for you ... I need you to rock a baby to sleep," he stated bluntly.

"Yeah ... well you know that's gon' cost you five," he said calmly. It wasn't nothing for Nootie to kill someone. $5k to kill someone was dirt cheap and it got even cheaper when one was dealing with desperate niggas in need of fast ends.

"Cool. I'll give you $10k if you do it solo. Where you gon' be? I'm gon' come through in say ..." He looked down at his simple, black and stainless-steel Rolex to check the time. "In an hour and run down the game plan."

"I can handle that. I'll be right at Broad and Erie. My sister live right around the corner. Make sure you have half that bread with you."

"Cool, see you then."

Mann terminated the call and sat back in satisfaction. Soon Yosohn would be out of his way. The streets talked, and most of the hood knew Kiesha had set Hakim up to be robbed and killed. Both Yosohn and Mann knew this. Yosohn had just put money on all three of their heads. Unfortunately for the two brothers, no one had given them fair warning. This was their silent warning. Since Nootie was going to be looking for Yosohn, he would possibly have a slim chance at survival. The hit would be unlikely carried out if Yosohn came up missing. It was every man for himself as far as he was concerned. For now, he would use the crash dummy to get Yosohn out of his hair. It was no longer just about a female. Yosohn had disrespected him, and he would see that he paid the price: with his life.

THE NEXT DAY, SERENITY HAD JUST STEPPED OUT OF HER AUDI when she heard her phone ring. She glanced down but decided that she would answer it later since she was in a hurry to sign in at her Obstetrician's office. Not too much had changed over the past couple of weeks. The baby was healthy, and she was putting on the proper amount of weight for a healthy pregnancy. As she walked, she reached down and rubbed her swollen belly. Everything seemed like it was moving so fast. School was almost over, and summer was also quickly approaching. Everything was good.

After signing in at the front desk with a plump white lady, Serenity took a seat on the large, brown leather sofa in the waiting room. She reached over to the coffee table to retrieve a copy of an Essence magazine to occupy herself until the doctor called her in. She knew it would probably be at least fifteen minutes before she went back so she made herself comfortable. After sitting for several minutes Serenity felt the rumbling vibration of her phone. She dug it out the bottom of her purse and saw that it was an unknown number. Without hesitation, she accepted it.

"Hello," she answered.

Jocelyn took a deep breath on the other end of the phone. "Bitch where ya man at?" she asked angrily.

Serenity already knew who it was, but she still asked, "Who is this?"

"Bitch you know who it is. I'm looking for ya man … my baby daddy … oh I'm sorry…" she laughed. "*Our* baby daddy. I bet you didn't know I was six months pregnant," she taunted.

Serenity didn't utter a sound. She was shocked. She had nothing to say.

"I guess da cat got ya tongue. Tell ya fuck ass nigga I want my money!" she added to generate a response from Serenity.

"What money?" Serenity whispered, peering around nervously to make sure no one heard her.

"Ya man been giving me $5k a month, and this month his ass is late. Tell him I want my money, or he'll see me and his daughter in court in a few months."

Jocelyn hung up the phone. She already knew Yosohn wasn't going to give her any more money. Contacting Serenity was merely out of spite. She knew she would really have to see Yosohn in court. Hopefully, that was the only place she saw him...

"Serenity Smith," a Spanish medical assistant called from the entrance to a backroom.

Hearing her name being called, Serenity slowly stood up to head to the back. She felt a little dizzy, but she proceeded anyway. She needed to have a sit down with Yosohn.

SERENITY WALKED OUT OF THE DOCTOR'S OFFICE KNOWING what she had to do. After meeting with her doctor, she was told she had high blood pressure. Since she was fine the previous visit, Serenity determined that it was most likely stress-related. With high blood pressure, her baby was at risk. No one was more important than Heaven and the baby that was growing in her stomach.

She needed a break. She had to get away. Instead of going to her sister, Shyanne's to pick up Heaven, she went home first. When she pulled up, she saw that Yosohn wasn't there. He had been hanging out a lot more lately after he found out she slept with his friend. She had been trying to talk to him but for the most part, he had been shutting her out. She understood; he was hurt. Serenity looked at her beautiful new house and held back tears. Despite how much she loved it, she was going to have to leave it. She went in and got Heaven's favorite doll. She didn't even bother to pack a bag. She planned to just buy what she needed. Nothing was worth her sanity or the well-being of her children.

She backed her car up from the paved driveway and told herself the trip was temporary; she would see her house again soon. She was headed to a peaceful place in Jersey: her fathers'.

CHAPTER 25

Yosohn didn't have any friends. After Hakim's passing, and Mann's deceit, he'd become a loner. So, he sat in his favorite Clock Bar and made small talk with the bartender. He was on his third drink and he was beginning to feel the shots of rum wreak havoc on his bladder. Holding his urine, Yosohn continued to think about the past day's events. Jocelyn was still calling him with threats and he and Serenity were barely speaking. It wasn't like she hadn't been trying to communicate with him; he was just being stubborn.

Every time he looked at her, his mind couldn't help but create fictitious scenes of her with Mann. *Did she moan with Mann when she was with him? Did she touch Mann like she touched him? Did she kiss Mann like she kissed him?* The dreadful thoughts consumed him every time he looked at her. He wanted to move past it, but he knew it was going to take some time.

Yosohn ordered another shot of rum and got up to go take a leak outside. The bathroom inside of the Clock Bar was despicable. Yosohn preferred to take his chances outside with mother-nature. As Yosohn pushed his way out of the dirty fingerprint stained glass, he noticed a tall light-skinned cat on the corner talking on his cellphone, as well as a washed-up fiend trying to flag down passing cars. She spoke undecipherable words to Yosohn, but he didn't bother to turn around. The fiend who appeared to be in her late twenties, was dirty and had long been stripped of her beauty by the streets.

Yosohn made it to the back of the bar and unzipped his pants so he could relieve himself on a pile of old garbage. As he washed down the trash in urine, he heard a familiar sound close by. Similar to the sound of a gun cock. Yosohn reached in his waist for his burner and spun around. It was too late to draw. He now stood face to face with the person who was allegedly responsible for the death of his friend Hakim.

As Nootie squeezed the trigger of his firearm, Yosohn rushed him, dropping down low to avoid the bullet. The attack sent Nootie to the ground and Yosohn on top of him scrambling for the fallen gun. Yosohn had dressed for the warm weather, so his exposed knees and elbows violently scratched the pavement as he used all his strength to grab onto the gun that was a few inches from him. When he reached it, he turned around and pulled the trigger. The bullets ripped through Nootie's chest, sending him to the ground in a heap.

Yosohn took off running. He had no time to panic unless he wanted to be locked away for the rest of his life. He tucked the additional firearm in his waistband and did his best to exit the back of the building. He needed to blend in with the pedestrians traveling the busy street. Sweat coated his forehead as he walked briskly.

When he reached his car, he quickly started it up and headed back to his home. It was a close call; Nootie had caught him slipping. He prayed the cameras in the vicinity didn't catch what happened. If so, he would need to retain the best lawyer in the city. He reached in his console and commanded his phone to dial Serenity. After multiple rings, the voicemail picked up. He tried again. Same thing.

"Siri, call Nikki," he commanded. Nikki picked up on the second ring.

"Hey, Yosohn. Wassup?" she asked in a groggy tone like she had been sleep.

"Nikki! Listen, some shit popped off. I need to stay at ya crib tonight."

"Okay," Nikki replied hesitantly. "Are you okay? Everything alright?"

"Yeah, I'm good ... Listen, I can't say anything over the phone but I'm on my way there now ... Have you talked to Serenity?" he asked as he continued down the cracked city streets.

"No. Why?" she asked concerned, and now fully awake.

"She not picking up." Yosohn didn't want to go into details about him and Serenity with Nikki. He just needed a safe place to stay until he figured out what his next move would be.

OVER A WEEK HAD PASSED AND YOSOHN HADN'T HEARD anything from Serenity. He didn't know what was going on and he was worried sick. After staying at Nikki's house for several days, Yosohn decided he was good to return home. Although people had heard the shots ring out, no one had come forward with information yet. At least that was what he heard through his bartender acquaintance. He still wasn't sure how Nootie had found out he had put money on him and Teddy. That was the only reason that he could think of Nootie aiming for him.

Yosohn didn't bother to call Serenity again since her

number had been recently changed. It just didn't make sense to him since everything in the house was still intact. Serenity hadn't taken anything. Yosohn looked around and saw unpacked boxes strewn around the house. Once again, his life was a mess, and this time he wasn't even sure why. He'd called Gina and Serenity's sisters, but they didn't give him much information. They told him she was safe and not to worry. Unfortunately, they also didn't know where she was.

Yosohn sat on the couch and stared at the wall. He wanted to drink and smoke to take away the stress on his mind, but he couldn't. Nootie had only been dead about a week. Yosohn knew it was only a matter of time before his brother Teddy came looking for action. He had to be on point and ready. He rubbed his hand against the gun on his hip. He was prepared either way. Just because he had a little money didn't mean he forgot what the streets were about.

CHAPTER 26

Serenity paced her speed at sixty-five down the turnpike. Heaven was with her dad at his house in Jersey, and she was headed back to Philadelphia for dinner at Naomi's house. Naomi had practically begged her to come by and fill her in on what was going on with her and why she was staying way out near the shore. Although her mom knew where she was as well as why, she made her promise not to tell the rest of her family. She would tell her sisters when she felt it was the right time. She didn't feel like hearing all the questions, nor the *"I told you so's."* She also knew Shyanne looked at Yosohn like a big brother and would spill the beans if he pressed her.

Serenity was focused on keeping her blood pressure and stress level down by relaxing and doing essentially nothing. Susan was handling the laundromats for her while she oversaw the paperwork remotely. For the most part, she had been in Jersey shopping, eating, and hearing old stories from her dad. Serenity took exit 6a for Philadelphia off the New Jersey Turnpike and after another thirty minutes of driving, she was at Naomi's Northeast Philadelphia home. Serenity got out her car and approached the building. Naomi swung open the door before she could even knock.

"Hey, boo! I missed you," she screamed, before giving Serenity a big bear hug.

Serenity giggled. Naomi was always so hype.

"I missed you too," she replied. "It smells good. What we eating?" she asked greedily. Serenity was starving after the nearly two-hour ride.

"Girl … I made some chicken fettuccini alfredo with broccoli. Extra cheese *and* sauce, just how you like it." Serenity smiled. She knew her too well.

The two sat down to eat, and Naomi begged her to tell her what had been going on that prompted her hasty decision to leave. Serenity didn't really want to tell her the whole situation especially everything that led up to the move but decided she would be completely honest with her close friend to free her burdened conscience.

Naomi hadn't brought up Mann since the day they ate lunch with Shameka. She had been seeing a new guy and often gushed about him. Serenity believed it was safe to assume that Naomi was completely over her little crush and thoughts of Mann.

Unfortunately, she thought wrong. As she confided in her best friend about what really occurred between her, Mann and Yosohn, Naomi stopped her right in mid-sentence.

"You fucked Mann?" she asked, her mouth hanging open.

"Naomi, we were drunk. He was so aggressive, and shit just happened," she admitted, a little ashamed. She was hoping her friend wouldn't judge her based on that one mistake.

"You knew I liked him though," she countered like a teenager, instead of the thirty-year-old woman she was. For some reason, Serenity expected her to be understanding; unfortunately, Naomi wasn't trying to hear it.

"That's trifling, Ren. I was talking to the nigga and he was one of Yosohn's closest friends," she added, doing her best to make Serenity feel bad.

"Look, Naomi, at the end of the day, what I did was wrong. I figured I would come to you and tell you like a woman instead of letting you find out any kind of way. You said y'all were talking ... but a couple phone calls and a double date doesn't exactly make you two as an item. I don't have to sit here and lie about the nigga staring at me around my house, flirting with me, and he basically pushing himself on me when he felt he had the opportunity." Serenity deliberately left out the part about her flirting hard too. "He even came to the laundromat multiple times. He clearly was checking for me long before. I can't help that. What I did was wrong ... *yes*. But do I think that stopped y'all? *No*. If he was interested, he would've made something happen. You sure as hell was more than willing," Serenity added, unintentionally making Naomi seem like a thirsty broad.

Naomi peered at Serenity for a moment. Her long eyelashes seemed to flutter while she searched for a response.

"On some real shit ... like I said before, you're trifling. It's not enough for you to have a big ass house and a paid ass nigga. You want to fuck his friend too? Chicks like you kill me," she scoffed, shaking her head.

"Why you sounding like a hater?" Serenity asked puzzled, while calmly taking a sip of the iced tea Naomi had given her with dinner.

"I ain't no hater, I just can't stand chicks who got it all, and it's never enough. Bitches like me who want a good dude, can't get one —"

Serenity cut her off while she spoke. "What makes you think Yosohn's a good dude? Because he takes care of me? Because he has money? Do you know what I go through?

Dealing with the bitches he's fuckin or has fucked in the past," Serenity asked, her voice cracking. "I just had a bitch tell me the other day she was six months pregnant by this nigga," she admitted. That' why I left. That's why I went to my dad's in Jersey. Because I was stressed the fuck out. My blood pressure soared through the roof and my pregnancy is in jeopardy. So, fuck all that good nigga shit," she said bluntly with tears lining the brim of her eyes.

"You just don't get it do you?" Naomi asked, shaking her head and dismissing Serenity's sob story. She would take Yosohn any day. Fuck what Serenity was talking about.

"I guess I don't," Serenity paused. For a second, she thought about holding off on speaking her true feelings, but then decided against it since Naomi didn't hesitate to speak hers.

"You know … maybe if you stop being so aggressive and coming off as desperate, then maybe you might be able to get a man. Acting thirsty obviously doesn't help. Maybe that's what happened with Mann."

"No … you fucked Mann, that's what happened!" Naomi said, losing her patience. She'd had enough of her self-absorbed friend who thought it was okay to mentally attack her in her own home.

"So, it's *my* fault?" Serenity asked in disbelief, whipping her head around to face Naomi. "Girl, bye. You were the one —not me, letting the nigga watch you stuff ya damn face at the crab truck. You were the one throwing the fuck up after piling liquor on top of it. Real fuckin' attractive, Naomi. Keep it real. You have issues within yourself. *That's* why you can't get a man. Instead of blaming me for stepping on your toes, you need to start addressing the real issues."

"So, what are you saying, Serenity? Issues like what? My weight?"

"Naomi, you know what your problems are." Serenity

glared at her. Naomi was ready to start the pity-part bullshit and she didn't have time for it. "You don't need clarification from me. And, frankly, you make shit problems when they don't have to be. You're a beautiful girl despite your weight."

Naomi had far more than weight issues she was dealing with. She was flat out envious of her friend. In Naomi's eyes, she had the babies, the man, and the big, beautiful house. She was gorgeous *and* confident. She had no trouble getting any man. *So why screw the man, she knew I wanted?* Naomi thought to herself bitterly.

To be rejected was enough, but to be rejected for her friend was even harder. To top it off, Mann was damn near infatuated with Serenity. Obsessing over her like she was some sort of precious treasure. It was a cold case of jealousy, and it made Naomi angry and full of spite.

"Well, Serenity, right now my problem is *you* and I think you should leave," she suggested.

"You putting' me out ya house?" Serenity asked Naomi in disbelief. When Naomi didn't respond, Serenity grabbed her keys and began to depart. She looked back at Naomi, but she had walked off to her bedroom. Serenity knew what she did was wrong, but Naomi was angry for all the wrong reasons. She always thought her friend was happy for her, not jealous. The more time passed, the more she was learning people were never who they portrayed themselves to be.

CHAPTER 27

Yosohn pushed the silk sheet off his brown, chiseled body and got out of the bed. After throwing on a t-shirt and basketball shorts, he went downstairs to deactivate the alarm. Although it wasn't that late he was in bed trying to rest his tired, sleep-deprived body. However, that was interrupted when he received a call from Naomi. She claimed that she had some information about Serenity. One of the handful of people he reached out to initially when looking for her, he felt a sense of relief when she called him. Yosohn still didn't know what was going on with Serenity, but he was hoping Naomi could tell him that tonight. He watched as the headlights of Naomi's Toyota Camry lit up the front of the house when she pulled up. After opening the door and allowing her in, he headed to the kitchen so he could pour a light drink and find out what she knew.

"Thanks for calling me. Wassup?" he asked anxiously, while taking a small sip of rum and coke he had poured.

"Well, Serenity called me and she's okay. She's in Jersey at her dad's house." Naomi sat her purse down and made herself comfortable at the kitchen island.

"Why the fuck would she be all the way up there?" he asked with raised brows.

"Jocelyn called her. Said she was six-months pregnant or something?" she asked Yosohn. Yosohn shook his head from side to side. He should've known Jocelyn had something to do with it.

"The bitch is lying," he said calmly, sitting his glass down on the granite countertop in the kitchen. "What doesn't make sense to me is why Serenity would just pick up and leave without saying nothing. She usually would've come to me and talked to me."

"Well, when Jocelyn called her, she was at the doctor's office. Her blood pressure was high, and she became a high risk for a miscarriage. Yosohn ... to tell you the truth, I don't think Ren is coming back."

Naomi wasn't certain but she figured she'd create the narrative. Yosohn took a deep breath and let everything she said sink in. He couldn't believe the bullshit he just heard.

"Thanks Naomi. At least I know she's ok. Everybody else shut me out, but at least you gave me some peace of mind." Yosohn tried to give Naomi a quick hug to express his gratitude. However, when he hugged her, she didn't let go. Instead, he felt her lips pressed against his neck and her tongue slither across his skin causing a jolt to his dick. Naomi pressed her big, soft body against his. He couldn't lie, it felt good, but she was off limits.

"Yo, what are you doing?" he asked, pushing her away, his face frowned. He looked at her and lust-filled her eyes. He couldn't help but also notice sadness and desperation.

"Yosohn baby, Serenity's not coming back. I can take her place. Nobody has to know," she stated, approaching him and rubbing his chest. Her left hand slid down to the bulge in his pants. "I can be your sneaky link."

"Yo, are you fucking crazy? What the fuck is wrong with you bitches? Get out!" he yelled, surprising her.

He had enough shit to deal with and Naomi was trying to make it worse. He was getting his girl back and fucking her best friend behind her back was sure to eliminate that if she found out. Yosohn was tired of the games. It wasn't worth it. No bitch was. He wasn't sure what caused Naomi to come with the treachery, but he wasn't taking the bait.

Naomi just stared at Yosohn and the look he gave her made her feel like even less of a woman. Not only had she been rejected by Mann for Serenity, she had also been rejected by Yosohn. She practically threw herself on him and he still didn't want to touch her. The jealousy she possessed for her friend had surfaced full force and she knew their friendship was essentially over. She quickly spun around and fled the house ashamed and humiliated.

Yosohn huffed in aggravation before pouring himself another drink and throwing on his black Jordan Retros. He was about to handle some shit he should have handled a long time ago.

YOSOHN PRESSED DOWN ON THE GAS PEDAL AND SPED FROM Chestnut Hill to Northeast Philly. There was no emergency. He was simply angry and eager to confront Jocelyn. He was so furious that he was shaking. He did his best to stop his hands from trembling on the steering wheel while he drove. He'd tried to be nice. He'd tried to talk some sense into Jocelyn. But it didn't work. Instead of owning up to her wrongs, she'd laughed at him. Actually laughed at him. All he wanted to do was put an end to the games. All he wanted to know is why she had called Serenity and told her that she was pregnant. Why? She claimed that she was going to let the court handle it, but she didn't. She'd destroyed his home once again.

Yosohn was sick and tired of being played with. He was at his breaking point. The death of his friend. The death of his friendship. The death of his relationship. He was tired of losing. It was time for other motherfuckers to start paying the price. It wasn't going to just keep being him. Yosohn knew he hadn't been the best. But he damn sure hadn't been the worse either... but he could be. One thing for sure... He was about to show Jocelyn that playtime was over. He was not the one to be fucked with.

CHAPTER 28

"What did I tell you?" Yosohn demanded, approaching Jocelyn in his dark hoodie like the Grim Reaper. She was too terrified to speak, so she remained quiet. She'd never seen Yosohn that angry before. She knew that he was pissed when she laughed at him and hung up the phone, but she never expected him to come by.

He'd come by unannounced. A simple knock at the door. When she went to answer it, he barreled through it with murder in his eyes. She'd never felt scared around Yosohn. However, tonight she did. When he came through the door, she tried to run, but he knocked her down. The look in his eyes spoke volumes. His intentions weren't good. She sat quietly in fear. She didn't want to say the wrong thing.

"Oh, you quiet now?" he questioned, cocking back his foot and kicking Jocelyn while she was still on the ground and trying to escape him. Pain coursed through her body causing her to scream out and shake violently in terror.

"Shut the fuck up," he growled, grabbing a handful of her twists and yanking her up to her feet. He spun her around to face him, her head tilted back at an odd angle. Tears formed in her eyes and quickly slipped from the corners. She didn't recognize Yosohn. He was downright terrifying. She had to find a way to get away from him.

"Yosohn, I'm pregnant. Please let me go," she begged through teary eyes.

"Bitch, I don't give a fuck. Fuck you and that baby," he spat with zero compassion. "You fucked up my life," he accused through clenched teeth, before shoving her onto the thin, dusty mattress. He looked down at her in disgust and couldn't help but wonder how he had allowed himself to fall victim to her sexual prowess. How he managed to let a hoe like her come in and dismantle his relationship and life he'd worked so hard to build.

Seizing the opportunity to defend herself, Jocelyn scrambled away and grabbed a lamp that was nearby on the nightstand, hurling it at him. Yosohn ducked, and it collided into the wall, shattering. Rage choked him, and he rushed over to her and grabbed her by her throat. He was sick of her and her outlandish antics. He wished he had never met her. She had caused so much turmoil in his life when he had done nothing but be honest from the beginning.

Now all he wanted to do was the right thing, but everyone was out for themselves. Everyone was willing to use him as a pawn to achieve satisfaction for themselves. He was going to put an end to the nonsense *tonight*. With *everyone*. He didn't care about the consequences. Everyone who had crossed him, was going to pay. Yosohn looked down at Jocelyn while she squirmed underneath him from the weight of his body and pressure to her neck. He pressed against her to keep her still and used both hands to apply immeasurable pressure to her throat. She kicked and writhed on the bed, but he was too strong. Clawing desperately at his hands, she struggled for air, but it was to no avail. Weakness was overcoming her, and Yosohn had transformed. He had been sent to call her home.

Yosohn's former, perfect life flashed before his eyes as he continued to strangle Jocelyn. He thought of all that he had, and all that his life was before she had come into the picture. He cursed the day he had met her. He saw nothing through his pupils. The sounds from Jocelyn, became muffled and distant … until finally, they stopped. Yosohn's heart hammered vehemently in his chest, and before he realized it, she was still. *She was dead.*

For a few seconds, Yosohn stood blankly and stared at Jocelyn's still body. Then reality quickly set in and he realized he had to get the fuck out of there. He had just killed someone, and he was about to go the fuck to prison if he didn't jet.

Yosohn backed away and slowly opened the door. He turned the knob and nervously peeped out the door. The coast was clear, so he made a brisk, quiet exit into the hallway and headed for the stairs. He didn't care about fingerprints since his would be one of many in the highly traveled room. As Yosohn fled the scene and headed back to his truck around the corner, he didn't bother to look back. He didn't need to. One problem down, another one to go.

Bianca's room was only a few doors down from her best-friend Jocelyn's. She had heard some unusual sounds and went to go make sure things were okay. After quickly throwing on her robe, Bianca walked down to the room and tapped on the door.

"Jocelyn, open the door bitch; it's Bianca."

When there was no response, she grew worried. Bianca slowly turned the knob, expecting resistance from the lock.

Maybe she'd finally taken her advice and stopped leaving her door ajar. To her dismay, it wasn't locked. She looked down and noticed the space between the door and the latch. As usual, it was ajar.

Bianca entered the room and for a moment, her world seemed to run in slow motion. However, once her eyes completely processed the sight in front of her, she sprang into action.

"Jocelyn!" she called, running over to her friend who was laying limp on the bed appearing lifeless. She was lying stiff in the middle of the bed with her arms and legs sprawled out wide.

Bianca called out to Jocelyn several more times while she smacked the sides of her cheeks to see if she would come to. She didn't know how to check a pulse, so she felt her chest to see if her heart was beating and then stuck her hand under Jocelyn's nose to see if she was breathing. There was nothing. Bianca immediately began screaming for help.

"Help me!" she yelled, before grabbing the motel phone off the dresser and calling 911.

"911, what's your emergency?" the operator asked.

"My friend isn't breathing, and I can't feel her heartbeat! Please help me and hurry! She's pregnant!"

"Try to calm down, ma'am. Can you tell me where you are?"

"At the Sleep Inn on Roosevelt Boulevard in Philadelphia! Please hurry!" she frantically demanded while checking Jocelyn's chest again.

"Try to stay calm ma'am. Help is on the way."

MANN WAS PISSED WHEN HE FOUND OUT NOOTIE WAS THE person they found outside of the Clock Bar. He care that he was dead; what bothered him was that Yosohn *wasn't*, and he had paid Nootie's simple, unreliable ass $5,000. He wasn't gon' sweat it though. He would make other arrangements.

Mann continued to cruise down Old York Road in his new BMW and stared at all the prostitutes who lined up the streets. His mom used to work the same strip. He watched several of them attempt to wave down car after car, with one finally stopping an elderly man looking for a quick sexual fix. He shook his head and silently wished he could open fire on the whole block without going to jail. Mann hated prostitutes, especially strung out ones who chose to neglect their children for a temporary feeling of nostalgia. Mann turned into Hunting Park and made his way to the parking area to watch a game of hoops. A couple of guys from his team were meeting down there to shoot the shit and smoke weed.

Everybody hung out at the park when there wasn't anything to do, and paid niggas like himself were like God's when they pulled up in their foreign cars. As Mann pulled into the park, he just so happened to glance over to Cayuga Street that was parallel to the park. He spotted a young boy named Slay, who slung weed for him. He was posted up at the window of an SUV. When Mann looked closely, he realized it was Yosohn in his Range Rover.

Mann reached under his seat and grabbed his gun. He figured he wouldn't get a second chance. Instead of parking, Mann continued up and headed out the park. He figured he would bend the block and come from behind, since Yosohn was facing the opposite way. As soon as he got close enough, he was going to light his ass up.

After stopping to a light, Mann turned onto 10th street and u-turned onto Cayuga Street. He slowly crept down the block towards Yosohn. Mann slowed his speed and raised his gun when he got close to Yosohn's truck. He rolled down the window and his young nigga pointed to him and mouthed some words. Mann immediately opened fire.

Pop! Pop! Pop!

～

YOSOHN WAS SITTING IN HIS RUNNING TRUCK, TALKING TO A young nigga he had met through Mann named Slay. He had pulled up on him to see if he had seen Mann around. Slay hadn't seen him in a few days; however, directly in the middle of their conversation, he pointed to the street and said, *"There he go, right there."*

As Yosohn turned to face the street, he spotted Mann with his gun extended out the window.

Pop! Pop! Pop!

Mann fired repeatedly into Yosohn's truck, instantly killing Slay with a random bullet to the eye. Yosohn tried to duck, but the bullets ripped through the interior of his Range Rover. Desperate for an escape, he frantically grabbed the door handle as the bullets continued to fly. As he scrambled to exit the truck, Yosohn felt a bullet rip through his stomach. The pain from the hot lead was enough to bring him to his knees.

Yosohn managed to get the door open and as he slid out of his truck, he felt another bullet strike his back. His lower body went numb as he tumbled to the hard pavement. The shots eventually stopped, and he heard Mann peel down the block, leaving nothing more than the smell of burnt rubber behind, along with two fallen bodies. Yosohn could no longer feel the pain as he slipped out of consciousness. He watched his blood leak onto the ground as he eventually faded out; his gun still attached to his hip.

～

SERENITY GOT THE CALL FROM HER MOM NEARLY ONE IN THE morning that Yosohn had been shot. Luckily, she wasn't far. After Naomi put her out, she didn't feel like driving back to New Jersey, so she booked a room in downtown Philadelphia. She'd been told that Yosohn had been transported by paramedics to Temple Hospital. Using his cell phone, police contacted who they believed to be his next of kin. Gina's name was listed under Mom in Yosohn's phone, so they called her first. Serenity's sisters, Gina, Chris, and even her father Tate who was coming from Jersey, were all headed to the hospital. Gina had called everyone. It didn't look good.

Serenity pulled up to the hospital and illegally parked in front of the Emergency Room. They could tow the car for all she cared. Her mind was focused on Yosohn. She ran to the information desk and began rambling.

"I'm here for Yosohn Thomas. Is he okay? I'm Serenity Smith, his fiancé." Her mind and heart were racing a mile a minute while nausea enveloped her.

"Give me one-minute ma'am. He just came in," the older black lady at the desk told her. She quickly looked through the computers before getting up and heading to the back. She was only gone a minute, but to Serenity, it felt like hours. Her head was pounding, and she was beginning to get lightheaded. The suspense was killing her. She wanted to know what happened. Where was he shot? Was he going to be okay? Who was he with? Who did it? So many thoughts were running through her head. The lady from the desk soon returned, but she had brought company. She was accompanied by an African American, silver-haired, distinguished looking doctor in blue scrubs.

"Miss Smith?" he asked, not sure what to call her. The patient's last name was Thomas, but he was informed that his wife Miss Smith was present.

"I'm Miss Smith, Yosohn's fiancée; is he okay?"

The doctor looked at her solemnly and carefully chose his words. "Yosohn was shot multiple times, once in the stomach and once in his back. The bullet to his back damaged his spinal cord. The doctors are doing everything they can to save his life right now ... but to be honest the chances of him surviving are slim ... If he does survive, he could very well be paralyzed. We're doing everything we can to help him."

Serenity put her hand to her chest and tried to digest what the doctor said. It was too much. The hospital was too bright —the lights in the ceiling too hot. She felt faint and her knees buckled underneath of her, sending her to the floor.

"Are you okay?" the doctor asked her, crouching down to look at her.

"Get a wheelchair," he yelled, after getting a glimpse of her blood-soaked leg.

"Ma'am, how many months are you?" he asked with an authoritative tone.

"I'm five. Ughhhhhhh!" she yelled out. Unexpected pain exploded through her abdomen.

"Get her to the back! Hurry up!" he yelled to staff members around him.

"Ughhhh!" Serenity screamed again when she felt pain rip through her body. This time she also felt it in her back. Serenity felt warm fluid run down her leg. She was going into labor.

"Oh my God! Oh my God!" she screamed. "My baby's coming! It's too soon. Please make him stop. Ughhhhhh!" she yelled.

Several nurses rushed out to assist while doing their best to calm Serenity down. While they aided her, she felt faint again. Bright lights flashed in front of her face, her chest felt heavy and she suddenly slipped into darkness.

CHAPTER 29

Serenity was heavily sedated to manage her pain; however, she was still able to recognize the doctor when he walked into the room. Gina, Chris, and Tate surrounded her bedside as she blinked her heavy eyes and tried to make out what the doctor was saying. She couldn't determine whether they were talking about Yosohn or her baby. Finally gathering up enough energy to speak, she whispered out, her voice faint.

"Where's my baby," she mumbled. With the medicine flowing through her system, she didn't remember much. She did however remember that she was forced to deliver her baby early. With the little strength that she had, she reached down and touched her belly. Sure enough, he was out. She wanted to see him. When no one answered her question, she repeated herself.

"Where's my baby?" she asked again.

With tears filling her eyes, Gina shook her head from side-to-side and responded with heartbreak.

"Serenity baby ... I'm sorry honey, but he didn't make it."

Serenity didn't even bother to ask what that meant. She

already knew. She had only been carrying him five months and his body wasn't developed enough to be out in the world. She closed her eyes and the pain she felt nearly took her breath away. It was like being hit in the chest with a ton of bricks. The pain was indescribable. Her baby was dead. She hadn't even had the honor of meeting him yet. *Why me God?* she thought. She'd struggled so long to have a baby with Yosohn. For him to be snatched away felt cruel and unfair.

With tears streaming from her face, she asked, "Is Yosohn okay?" Although the drugs slowed her body down, her mind still struggled to keep up.

Gina looked at Chris, and Chris glanced at Tate. Tate nodded his head for her to go ahead and tell Serenity what was going on.

"I'm sorry, baby, but …" she cried out.

She threw her head into her palms and sobbed. It was all too much for Gina and she had no idea how Serenity was going to cope. Her family would see her through.

CHAPTER 30

The doctors hadn't expected Yosohn to survive through the night, but by the grace of God, he did. The bullet that tore through his stomach should've killed him, while the bullet through his back should have left him paralyzed. Neither of them did either. It was hard for Gina to initially explain to Serenity that Yosohn was in a medically induced coma and not expected to live through the night. She was having a hard time digesting the news herself. When he pulled through, it was a blessing for the small family. However, it was a bittersweet moment since he would not be accompanied in life by his child. Serenity was thankful that Yosohn still had a chance but devastated because her sweet boy would not. She felt defeated. She felt when it rained it poured, and she seemed to be the only one getting wet.

SERENITY OPENED HER EYES IN THE DARK HOSPITAL ROOM AND slowly peered around. Although she couldn't see much, she did manage to make out the glimmer of the streetlight far away. What she would forever see in her mind were the vivid images of her baby and his headstone. She would never be able to erase those images. She had named him Jahkee Yosohn Thomas. She could still see him. When she finally got to see her baby, she was at a loss for words. He looked like Yosohn but had her full lips. His fair skin was pale, and he weighed less than a pound. She remembered cupping him in her hands and staring down into his closed eyes. She had watched and waited, hoping they would flutter, and he would come back to life. She cherished and would still envision every moment she had spent with him. In her head, she could still see his name crystal clear on his black, granite headstone shaped like a tricycle. He had just been buried a week ago in an extremely quiet ceremony, reserved for only a handful of immediate family.

While Yosohn lay in a medically induced coma at Temple Hospital, Serenity laid their sweet baby to rest. She told herself she had to be strong, but her heart rebelled. She often cried day and night. From the time she pushed his small dead body out of her own, until the time they covered his casket with dirt, she cried non-stop. She didn't understand what she had done to receive such a harsh hand. She wanted to scream and question God, but she wouldn't dare. She felt she had been blessed in so many other ways and had no right to question why He did things the way He saw fit. Serenity was without a doubt angry, but she refused to be bitter. She promised herself that pain would make her a better person. She would cherish everyone in her life. Nowadays, when she breathed, she would breathe deep. When she hugged Heaven, she would hug her longer and harder. When she sat quietly by Yosohn's bedside, she would stroke and kiss his hand a tad bit more gently.

Despite what she had been through, she still loved Yosohn and would see him through recovery. However, when it was all said and done, she seriously contemplated leaving him. She had already found a condo community in New Jersey, close to her father. She planned to dissolve her and Yosohn's businesses and walk away with a newfound sense of freedom. She thought about how she had come to the decision.

Not even twenty-four hours after Serenity lost Jahkee, and Yosohn lay recovering from emergency surgery, two rookie detectives showed up. Their arrival and upcoming revelations would further influence her decision to leave.

The lack of qualified candidates applying for the infamous Philadelphia Police Department was the main reason the two inexperienced detectives had arrived at the private room of the quiet hospital that day. They were new to the homicide department and had only been on a few cases; however, they were eager to take on the case of a pregnant dead prostitute, as they knew that it would bring a huge amount of publicity and give them an opportunity to make a name for themselves.

The taller of the two Caucasian detectives did all the talking and introduced himself as Detective Devin Mason. He reeked of AXE cologne and was poorly dressed in his oversized gray suit, that swallowed up his lean frame. The other detective, Officer Edward Bohn was the opposite. He instead, was short and round. He reminded Serenity of Santa Claus; however, instead of wearing a jolly smile, his face was coated with an icy frown.

"What can I help you with? I already spoke to multiple officers and already told them I don't know what happened," she huffed, with wrinkles quickly forming in her forehead from irritation. She was tired of the questioning and just wanted to be left alone. She now wanted to sit quietly, mourn the loss of her child, and pray that Yosohn's surgery had been completely successful.

"I'm sorry. I don't quite understand. We're in charge of a

homicide investigation and need to ask Yosohn Thomas some questions," Detective Mason stated.

"*Homicide?*" Serenity quickly asked, with a puzzled look. She was confused. Yosohn wasn't dead. "Excuse *you*." Serenity stated abruptly, with an angry glare.

Detective Bohn had walked off and was slowly pacing the room while looking around suspiciously.

"If you don't mind, I need you to stay over here," Serenity demanded. She didn't trust cops and she needed them to stay within eyesight. Detective Bohn didn't respond as he walked back over to the entrance. He stood quietly by his partner.

"We're investigating the murder of Jocelyn Rodriguez. She was Mr. Thomas's estranged pregnant girlfriend," Detective Mason continued. He searched Serenity's eyes for any sign of emotions.

Although rookies, the detectives had done quite a bit of research. They knew Yosohn had been recently injured in a shooting and knew that his long-time girlfriend would be right by his bedside in a very vulnerable state. They weren't sure if she knew about his alleged love affair, but they did know that she could be an incredible asset if she did.

Serenity took a silent deep breath and waited before responding. Her stomach felt as if it were in knots and her mind struggled to quickly absorb what she had been presented with.

"You want to question my fiancée about a murder?" she asked sarcastically when she finally decided to speak.

She did her best to control her facial expression. She was truly shocked. Her lip twitched in anger. She wasn't angry at the detectives for doing their job; she was angry at Yosohn because the drama never ended. She knew the bitch Jocelyn claimed to be pregnant, but she wasn't prepared to think that Yosohn would take it that far and kill her.

"Yes," Detective Mason immediately replied, still searching her face for any indication of knowledge or guilt.

Serenity took another deep breath, this one loud and exaggerated. "Well as you can see," she pointed to the bed. "He's recuperating, and I'm tired, so I'd appreciate it if you stepped out. Yosohn is in no state to answer any questions at this time, and when he is." She paused. "He'll be accompanied by the best lawyer in the city."

She looked away from the detectives, pushed the cheap, flower-patterned recliner back, and pretended to attempt to go to sleep. She had nothing else to say.

"Well you tell him; he'll damn sure need it," Detective Bohn said, finally speaking again since he had formally introduced himself.

Serenity rolled her eyes, but in her heart, she knew that he wasn't lying. She wondered what kind of mess Yosohn had gotten himself into this time.

CHAPTER 31

Yosohn slowly peeled open his eyelids to see. His body hurt like hell and his eyes felt heavy and dry. It hurt to absorb the light that was seeping spilling into them. He turned his head to the direction of a humming sound. It was coming from medical machines and monitors that he seemed to be hooked up to. He quickly realized he was in a hospital. Which one, he was unsure of. He peered to his right side and saw Serenity nestled in a recliner fast asleep.

Yosohn sighed and closed his eyes back. He now remembered everything. Mann had shot him. He was lucky to be alive. He remembered the hot bullets ripping through his flesh. He also remembered watching blood flow from his wounds and his energy wane as he slipped out of consciousness. He remembered it all. Yosohn reopened his eyes and parted his lips to speak. His dry throat made it difficult. His words were distorted. It was almost as if he was whispering.

"Ren … b-b-b- baby," he struggled to mouth. She didn't hear him. He let out a weak cough and repeated himself.

"Ren," he started.

Yosohn's cough, as well as the sounds of him struggling to speak, caused Serenity to sit up. For a minute she stared around in confusion, struggling to adjust from being awakened abruptly. When she did, she attempted to process the image in front of her. She wiped her eyes to make sure it was real. It was. Yosohn was finally awake. He had been in a medically induced coma for a week.

Scrambling out of the recliner with excitement, Serenity anxiously pulled down on the assistance button behind Yosohn's bed. Words couldn't describe the happiness she felt to see Yosohn with his eyes open, alive and breathing. She couldn't help but cry as emotion, as well as the feeling of relief rushed her.

She had so much to talk to him about. She forced a dry swallow. She wasn't sure how to tell him she had lost the baby. She also thought about how she would tell him he would never walk the same again. She shook the thoughts out of her mind. It would wait until later. Yosohn's life as he knew it would officially change forever.

"You're extremely lucky Mr. Thomas. The bullet that penetrated your abdomen narrowly missed important organs." The doctor paused. He always gave the good news first. "Unfortunately, the bullet that we retrieved from your back did damage a small portion of your spinal cord. On the bright side, that is something that can be improved with therapy allowing you to manage it and live a full life. The quick actions of the paramedics and doctors saved your life, my friend. You're incredibly lucky. You escaped paralysis, as well as the need for a colostomy bag."

The doctor that was examining Yosohn wasted no time

informing him of how lucky he was to be alive. In fact, he believed that Yosohn was doing quite well after being shot twice, undergoing emergency surgery, and being in a coma for over a week. His recovery was phenomenal, and he was scheduled to be discharged soon. His walk would never be the same, but the way the doctors saw it, it was a miracle he would be able to walk at all, especially with no need for intensive physical therapy.

"Thank you, doctor. We appreciate all the care that you and your team have given to Yosohn. We are curious as to when he will be able to go home though?" Serenity asked.

Picking up his clipboard and straightening out his white lab coat, the doctor responded. "I'd say a few days. We want to keep an eye on his wounds and monitor him a bit more. Then he's all yours," he smiled.

"Thank you," Serenity said, returning the smile, before the doctor walked out. She pushed back her tangled hair and sighed. She was beat; she was hurting; but more than anything, she was relieved. The last week and a half had been a rollercoaster to hell, and she would be glad when it was finally over. Sitting up in her chair she quietly took Yosohn's hand before looking in his eyes. Yosohn was still resting on the bed and knew something was up.

"What's wrong," he asked hoarsely, growing concerned by her changing demeanor. Her peaceful look had been replaced with worry. He sensed grief. He painfully lifted his body up to sit up and face her.

"Nothing babe ..." She paused. She wondered if she should wait. She decided against that option. She had to know.

"Yosohn ... What happened that night you were shot? Who did this to you?" she finally asked, while peering intensely in his eyes. Light tears formed in her own eyes and threatened to spill out while she waited for a response.

Anytime she thought back to that night, emotions overwhelmed her.

Yosohn stared at her for a minute without responding. He didn't like to keep things from her, but he figured he had to tell her. The whole situation was a result of her infidelity with Mann. He didn't blame her for being shot, but he wanted her to be aware of what was going on, and that she could be at risk. Yosohn took a deep breath and told her.

"Ren … When I found out that you and Mann had …" He paused, took a breath and swallowed the lump in his throat. He hated to think about it. "When I found out that you and Mann had fucked around, I tried to reach out to the nigga, but he wasn't responding. I left him a message and things escalated from there."

Serenity didn't bother to ask what kind of message he meant because she was fully aware of Yosohn and his temper. She wasn't surprised.

"The next thing I knew, I was out near the park bustin' it up with some little nigga and he came through gunning," he continued.

He left out the reason for him being at the park. He didn't want her to know that he had been looking for Mann, and that he got caught slippin'. As Serenity listened to Yosohn she involuntarily chewed at her bottom lip. She couldn't help but feel partly responsible.

"Yosohn baby, I'm sorry," she started, but Yosohn wouldn't allow her to finish.

"Ren, on some real shit, I just want to put that shit behind us and move forward. I know why shit happened the way it did. I blame myself for that, because for every action there's a reaction."

"Yosohn, I have something else to tell you," she started, with tears in her eyes. For her, it was now or never. Yosohn looked at her nervously, unsure of what news she would deliver next. Serenity took a deep breath.

"I lost the baby," she continued.

"What? *How?*" Yosohn asked in disbelief. That wasn't what he was expecting to hear from her. They had been ecstatic about the news of her pregnancy. He knew she was devastated over the loss. It hurt him too, but he knew as a mother, her pain was different. He reached for Serenity's hand and took it into his. With tears forming in her eyes, she replied.

"The night you were shot my blood pressure went up really high and I went into labor right in the emergency room. With my blood pressure rising so quickly it put the baby in distress … He was stillborn," she replied solemnly. Tears slipped from her eyes and down her chocolate face. Yosohn went to speak but was disrupted by a knock at the door.

DETECTIVE BOHN AND DETECTIVE MASON TAPPED LIGHTLY ON the patient's door and then proceeded to enter Yosohn's room without waiting for an invitation. They had gotten the call from the cooperative staff at the hospital that Yosohn was awake and doing well enough to answer any questions the detectives had. As soon as they entered the room Serenity glared at the detectives while Yosohn looked confused. She hadn't even gotten to mention the two coming by, or the fact that they wanted to question him about a homicide.

"How are you feeling Mr. Thomas?" Detective Mason asked with a smile that lacked authenticity. He didn't really care one way or another. "I'm Detective Mason and this is my partner Detective Bohn. We're from Philadelphia Police's homicide department and we've come to ask you a few questions."

Yosohn immediately thought back to the night he was shot. Slay had been killed he figured that's why they were there. He adjusted his body and turned towards the door.

"Well I'm gon' stop you right their officer. I don't know who the gunman was. It was nighttime and I didn't see his face … Besides, you two niggas can do yo' own fucking job," he added, before turning back to face Serenity. Growing up in the gritty streets of Philadelphia, Yosohn also had a distrust and dislike of cops. Besides, he wasn't in a good mood. He had just been given bad news and was still trying to digest it. His girl had lost their child and he apparently had even missed the burial. Now just wasn't the time.

Detective Mason peered at Yosohn, unmoved by what he had just said. When it was all said and done, he was going to enjoy arresting Yosohn. From what he knew, Yosohn was a hoodlum who likely used his criminal revenue to turn himself into a semi-legitimate businessman. Despite his attempt to clean himself up, Yosohn still reeked of slums to him. He hated arrogant ghetto assholes and felt no sympathy for him as he lay in his hospital bed injured from gunshot wounds that he probably deserved.

"Actually Mr. Thomas, we're here investigating the murder of Jocelyn Rodriguez. She was strangled in a motel a little over a week ago. A motel that we were told you used to frequent regularly."

All the color drained from Yosohn's face. He did his best to maintain his composure and tone, since deep down, his mind was doing somersaults.

"I have absolutely no idea what you're talking about and I won't be answering any questions until my lawyer is available and present," he stated with finality.

He wasn't even going to pretend like he cared the bitch

was dead, because he didn't. Detective Mason paused for a minute but finally responded.

"You will definitely want to do that since by the end of the day we'll have a subpoena for a blood test for the baby she was carrying. Although Ms. Rodriguez is deceased, quick actions from paramedics saved her unborn child's life."

Yosohn glared at them silently. He was glad they couldn't read his mind because it was going a mile a minute with alarming thoughts. If he were in a dark alley, he wouldn't hesitate to snatch the breath from them both.

"We'll see you tomorrow, buddy, *with* that court order," Detective Mason joked, before the two walked out of the room.

Although they were disappointed that Yosohn refused to answer questions, they weren't surprised. That was typically the way things went during homicide investigations. Every now and then they would get the idiot that would tell on himself. It certainly made their job a whole lot easier. As the two detectives walked away from Yosohn's room and down the hallway, Detective Mason couldn't help but remember the cold look in Yosohn's eyes when he revealed the baby had survived He was a heartless son of a bitch and he would enjoy taking him down off his high horse.

～

"THEY CAME HERE A FEW DAYS AGO," SERENITY SAID FINALLY speaking, her tone revealing her anger. She glared at Yosohn. She was beginning to suspect that he had a lot more going on than he cared to admit. "What the fuck is going on Yosohn?" Serenity demanded to know. She no longer cared about him being in a hospital. She wanted answers.

"Man, I don't know what they're talking about," he insisted, maintaining his innocence.

Despite appearing confused, his mind was racing. He was sure he had put Jocelyn out of her misery when he left. He assumed the baby would die with her ass. He thought his problem was over that night. Never in a million years did he think his problems were just beginning. Yosohn knew he was a piece of shit. To say he was selfish would be an understatement. However, he didn't care. He just wanted his life back. Meeting Jocelyn was one of the worst things that had ever happened to him. His life had spiraled downward ever since he had met her. While silently in his thoughts, Serenity glared at him. Her eyes cut through him like daggers.

"Yosohn, I don't know what the fuck is going on but for whatever reason this girl is dead. Now I'm not gon' front like I give a fuck, because I don't. But I do pray that you didn't have shit to do with it." Serenity no longer knew what to expect from anyone anymore.

"Serenity … I don't know what they are talking about," he stated with finality.

He wasn't going to incriminate himself. Not even to her. While he knew Serenity loved him, he would never put his freedom in the hands of anyone. He trusted her on many levels, but murder --- He knew there was no way she was rocking with that. He also knew she was in a highly vulnerable state due to the loss of their baby. Serenity was good at putting on a tough face, but deep down inside, he knew she was hurting.

"Was that your baby she was carrying?" she asked, her eyes burning a hole through him. She had never spoken to Yosohn about the day Jocelyn called her when she was at the doctor's office. In her heart, she knew that the accusations Jocelyn made held some type of truth to them. Deep down she prayed that it wasn't Yosohn's baby; however, something inside of her told her different. Serenity knew eventually the truth would surface, and she had no idea how she planned to deal with it when it did.

"Hell no," Yosohn countered quickly. He could see the pain and doubt through her glossy eyes.

"Okay," she replied. Serenity knew that unless there was hardcore proof, Yosohn would never admit it. She wasn't going to run the issue into the ground. She would simply sit back and watch how things unfolded.

CHAPTER 32

Detective Mason and Bohn quietly sat in a state-supplied police van and listened to the live surveillance of Yosohn and Serenity talking in Yosohn's hospital room. They had gotten a court order to place a wire in the room while Yosohn was admitted. The conversation the two had was nothing that would deem helpful to their budding case. They spoke mostly to doctors and Serenity seemed to stay on the phone handling what sounded like business matters.

The two detectives didn't have much evidence to work with to identify Jocelyn's killer; however, Yosohn was still their lead suspect. They had no doubt in their mind that he was responsible for her death. Jocelyn's friend had proven to be instrumental in their premature case against Yosohn. Through Bianca, they had learned that he and Jocelyn quarreled about the baby she was carrying. They also learned that he had been giving Jocelyn $5k per month in hush money. Unfortunately, Bianca had not seen Yosohn enter or exit Jocelyn's room the night of her murder, and she also confirmed it had been a while since she had even seen the two make physical contact. It also didn't help that the motel she was murdered at didn't have reliable working cameras throughout.

Yosohn had done a good job of limiting his contact with Jocelyn. And while the information Bianca had given was enough to provide them with a motive, it wasn't enough to charge Yosohn with murder. With the bug in place, they hoped that Yosohn would incriminate himself in some way while speaking to his fiancée; unfortunately, Yosohn was remaining silent about the topic.

Pursuing Yosohn was becoming increasingly frustrating for the two detectives and they hoped to get a lead soon when they presented to him a freshly signed subpoena for a blood test. They already had the baby's DNA, and their request for Yosohn's DNA had been approved a few hours before and the two couldn't wait to present it to Yosohn in the morning.

MANN PUSHED NAOMI'S HEAD AWAY FROM HIS CROTCH AFTER releasing a stream of hot semen in her mouth.

"Swallow it," he demanded, after seeing her cringe.

Forcing a smile to her face, she gulped the cum down her throat and struggled to stop the gag that was begging to escape. Unable to contain it any longer, part of the liquid violently forced its way back up. She caught it in her hands and jumped up and ran to the bathroom. Mann laughed as Naomi ran off naked, her spiral curls bouncing.

Mann had been fucking with her since the night he shot Yosohn. Initially, he was unaware that she and Serenity had just bickered about him. Of course, Naomi would fill him in. Being the opportunist he was, Mann decided that he would use her to stay one step ahead. He knew that with her vulnerability and low self-esteem, Naomi would be easy to conquer sexually and eventually control. He had saw the signs when Serenity first tried to hook them up. He knew with a little work she would easily be his key to staying abreast to what was happening. Despite the fact he had no initial desire to be intimate with her, he called her up. After forcing himself to listen to her argue with him about sleeping with Serenity, he managed to convince her to come see him. The rest was history.

Immediately recognizing Naomi's intense jealousy for her friend and internal insecurities, he was able to manipulate her into thinking that he had been truly interested in her the entire time and that alcohol was responsible for him and Serenity hooking up. Within a week's time Naomi was head over heels and certain Mann was the one for her. Like the master manipulator and deceiver he was, he used Naomi like a pawn to stay one step ahead.

"Babe you got any more of that blunt left?" she asked, after returning from the bathroom. She climbed on top of him and kissed on his chest.

"Chill," he demanded firmly, growing agitated. "I have a few calls to make."

Naomi sucked her teeth and climbed off him.

"Here," he said, while passing the crack laced blunt to her.

He had been secretly placing the rocks in her blunts since he had been fucking her. He figured she would be easier to control if she was drug-influenced. It was working.

"You gon' smoke with me?" she asked, while eagerly taking the blunt from Mann. She reached over to the nearby nightstand and grabbed a lighter.

"Na, that's all you, baby. Enjoy yourself. I'll smoke later." He had no intention of smoking what she was smoking. He watched as she flicked the lighter and held the flame to the tip of the twisted poison he had given her. She didn't even notice the soft crackling sounds the blunt made as she pulled on it. It was the sound of the crack popping from the flames burning into them. Naomi hungrily inhaled and allowed the toxic smoke to penetrate her lungs, temporarily altering her state of mind. The intense euphoric feeling immediately rushed over her. Mann could smell the chalky scent of cocaine burning in the air. He had her and she had no clue.

"Babe, have you spoken to Serenity? How's Yosohn doing?" he asked.

Naomi rolled her eyes and blew a stream of smoke out of her plump lips. "He's better. She said he don't know who shot him, but I think she was lying," she coughed.

Mann never admitted, nor planned to admit to Naomi that he had shot Yosohn. As soon as he found out that he had survived the shooting, he began using Naomi as his information source. He told her that he and Yosohn hadn't been on the best terms, and that he had been laying low because he figured he'd be the first person that Yosohn blamed for shooting him. Mann was able to get in Naomi's head so well that she was beginning to believe that she was the Bonnie to his Clyde.

"Well, definitely stay close to her. Keep in touch with her. Once Yosohn is back up and moving, he may be looking for me. You know the streets make up wild stories. People saying I did it. Yosohn is the type to shoot first --- ask questions later. He may be paid, but he a street nigga at heart. Even though I didn't have shit to do with him getting hit up, he still probably gon' still lash out at everyone. His radars are definitely gonna be up," Mann explained.

He looked over to Naomi who seemed to be staring off into space with wide eyes and dilated pupils. The euphoria from the laced blunt was in effect and she was absorbing Mann's words like a sponge. Mann took his rough hand and trailed his fingers to the center of her thighs. Naomi's mouth parted and a pant escaped them. His touch woke her.

"I hear you boo. I got you," she finally replied. "I'm on point. If he's coming for you, then he's coming for me. We a team bae," she stated, before spreading her legs to make room for Mann's big bald head.

He took the invitation and dived into her full-figured wetness. Mann played the game to win, and if keeping her high and satisfied was what it took to stay on top, then so be it.

CHAPTER 33

Serenity slowly pushed open the door to her daughter's room and peeked in. Heaven was sleeping peacefully in her large, pink canopy bed that was fit for an Egyptian princess. She smiled before gently closing the door so she could continue her peaceful slumber. Walking back into the kitchen she sighed before sitting down at her dining table. She was exhausted from the chain of events that had taken place over the last two weeks. She wished she could snap her fingers and make all her problems disappear. However, she knew that she couldn't, so she would have to settle for a glass of wine for a temporary fix.

"So, what's next Serenity?" her mother Gina asked with genuine concern once she got comfortable at the table.

She had been in and out helping Serenity with any and everything she needed. She had even taken time off work to make sure she was available for her stressed and grieving daughter. Gina did her best to keep a positive attitude, but it was proving to be difficult. She was worried about her Serenity and had been stopping by every day while caring for

Heaven so Serenity could go back and forth to the hospital to see Yosohn.

Serenity scratched the top of her forehead and pushed away the loose strands of hairs out of her face that had fallen from her messy ponytail. She was frustrated, and it showed from her demeanor and sighs escaping her lips.

"I don't know Mommy," Serenity sighed. She knew where her Mom was headed, and she was trying to avoid the conversation. She cringed internally at the thought of her mother ranting for the next thirty minutes. These days, she was hearing it from everyone, including her father.

"Look, Serenity, baby. I'm not telling you what to do with your life because, at the end of the day, you are going to make your own choices. However, you really need to focus on you and Heaven. You are smart, pretty, and educated. When are you going to stop putting yourself through this?" she asked, referring to Yosohn and his seemingly never-ending drama.

Gina was also frustrated. She wanted answers, and she was tired of watching her daughter constantly go through unnecessary soap-opera drama with a man that was not her husband. Even if he were her husband, to Gina, Serenity was above the drama he subjected her to. Gina waited for a response, but Serenity didn't answer. She just sighed and picked up her half empty wine glass from the granite countertop. She took a hearty sip of red wine from her glass. Smacking her teeth at Serenity's stubbornness, Gina continued.

"What are you going to do if they come back with that subpoena for him to take a blood test?" Gina asked before pausing. "What are you going to do if the baby is his?" she continued, tilting her body and head to make eye contact with her daughter who appeared to be doing her best to avoid it. Serenity still didn't respond.

"What are you going to do if he's arrested and charged with murder? Shit, what are you going to do if whoever shot him comes back and tries to shoot him again?"

Gina continued to stare at Serenity while she in turn stared down at the table. Tears formed in her large brown eyes and trickled down her face. Seeing her daughter cry for the millionth time over the last week was a hard sight to watch, but nevertheless, she needed to hear the truth.

"I know you love him, but you have to think about you and Heaven. Whoever did this could come back, and either of you, *or both of you*, could get caught in the crossfire … I know you're grown but that is a risk I will not allow you to take," Gina argued.

She didn't understand what it would take for Serenity to wake up and see that her relationship with Yosohn was no longer healthy.

"For God's sake, you just lost your baby from being all stressed," she added so Serenity could see the merit behind her argument. "Do you plan to play step mama to a love child he made while with you?"

While Gina knew all too well the intense feeling of love, she didn't understand what exactly her child was holding onto. Serenity had literally cried for days over the loss of Jahkee. Yosohn was the reason behind Serenity's high blood pressure. At first, she hadn't told anyone why she left Yosohn; however, when she went into premature labor, the ER doctor would inform her family that her high blood pressure was stress-related. With her medical record available from her Obstetrician, it was all on file. When questioned by her family, she would go on to admit that stress was related to her high-risk pregnancy. Yosohn was the reason for everything: the cheating, the crazy mistress, and a possible baby. The headaches and the heartaches never ended. Growing frustrated, Serenity finally decided to respond.

"Mommy can you please just mind your business and let me handle this." She waved her mother off with her hand in frustration. "I know you care, but this is my life and I am going to live it how I want. I also know that you love me enough to respect that, without judgment."

She hated telling her family her business, and that was the reason many things her and Yosohn went through, she kept private. She hated people passing judgment on her or him. Gina took a deep breath and exhaled solemnly. While she was extremely frustrated, Serenity was right. She decided she would leave. She got up and leaned over to give Serenity a kiss on the forehead.

"Get some rest, baby, and call me. And call your father. He's been trying to reach you … Just know that whatever you decide, I'm with you."

While she didn't agree with many of Serenity's choices lately, she never wanted her daughter to feel that she was alone and couldn't come to her. With that said, Gina walked quietly out of the home. She and her husband Chris, were planning to see a movie later out at Plymouth Meeting Mall. Although she initially didn't want to go, Chris insisted that she go to take her mind off what was going on. The way he saw it, Serenity was going to make her own decisions and she had certainly made that very clear. There was no need to carry extra weight on her shoulders over someone else's choices.

As Gina's tires made the crunching sound from driving over her rocky gravel driveway, Serenity walked over and peered through the windows. She saw her mothers' vehicle drive off down the road of the gated community in which Serenity had returned to care for Yosohn. With her fingers clutching her glass, Serenity tossed the remaining wine down like it was cool water. For the past week she had struggled with what she planned to do. Losing her baby made her feel like she had hit rock bottom.

She had decided earlier that day when she looked into Yosohn's eyes, that if it came to light that he had lied about fathering an outside child that she would walk away from him and the life they shared. Losing her baby was one thing; but finding out that he fathered another baby right after, would be the icing on the cake. How could she accept another's child when hers had been taken? Yosohn had no idea how much pain he had caused her.

To her, he nor the life were no longer worth that pain. Before, the joy of expecting her son made it seem worthwhile, but now that was no more. Although she was hurt, she decided to be grateful. At the end of the day, she already had a beautiful child, a beautiful family, a well-earned degree, and enough money in the bank to open several of her own laundromats. She no longer needed Yosohn's bullshit. If that baby was his, she was leaving. That was her decision, and hers only. She wasn't going to explain that to anyone.

CHAPTER 34

"Yosohn, it's a court order and you have no choice but to submit to the blood test." Yosohn looked at his long-time attorney and shook his head in disgust. He truly wanted to smack the strands of hair from his head. He didn't understand what he was paying him for. He was supposed to be one of the best lawyers in the state. He didn't want to take a blood test. He was aware of the possibility that Eva could be his baby and he wasn't prepared to entertain that idea. If she was his, he didn't want anyone finding out about it, especially not the police. How could they just force him to give his blood? He was more than pissed; he was appalled.

"Fuck," he replied quietly. "What happens if it's mine?" he asked, refusing to refer to the baby as a person. He had only just recently found out her name. Yosohn was still in slight denial, although he wanted to be prepared for whatever.

"It doesn't mean that they will try to charge you with anything," John explained, doing his best to look at the cup half full. "Frankly, I don't feel they have sufficient evidence to charge you with anything at all. If they do decide to pursue a case against you then it would be purely circumstantial. The problem is, you do actually have a motive."

John got up and paced the room in frustration. He had represented plenty of rich guilty people and it never ceased to amaze him that they became frustrated when they were the ones who committed the crime. It was if they felt like the law didn't apply to them and that money should be able to buy them out of a situation. And that just wasn't the case all the time. In his heart he truly believed Yosohn did it; however, as his attorney, he didn't really care.

"She *was* blackmailing you. You had a lot to lose: a fiancé, a new baby, businesses. And suddenly... poof! She winds up dead." John threw his hands up after the statement for emphasis. "You already know how that looks Yosohn ... And these are all the things they are going to come at us with if they do decide to charge you. Purely circumstantial, but nevertheless, enough for a strong motive. The only thing that works in your favor is that she was in the prostitution field and she could have ruffled anyone's feathers. However, it sure as hell won't help if that baby she was carrying while she was murdered turns out to be yours." He stared at Yosohn somberly. This was serious and he wanted Yosohn to understand that.

Yosohn stared ahead blankly. The more John talked, the more he realized his life was going to shit. He'd tried so hard to build a respectable life, and now here he was ... preparing himself to fight a case for killing a prostitute. Yosohn hated that term. He knew Jocelyn probably slept around for money, but the term was so degrading. It bothered him even more that he could possibly be the father to a woman that held such a title.

"If it goes to court, we have a shot, but ... that's not a guarantee that we will win. It's going to look bad if that baby is yours. That's pretty much what everything is riding on at this time."

Yosohn shifted around in his motorized, leather wheelchair he'd been given at discharge. He was growing hot and uncomfortable. He was used to being in control. He knew he had lost that a long time ago. What John was saying was true and Yosohn didn't like the idea one bit. Worse came to worse; the district attorney was going to charge him with murder based on some circumstantial bullshit, and he would have to pay at least $100k to ensure he was well represented with the best team of lawyers in the area. He didn't have time to be sitting in jail over trash like Jocelyn. He also didn't want to spend that much of his money on a ridiculous amount of legal fees.

"Fuck it," he said out loud. He figured he would deal with it how it came. He had no choice. He had to be ready.

BIANCA WALKED UP THE SHABBY STEPS ON A QUEST TO REACH the gates that would take her into the Brooklyn hi-rise she was headed to. Broken beer bottles, random debris, and an old cigarette box blocked her path. She walked around it and made her way to the first floor, finally arriving at apartment three. She had been coming there for ages. She knocked lightly and waited. Jocelyn's mother Arima opened the door of the ran down apartment that had been home to her and her children for many years. The home held so many unpleasant memories that no one bothered to even visit. In her arms she held baby Eva.

Eva had been named in a haste. Rushed into the emergency room at 10:00 p.m., baby Eva was only two pounds, but was surprisingly in good shape after having been removed from her dead mother via cesarean-section before her oxygen supply was completely depleted. Eva had been lucky. A few more minutes inside of her mother would have caused her severe brain damage, and possibly death. Luckily her self-designated godmother Bianca, had been there to call for help, giving baby Eva a chance to make it.

"Hey, Miss Arima; how are you? Just coming by to check on you and the baby." She smiled and held out the large plastic bag she had tucked at her side. It was more diapers, as well as a few more outfits for the fast-growing baby.

"Thank you," Arima mumbled, while quickly taking the bag. She didn't bother hiding her agitation. She had been up all night with the crying child, and she had finally gotten her to sleep again before Bianca's knock. While Arima loved the child, she was none too pleased to learn that her daughter had been murdered in some old, nasty hotel room. She was most displeased with the fact that she would have to raise her baby.

Arima had raised all her children and hadn't gotten a penny's worth of credit for doing the best she could. Jocelyn had been especially defiant and ungrateful, and Arima wasn't surprised she had been killed. Bianca sensed her irritation and decided she wouldn't waste her time making small talk.

"Can I just give her a quick hold and hug so I can leave you two alone?" She smiled, doing her best to lighten the tension in the small room.

Bianca already knew how Arima felt about her daughter Jocelyn. Additionally, she was old and bitter, and Bianca couldn't blame her. Coming to the U.S. had done nothing for Arima but provide her with better medical coverage and a harsh dose of reality. With no education, she was thrust into a life of poverty and prostitution. A few years ago, she had been diagnosed with HIV and had been living like a hermit ever since. Bianca knew that it was only so long before someone had to step in and care for baby Eva. She decided it would be her. While Arima did her best, Bianca sensed her frustration with the newborn every time she came by. Eva would often be crying and would usually have on a wet diaper. This concerned Bianca since Eva had been born premature, and although healthy, needed special care.

It had been weeks since Jocelyn had been cremated and Bianca had been taking major steps to change her life. Bianca understood it could've been her lying dead on that dirty mattress. After all, they played the game together. Bianca played it to win while Jocelyn had been playing for keeps. Breaking the cardinal rule had cost her life. She was to never get caught up --- never fall in love, but she did. Unfortunately, she learned a very hard lesson. Looking in, many would say she deserved it. However, to Bianca, her punishment had been extreme and unjust.

These days Bianca was quickly making changes so she could turn her life around and eventually file for guardianship of baby Eva. Seeing Jocelyn dead, she felt a sense of responsibility for Eva. Jocelyn had been her main bitch and she wanted to do right by her child. She had just gotten a job as a Home Health Aide at a nursing home close by.

With some hard work Bianca would save some money and move out of her mother's apartment into her own so she could raise Eva up right. She was even thinking about getting out of New York. Maybe move to Jersey.

There was no telling how many years left Arima had in her, and with no father, Bianca was the closest thing to family as she would have. She would make it happen for both herself and Eva. She kept those thoughts in her mind before kissing Eva on her forehead and heading out. It was still early and the only reason she had come by at that hour was because she had to be to work by 10 a.m. As she bounced her way back out the building to catch the nearby sub, she pushed back her thoughts of her friends' killer. He was somewhere living it up with his perfect life, while her late friends' body lay cold in a box.

CHAPTER 35

S erenity parked Yosohn's car in front of the District Attorney's office that was located downtown. After helping Yosohn get out of his wheelchair and in the car, she sat quietly and waited for him to tell her how the meeting with his lawyer went.

"So, what happened?" she asked after a minute of silence.

He seemed as if he didn't want to talk about the situation, but Serenity didn't care. Just the day before, he had been served at their home with a subpoena for him to take a blood test for Eva. Since then, Yosohn had been quiet. To Serenity, that was merely a sign of worry. She didn't need Yosohn to confirm that the baby might be his because she could sense that fact in his demeanor. Since she met him, Yosohn had always been confident. These days, he seemed stressed out while his mental state, along with his physical state, seemed fragile. That was a far cry from the Yosohn she knew.

What Serenity didn't know was that Yosohn was terrified. He could handle the fact of being Eva's biological father. He had the means to provide for her and could pay whatever child support they ordered. If only it were just that simple.

What Yosohn could not handle was the fact that Serenity was most certainly going to leave him for good if he was the father. He had just got her back. He loved her and he didn't want to lose her. On top of that, he had just been shot, and could very soon be fighting a murder case. Yosohn was a nervous wreck, but he still tried to keep a brave face. There was a lot riding on that paternity test. Hitting rock bottom would be an understatement if the test determined that he was the father. He would need Serenity more than ever, but more importantly, he would need God.

"Well." He paused. "I didn't have a choice but to take the test. It was court-ordered." He sighed then continued. "So, my lawyer met me up here so I could take the shit. In a few days that jawn will come back. John says that's basically what they're waiting on to decide whether they're going to try and charge me. Of course, they're not gon' tell us that, but John not stupid and he keeps me hip to the procedures and tactics they use."

Serenity looked at Yosohn.

"Yosohn if for any reason you believe this is your baby, please keep it real with me," she begged. She had asked him the same question repeatedly, but he always told her the same thing. She stared at him, eyes wide and intense. He avoided her gaze, choosing to look straight ahead.

"It's not mine, Serenity," he said with irritation as he scratched into his freshly tapered beard.

Yosohn wouldn't dare admit to the possibility. He could only pray that the paternity results came back in his favor. He had no idea what he was going to do if the test revealed he was the father. He wasn't sure how he was going to tell her. If given the option, he would hide it and take it to his grave.

Finally pulling up to their home, Serenity got out, her backless gold jumpsuit clinging to her shapely body. Since the birth of their deceased son, her already voluptuous frame had filled out even more. Her breasts were fuller, her hips wider, and her backside even more shapely. Walking around to the passenger side, Serenity went to help Yosohn out of the car. Although he used a wheelchair to make it easier to get around, he was making excellent progress. He still had some pain, but with the proper rest, the doctors expected him to have most of his strength back in a few weeks.

After getting Yosohn settled in, Serenity walked to the bathroom. She sat on the toilet and took a deep breath. Tapping her feet against the slate gray tile, she groaned lightly. She was still having cramps and bleeding from Jahkee's birth. After cleaning up, she stood up. She washed her hands and then proceeded to pull some Tylenol out of the cabinet. Cupping her hand in the faucet to drink water, she quickly threw the pills back.

Sitting back on the closed toilet seat, Serenity placed her head in her hands and closed her eyes. It was her way of finding momentary peace: peace from all her problems with Yosohn, her family, and the constant thoughts of Jahkee. She had no time to mourn and no time to wallow in self-pity. She had Heaven to take care of and a business to run.

Both had been tremendously neglected over the last few weeks. She planned to make it up to Heaven with her undivided attention and a mini vacation. As for Susan, she planned to give her a well-deserved surprise bonus. After working longer days and handling all the paperwork and inventory, she certainly deserved it.

Breaking away from her thoughts, she reached and grabbed her vibrating phone off the sink. It was Shanita.

"Hello," she answered.

"Hey. How you feeling?" Shanita asked, always full of concern.

"I'm okay. Just got in from the District Attorney's office

and now my damn stomach is hurting from cramps," Serenity complained.

"Ugh … Well, did you take something for it? And what did they say when y'all went up there?"

"I took a Tylenol and honestly I don't know exactly what was said because Yosohn insisted that he go in alone. He claims his lawyer says it's best. The less I know, the better apparently," she scoffed. "I think he's hiding shit from me and doesn't want me to sit in on meetings with his lawyer because he is able to speak more freely. I ain't gon' worry about it though, because the truth will definitely surface; it always does."

"I couldn't have said it better myself … Well, the reason I called you is because I cooked. I made some meatloaf, mashed potatoes, and peas. I can bring you a plate or you can go get Heaven from Shyanne's and y'all can come eat over here," she offered.

"I will be by there shortly. I gotta pick up Heaven anyway. I've been seeing her on and off for the last couple weeks … I don't want to keep pushing her off on anyone and I know she feels neglected," she said, sighing for the millionth time that day.

"Heaven understands and everyone loves her. She's like one of our own so it's not a problem at all. Don't ever think that … But look, come get this food. I'll wrap Yosohn up a plate also for him to eat later."

"Thanks, Nita. I'ma check on Yosohn and then I'm on my way."

"Ok," she responded. They both hung up and Serenity exited the bathroom to go check on Yosohn. He was fast asleep in their king-size bed, with the sports channel still playing loudly. She could never understand how he slept through so much noise. Giving him a soft kiss on the cheek, she grabbed her keys and left.

After driving for a few minutes, Serenity took the street that allowed her to enter onto the expressway. Shyanne stayed way out near West Philly in Wynnefield, a racially diverse, middle class section of the city. It was quite the distance during mid-day traffic, and out of the way from the Mt. Airy neighborhood that Shameka and Shanita lived in. Their neighborhood was just next door, a few minutes away from her own in Chestnut Hill.

"What the fuck!" Serenity yelled out unexpectedly while she drove. She had run over something in the road and her truck was now riding ruggedly and making thumping sounds over the roadway. She immediately recognized the sounds as a flat tire.

"Fuck," she muttered through gritted teeth. She immediately hit her flashers and pulled over on the narrow shoulder to avoid damaging the rim on her truck. She grabbed her phone and called AAA. She never used them, but they religiously took nearly $200 dollars from her bank account to give her and Yosohn peace of mind on the roadway. She ignored the automated messages and patiently waited on the line for a live representative.

While waiting, a black Ford Crown Victoria pulled up behind her. As the stranger exited the car, Serenity quickly looked to see if any more speeding cars were approaching. The expressway she was on was a dangerous one and there wasn't much space to walk. He could approach at his own risk, because she wasn't going to dare step foot out of her truck. The stranger approached the passenger's side window away from the roadway and knocked on the glass.

"You need some help?" he asked. He reached in his pocket to his wallet and pulled out his badge. He was a cop. He didn't look like one. Serenity rolled down the window and smiled.

"Yes, thank you. I do. I got a flat tire. I called AAA but they still have me on hold," she responded.

She noticed how handsome and ordinary he looked. Not that cops didn't look like regular people, but he looked like they could have grown up together, or perhaps could've lived down the block from her as a child. For some reason when she thought of cops, she thought of fat, white men or boring up-tight black men. This one was neither.

"Oh, that's easy," he smiled, his large brown eyes crinkling at the corners. He had a chocolate complexion, not as deep as hers but still very rich. He had bushy eyebrows that would benefit from a good pluck, and full luscious lips. He caught her staring and asked, "So, do you have a spare?" He said it like he had asked already. "I can swap it out for you in five minutes."

"Aww, thank you so much … And yeah, I have a spare. It's in the back," she answered with a smile. "By the way, I'm Serenity," she stated. She figured it was courteous to at least give him her name. After all, he was helping her out.

"Nice to meet you, Serenity. I'm Razul," he added, before taking off to the side of the car to tend to the flat tire. Serenity looked over and saw that he had on normal street attire. Blue jeans and a gray polo, paired with gray New Balance 990's. It was something about his plain, rugged manliness that sent chills to her body. After ten minutes of funky noises and the car going up and down, Razul was finished.

"Thank you so much. I really appreciate it," Serenity told him. Her eyes darted around for her wallet. She spotted it on the edge of the seat and quickly dug out $20 to give him.

"Here you go. I want to give you something for helping me out," she offered, extending her hand out so he could take the money.

"You're good sweetheart. I would never take money from

a woman." He smiled and couldn't help but notice how pretty she was. Something about her deep Hershey-bar complexion seemed exotic to him.

"Aww, well thank you again. I really appreciate it."

Razul hesitated for a minute but then decided to go ahead. He looked at the traffic whizzing by him and remembered that he *was* on the side of the highway.

"Umm, I did want to know something though." He smiled and paused. "I was hoping that I could take you out some time … sometime soon," he added.

"Uhhh, I don't know," she blushed. As she did that, Razul noticed the large, sparkling engagement ring on her finger.

"I mean, it's harmless," he said, doing his best to persuade her without acknowledging her future union. He didn't see a wedding band, so she was still technically up for grabs.

"It doesn't have to be dinner. Maybe we could have a drink … meet somewhere very public. I just want to see you again … as new friends."

"Okay," Serenity agreed, surprising herself by her quick response. She knew it wasn't the smartest idea but figured she could use someone new to talk to. Yosohn would flip if he found out. She looked at Razul and figured, what Yosohn didn't know wouldn't hurt him. He had more than his share of fun anyway.

The two exchanged numbers and Serenity drove off, all the while, her mind drifting back in thought to the mysteriously not-so plain cop she had just had the pleasure of meeting.

CHAPTER 36

Mann hit his key fob to lock up his cream-colored, late model BMW. He had just exited it to run into the gas station.

"Yo, let me get twenty on three," he said, speaking loudly to the clerk, who was behind a massive bulletproof encasement used to secure the cash as well as the lives behind it.

She nodded her turban wrapped head and quickly accepted his money through the designated space. Mann quickly hurried out of the tightly packed store and proceeded to pump his gas. He had several things to do and wasn't trying to be all night doing them. His new connect was supplying him with the best weed around and it was moving like crazy. After his massive come up off Dodda, he was doing triple the numbers he once was with Yosohn. This kept him literally running around night and day to pick up money from spots all over the city.

After gassing up his car, Mann hopped in and turned onto Cayuga street off Broad Street to exit North Philly. He had some money to pick up at a few spots in West Philly and then he was headed home. All else could wait. As he cruised down the expressway he reached over and grabbed his bottle of Hennessy he kept tucked on the side of his plush leather seats. Since his grandmother had passed, his headaches grew worse and so did his drinking. To him, alcohol eased his pain. Helped him cope. He got through most of the day self-medicated and slept through the night with the assistance of sleep aids and Tylenol. Although he was seeing more money than he ever had in his life, he was in a poor state mentally. His primary concerns and thoughts revolved around getting rich and keeping tabs on Serenity through Naomi. He wasn't even so much as worried about Yosohn anymore. If he was going to retaliate, he would've been done it. In Mann's opinion, legal life was making him soft. For now, he would keep quiet and wait everything out. It was all a tactic before the storm came.

YOSOHN WATCHED AS SERENITY ROCKED, SWAYED, AND struggled her way into her favorite pair of True Religion jeans. While he wanted her to go out and enjoy herself, he couldn't help but feel jealous at the thought of a bunch of dudes eyeballing his chick. It had been over a month since he had been shot and he was still making progress. Although his wounds were nearly completely healed and his body was on its way back to being strong, his sexual performance wasn't all the way back. With wounds to his back and stomach, he couldn't fuck her missionary. With Serenity bouncing up and down on top of him, he was barely going two minutes. Not only was it embarrassing, it was also frustrating to him because he felt like he couldn't completely satisfy her, which in turn fueled his current feeling of insecurity.

"Where you say you and Naomi was going again?" Yosohn asked.

"Mojo's … for the last time, Yosohn," she lied. "Why don't you get you some rest babe and relax," she said, doing her best to calm his nerves, before leaning over and giving him a kiss on the lips.

"What time you gon' be in?" he asked, disregarding her request.

"I don't know. I'll probably only be gone a few hours." She smoothed on her final coat of lip gloss and smiled wide. "I won't be gone long. I promise … It's a bowl of Jambalaya in the microwave if you get hungry and I'll call you in a little bit."

"Aight," he responded dismally. "Have fun," he mumbled sarcastically as he used the remote to flick through the channels on his 80-inch, wall-mounted plasma television, a gift he was given by Serenity after his arrival from the hospital. Knowing he would be weak and probably still somewhat bedridden, she picked it up.

"Thanks, boo. I will," she responded before walking out.

"YEAH GIRL. I GOTCHU," NAOMI LAUGHED LIGHTLY INTO THE phone. "If for any reason he calls me, you ran to the bathroom," she repeated for the second time as Serenity requested. "Then call you," she continued, knowing full well that Yosohn would never reach out to her after what happened between them … Or rather, what *didn't happen* between them.

In a way, she was glad nothing happened since she ultimately got the prize: Mann. In Naomi's eyes, he was the real hustler of the two. Mann had the vision; Yosohn just had the money. Now it was her man that was on top.

"What the hell are you up to anyway?" she laughed

jokingly, as Mann sat beside her with curiosity running through him.

"Okay, boo. Aight. Bye, girl," she said hurriedly before hanging up.

Mann sat silently with curiosity killing him. He did his best to avoid appearing nosy.

"Umm, hmm, her ass is up to something," Naomi said aloud.

"Why you say that," asked Mann.

"That bitch ain't never call me and ask me to cover for her with Yosohn. Talking about … tell him she going to Mojos, when her ass is really going to Sonix's. Sounds like she creeping to me." She laughed, doing her best to make Serenity sound like the whore she really was.

She was only putting up with her ass because of Mann. She didn't need her anymore, and their friendship was nonexistent. It had clearly been destroyed by jealousy.

"Damn … That would be crazy if she was. Yosohn just came home from the hospital," he said, growing angry at the thought of her being with someone else, whoever it was.

He didn't understand why he was so hung up on Serenity; he just was. Even if she was out creeping on Yosohn, he felt that Yosohn deserved it. The problem for Mann was, he felt like she was also creeping on him. What they shared that one night was far from over. Serenity was now his obsession, and he would stop at nothing to get her.

CHAPTER 37

Serenity walked into Sonix Restaurant and Lounge and peered around. It was dimly lit with rustic colors and a fireplace. It was very upscale and cozy. Razul waved to her from the corner. She smiled and walked over to him. It had been only two weeks since he changed her tire and they had been texting non-stop since then. Very quickly she had grown extremely attracted to him. Not only was he handsome: he was single, never married, and had no children. She also admired his drive and work ethic, as he often worked sixty hours a week as a Police Sergeant with The Philadelphia Police Department in the Narcotics Department. He wasn't well off, but he was secure and hardworking, and she respected that. Serenity greeted Razul with a light hug and sat down in the high top, wooden chair beside him. He smelled good. The cologne he wore was sweet with a woody scent.

"You look nice. How are you?" she asked, while checking out his attire. He had on a signature black and white Adidas tracksuit, and classic white shell tops. He was handsome indeed.

"Thanks. I try to be comfortable. And you of course look beautiful," he said with admiration. Serenity looked casual but stunning, in fitted jeans and a black half shirt. Her neck sparkled in gold while her waist-length Malaysian hair bounced around freely.

"Thank you. Can I get a Sangria?" Serenity asked the bartender, who had placed a napkin in front of her as soon as she arrived. The bartender took her order and walked off. Serenity went in her mini Lady Dior bag and pulled out her matching wallet, but Razul stopped her.

"I got it, sweetheart. You don't have to pay for anything when you're with me." While Serenity thought the gesture was sweet, she also found it unnecessary. She could pay her own way.

"Thank you. That's nice of you. I'll let you pay this time and next time I'll pay. I'm all about equality," she laughed lightly.

"You never told me what it is you do … If you don't mind me asking."

"Why? You ready to lock me up. You think I'm selling drugs," she laughed jokingly. "Na, I'm just joking. I actually co-own a small chain of laundromats in the city," she replied modestly.

"Niceeee," he said with a smile. "So, you can go ahead and pull that purse back out baby girl," he laughed, causing Serenity to laugh out as well.

"Nope. You offered," she said with a smile.

"So how was work today and if you don't mind me asking, what made you want to be a cop? No offense, but growing up, you seldom heard little black boys past ten years old talk about being a cop."

He smiled. That was one of the things he liked about her. She was inquisitive and not self-absorbed. She could hold a conversation that wasn't limited to reality shows and entertainment. He figured he would go ahead and give her his story.

"Well, when I was fifteen there was a so-called drug drought. The War on Drugs had been implemented and they were doing a good job ridding the streets of drugs. However, with a decrease in the available supply of drugs came higher prices and a lot more frustration on the streets. Blocks weren't doing the same amount of numbers and things were dry all over the city. Turf wars ensued. During the time, we were smack dab in the hood. Right in the center of every-thing … Shootings were happening damn near every day. I asked my mother could I get a part-time job so I could bring home an extra, you know, four to five hundred a month. I figured it would help us afford more rent so we could move to a better neighborhood. She wouldn't allow it. I was one of the best ballplayers in my school and an A/B student. I could have easily gotten a full ride into a decent college. She wanted me to focus on that. So, instead of me getting a job, she found a second job close by our house. The job was night shift. As dangerous as it was to be out at night during those times, she still took it. I told her I would meet her at her bus stop and walk her home every night she worked. One night I had a game and it lasted longer than I expected. I rushed to meet her, but I was too late. The one night I didn't show up." Razul paused for a minute. Thinking back to that time always made him sad.

"There was a shootout, and my mother was gunned down; mistakenly shot and hit by a stray bullet. Tore me to pieces. Immediately though, I knew she would not want me to be bitter; she would want me to be better. So," he exhaled. "I went to college and majored in Criminal Justice. Took a job with the police department right after. My goal is to get as many drug dealers off the streets as I can. Not just by arresting them and sending them to prison; instead, educating the ones who still have a chance. Every little bit counts right," he smiled.

"Wow," was all that Serenity could initially say. Razul was something special. A different kind of man she was used to. "I'm sorry to hear that happened but I commend you for making a positive contribution from something negative."

"It's all a choice … I speak at the jail and schools from time to time, and I try to instill that in these young boys. You have a choice out here no matter what circumstances you come from. Education can take the poorest person and turn them into something completely different. These kids just don't understand that. Instead, they sell drugs and look up to those that glamorize that life. Do you have kids?" he asked.

"Yeah, a little girl," Serenity beamed.

"I want some. Not until I'm settled though. I want their childhood to be completely different from my own.

"I understand that. I can't lie, I had my daughter early, but I have a great family and failure was not an option. I grew up decent, and I'm proud to say that I am able to separate her from that world you speak of."

Serenity thought that Razul was too good to be true. There was always a twist. She wasn't going to look for it because she always did her best to see the good in people and be optimistic; however, she wasn't going to sleep on him either. Ironically, he felt the same way.

MANN SAT IN A CORNER OF SONIX'S AND INCONSPICUOUSLY watched from across the room as Serenity conversed with some nigga he'd never seen before. As soon as Naomi had gotten off the phone with her, he made an excuse to rush out so he could beat Serenity to her destination. Although Naomi had been suspicious, she didn't dare question him.

Mann could be quick-tempered at times and since she enjoyed being with him, she wanted to stay on his good side … for now.

He continued to watch Serenity and the unknown male. A million questions ran through his mind. He wanted to confront her right then and there but knew it wasn't the right time. He would do it later, and when he did, she'd better have her story straight. To him, Serenity was the ultimate game player. From using him to get back at Yosohn, to trying to flee him like he was a pesky nuisance, to hanging out with a completely new nigga. She seemed to be scattered. If one situation was played out to her, she was onto the next. He hoped that she wasn't the scandalous hoe that Naomi claimed she was. Unfortunately, as time went on, claims about her character and conduct didn't seem to add up. She was into games. Problem was, *he wasn't*.

"THE RESULTS CAME BACK POSITIVE, YOSOHN." JOHN REACHED up, adjusted his tie, and cleared his throat before cautiously announcing, "You are her father," he stated quickly while Yosohn sat before him stunned.

Before he could respond, Serenity quietly got up and unexpectedly slapped Yosohn across the face so hard, it created an echo in the room.

"Fuck you, Yosohn, "she spat, before storming out of John's office.

Serenity was done. She felt as if she had been hit in the stomach with a baseball bat. She had been betrayed. Presented with a woman's worse nightmare. *A baby*. She had to let it digest. *A fucking baby*. She'd had enough of his shit and was taking back her life. She was moving forward. For the past seven years, Serenity had been multiple things rolled up into one. She had been Yosohn's lover, his confidant, his nurse when he was ill, and more importantly, his biggest and almost only support system. What she would no longer be, was his fool and his punching bag. While the blows he delivered to her were not physical, they were indeed emotional. She'd had enough.

Yosohn's face tingled from the forceful slap, while his heart sank to the floor. He didn't bother to run behind Serenity as he knew it would be pointless. He fucked up. He'd made mistakes. He didn't even know what to say to her at that point. It was like Deja vu all over again.

"What's next, John?" Yosohn asked softly. "Is this enough for them to try and prosecute me?"

"I can't say for sure, Yosohn. I don't know what else they have, or what other information they've acquired ... What I do know is that, we won't give up. If they come for you, I'll give them the best damn fight they've ever seen," he assured him.

Clearly frustrated, Yosohn hunched over and buried his head in his hands. He wished he were still a kid, all alone in the bathroom of his group home dorm. There he could cry silently and alone. Ever since he was little, he suppressed his emotions. He learned to cope with being alone mentally. His heart ached because Serenity had freed him from that feeling. She had helped him open up and showed him that he was not alone. Now she was gone, and the only person he had was his lawyer John, who was sitting in front of him pretending to be a friend. If the money ever ran out, he'd be gone too.

"John, I don't want to fight, man," he said revealing his growing weakened mental state. "How much to make this go away?"

John looked at Yosohn and worry shown on his face. "I don't know, Yosohn ... I can't bribe anyone. I could lose my license … What I can do is talk to a few people and see if I can get a favor for a favor. We'll discuss prices later. Ok, buddy?" John stated getting up from his large executive style desk and patting Yosohn on his tired back.

"Ok, John." He was counting on him.

CHAPTER 38

"**Y**ou're fucking shitting me," Detective Mason shouted angrily a week later. He'd just been handed a notice by his supervisor and he had to admit, he was floored. "Read this shit," he said before passing the paper over to his partner.

Detective Bohn took the paper and quickly read it. He immediately began to shake his head in disapproval and disappointment. Yosohn Thomas had been officially ruled out as a suspect in the murder case of Jocelyn Rodriguez. He was reading and holding the dismissal notice. The prosecutor had determined that there just wasn't enough evidence to move forward. They were no longer to question or bother Yosohn Thomas, or anyone associated with him.

"You know Bohn, I took this job to help catch bad people and see that justice was served. But every day I come here, I learn more and more that the city of Philadelphia's judicial system is based on who you know, and how much you can afford to pay. In just a few short years, I've seen rich assholes get off too many times to count. What are we here for?" Mason asked, not expecting an answer.

He couldn't answer the question, and neither could his

partner. It wasn't the first time, and they knew it surely wouldn't be the last.

~

AFTER HEARING THE NEWS FROM JOHN THAT HE HAD BEEN ruled out as a suspect, Yosohn was elated. John never mentioned or planned to tell Yosohn that he knew the prosecutor from undergrad. He never liked to reveal his sources and only called upon them when he truly needed them. A little convincing that Yosohn's wasn't their guy, and the reality that it wasn't worth the public circus to try a rich business owner for murder of a poor prostitute, with a criminal history, his prosecutor friend decided not to proceed. John played on the fact that the risk was huge for his career, as Yosohn had enough money to hire bull-dog attorneys that would literally rip through the prosecution team with their weak circumstantial evidence,

It also helped that an all-expense dinner to an elite reservation-only steakhouse downtown was gifted to the prosecutor and his wife. It was a small cost for John, as lawyers often scratched one another's back. However, it was a large cost for Yosohn. $50k for the paperwork stating he was no longer considered a suspect and would not be furthered investigated. Anytime John went out of his way, it didn't come cheap. Yosohn didn't mind.

"Thanks, John. I'll have that money transferred to your account by the end of the day." Yosohn paused but decided to finally go ahead and ask his counselor and legal advisor the question that was plaguing his mind. He was determined to do the right thing moving forward.

"John, what about the baby … My uhm." He paused, "My daughter. I want to know where she is."

"Oh, last I heard she was a ward of the state … Why do you ask? Are you thinking of getting custody?"

"Yeah," Yosohn responded, quietly. "She's mine, and I'm going to take care of her." Yosohn had decided, and it was final. He was going to start being a real man. Besides, she was his only real blood relative nearby. She was all he had. He had lost so much. He didn't want to lose anymore. He didn't want to hurt anyone else.

"Well then … Good for you, Yosohn. You know I'm with you no matter what. Listen. I have a good friend that works in that field. She handles custody hearings and works mainly in family court. I'll send you her number. She's definitely the one that can help you get your little girl."

"Thanks, John."

"Ay, don't mention it. And, Yosohn. Good luck, buddy. Stay out of trouble."

"No doubt," he responded, before ending the call and sighing.

John's phone call was the only good thing that had happened to him all week. Serenity had left him. She hadn't even bothered to pack her shit. He was sure she had gotten all new things, as there had been a ridiculous amount of charges totaling $10k on his American Express card. He was sure that had covered new wardrobes and furniture. He figured he would let her do her thing. He was the one in the wrong.

The first night after finding out he was the father to Jocelyn's baby, he felt like shit. He didn't want a baby by her. He didn't know any nigga that would want a baby by a prostitute. He had discovered her lies through his lawyer and police reports. She had never danced. She sold her ass. She was the lowest of the lowest, and sadly, he fell right under the same umbrella. His life would never be the same. He didn't expect it to be. His first thoughts were that he didn't want anything to do with the baby, but then he remembered Jocelyn saying that she wasn't close to her family. His heart was cold but not that icy. After all, Eva was his flesh and blood. He made a long and conscious decision that he would do right by her. He would do everything in his power to get Serenity and Heaven back but if he did not, he would have his own daughter, Eva in his life.

CHAPTER 39

S erenity waited at Zeppi's Bar, a quiet lounge that was tucked away on the Northeast Side of the city. It had been weeks since her and Yosohn's split and although saddened that their relationship had ended, she was happy with her decision and her life at that point. Feeling warm and excited, Serenity lightly fanned herself. She felt a light coat of perspiration build up on the tip of her nose.

"Here you go," the bartender said, as she slid another Long Island Iced Tea in front of her. It was her second and she silently vowed it would also be her last. She didn't want to be drunk.

"Thanks, she responded quietly, as she slid a bill towards the bartender.

"Hey, babe," Razul said in his masculine voice, surprising Serenity with his sudden arrival. She had been waiting for him but hadn't seen him when he came in.

"Hey you." He planted a soft kiss on the side of her neck, causing her to blush.

"How long you been here?" Razul asked.

He smiled and showed his pearly white teeth. His beard

was neatly tapered, and he had gotten a little darker since the summer had begun. He was looking Michael Vick good.

"Not too long." She smiled. "I'm glad to see you." She was tipsy and the sight of Razul always made her heat up.

They had been seeing each other consistently and it was safe to say that they were feeling one another. Although Serenity was the one who initially wanted to take it slow, she had decided she was finally ready to go to the next step of intimacy with him. He didn't know it yet, but it was happening when they left. He had the next few days off and she had agreed to hang out with him for the evening. It was summer and Heaven was away enjoying the shore with her father Tate.

After sitting down, Razul leaned over and gave Serenity another quick kiss. As he pulled away, she frowned. Her gaze was fixed near the entrance. Her mood instantly changed. She made an internal vow that she wouldn't engage in the foolery.

"Here we go with the bullshit," she sighed underneath her breath.

YOSOHN GREW ANGRY AS SOON AS HE ENTERED THE LIGHTLY occupied and dimly lit lounge. He had spotted Serenity with a male unknown to him. He took a deep breath and fought to contain the rage touring his body.

"What are you doing?" he asked Serenity, as he approached her with his now signature limp. The average person would mistake it as a bop but for Yosohn it was a constant reminder that he'd been shot.

Serenity met Yosohn's angry gaze. She wasn't surprised. She figured that Yosohn would go through whatever lengths to get her back. She did her best to hide her anger. She wasn't going to give him the satisfaction. Especially, considering that she was grown and no longer needed to answer to anyone.

"I'm minding my business. Why are you here, Yosohn?" she asked, coolly.

"What the fuck do you mean, *why am I here?* I've been calling and texting yo' ass for damn near three weeks and you been ignoring me. Now I see why … You out here being a fucking whore!" he yelled, no longer able to control his temper. "First you go fuck Mann, and now this shit."

Serenity balked at Yosohn's public tirade. "You act so fucking dumb … So, you following me now?" she asked. "I don't have time for this shit," she spat coldly, quickly looking to Razul to signal her departure.

She was embarrassed, and she wasn't doing the public fiasco with Yosohn so she could look like a ghetto buffoon in front of dozens of people

"Yeah I followed you. And I ain't trying to hear that shit. You ain't going nowhere till you talk to me like a fucking adult," Yosohn demanded, reaching for her arm.

As he grabbed at her, Serenity snatched back and Razul quickly jumped up and moved her out of the way to stand between them. It was mostly out of reflex, but he still felt like he had to do it.

"Yo, why don't you just go ahead. She told you she wasn't interested in talking to you," Razul calmly stated, his eyes locking with Yosohn's.

"My nigga …" Yosohn took a deep breath. "I don't know you, and don't care to know you. This is between me and her. I'm just gon' leave it at that," Yosohn said firmly and with finality.

His patience was already nonexistent, and it was especially short for the man in front of him. Yosohn was a street nigga and grew up witnessing some of the toughest dudes kill and be killed behind nonsense. It was something he strived to avoid so he chose his words carefully. He didn't make any demands or indirect threats. He simply did his best to be calm. He wasn't trying to challenge the stranger. He didn't want things to escalate, as he knew his own temper very well. He just hoped the man in front of him used his better judgment the same way he was. All Yosohn knew was, he was far from pussy, and if the man before him were to get out of line in any way, he wouldn't hesitate to put his gun on him. It had been a long time since he had to, but these days anyone could get. He was in no physical shape to fight the equally large man in front of him. If he knew what was best, he'd fall back.

"I don't know you either, but she's with me right now," Razul responded, matching his icy gaze.

Yosohn's eyebrows went up. "Is that right?" he asked, looking to Serenity. She couldn't have moved on that fast. If she did, that certainly said volumes about her character.

"Yosohn just go please," Serenity begged, feeling both irritated and angry. She never enjoyed conflict or confrontation, and the situation before her was making her highly uncomfortable.

"I'm not leaving until you talk to me," he demanded.

Razul's irritation increased and he figured he would have to call up a friend from the nearby precinct before things turned ugly and escalated. He was off duty, and from what he could sense, Yosohn was going to be an issue. The desperate man before him had no intention of letting up.

Feeling defeated and left with little choice, Serenity agreed. "Razul give me a minute okay. I'm going to step outside and talk to him," she said, throwing her hands up.

Yosohn shot Razul a dirty look and the duo proceeded to head outside in front of Zeppi's.

"Wassup?" Serenity asked impatiently. She wanted him to make it quick and get to the point.

"Why you ignoring me, Serenity.? Everybody's ignoring me. I called your mom, your sisters, and you. Nobody has been picking up for me. Nobody has been answering my texts or voicemails … It's like that?" he asked in disbelief. They were like his family and it truly hurt him that they had all turned their back on him.

"Yosohn, they are *my* family. What do you expect? You literally fucked up seven years in twelve months. It's over. They love you, but out of respect, they are distancing themselves."

"Why are you doing this?" he asked, as if things were her fault. "This is crazy. Serenity, baby, we can work this shit out," he pleaded. He knew he sounded like a punk, but he didn't care. He was desperate.

"No, we can't, Yosohn. And stop fucking saying it," she said angrily, her lip quivering. It was that quick. He always had a way of drawing emotion out of her. That was exactly why she wanted him to stay away. She loved him to a fault.

"You had a baby with her," she reminded him angrily, her tone low so no one would hear them. "I can't accept that … I will not accept that," her voice wavering. She did her best to contain the tears that never seemed to deplete. "For the last year I begged and pleaded with you to fix that shit," she said, referring to his affair. "I did my part. I even gave you the opportunity to be honest, and you did not. Why the fuck should I stay with you and help you raise another bitch's baby?" she asked.

She had heard; Nikki had told her that Yosohn sought legal custody of his love child. However, his attempt at trying to do the right thing wasn't impressive to her. It was painful, and she wanted no parts of it.

"Because I helped you do the same fucking thing. And

don't fucking act like you a saint. You did some fucked up shit too," Yosohn replied selfishly. She knew exactly what he meant. However, she couldn't believe the nerve of him.

"Heaven's father is dead, Yosohn. He was gone before we even got together. When you and I met, Heaven and I were a package, and the circumstances were different ... I didn't have Heaven during our relationship. I didn't go out and make her on you. And furthermore, like I always say to yo' ass, one time is a mistake, multiple times is a choice. What I did was a mistake."

"So, why the fuck you in here with that nigga?" he demanded to know.

Shaking her head in disgust, Serenity began to walk off and back into the lounge. Yosohn grabbed her arm. Although she snatched away, she slowed down and stopped.

"Ren, baby ... I am sorry. I fucked up ... I live with this shit every day. You're like my other half," he admitted in desperation. He figured he didn't have shit else to lose, so he chose to speak from his heart and beg her for forgiveness.

"You're everything to me. Please. I don't want to be without you. I swear I've changed." He stared directly into her eyes so she could see his sincerity. "I'm trying to make better choices. I know I hurt you ... I know that. But I love you a lot. And I don't want to be with anyone else."

He wanted to make excuses. He wanted to tell her that Jocelyn had played him, but it was pointless. He knew she wouldn't want to hear it. The only option he had, was to play on her emotions and the fact that she loved him.

"Yosohn," Serenity began while shaking her head in dismay. Her black shiny hair moved with her. She quickly wiped at it. She was disinterested in what he had to say. She didn't want to participate in the bullshit anymore. The topic was not only emotional for her, but it was pointless.

"It's over, Yosohn," she said slowly and sadly. "Please don't make this harder than what it has to be. I love you. I probably always will … but I deserve better."

Tears quickly formed in her eyes and spilled down onto her face. She wiped at them with her French manicured hand. She didn't want any stupid tears getting in her hair. Besides, crying wouldn't get her anywhere. It never had with Yosohn.

Yosohn let go of her arm and peered at her solemnly before speaking. "Na," he replied, while shaking his head in disagreement. He was done begging her ass for the night … but it wasn't over. He wasn't giving up yet. He turned around and walked back to his car that was parked in front of the restaurant. Begging wasn't getting him anywhere and his anger was only escalating. Rejection of his apologies was fueling his fire, and to add salt to his wounded heart, she was on a date with another man. He figured it was best for him to leave before things escalate. He wasn't ready to give up though. He just had to show Serenity he was a man that had changed.

Serenity shook her head sadly and walked back into the restaurant without looking back. She didn't know what Yosohn meant, but what she did know was, he was going to be persistent. He always had been, and that was one of the reasons she had stayed around so long. Things were different now; that chapter of her life was closed, and Yosohn was just going to have to accept that.

CHAPTER 40

S o, back at the restaurant; what was that about?" Razul asked as he plopped down beside Serenity on his spacious microfiber sectional.

He moved a few pillows so they could be close, then he wrapped his arm around her and pulled her into him. He kissed her softly on her cheek to relax her. He sensed she was bothered. After the verbal exchange with Yosohn, Serenity had returned inside the restaurant. While Razul noticed she seemed bothered, she still proceeded as if nothing had occurred. They quickly left at her suggestion and they were now back at his place to watch a movie and chill.

"That was Yosohn," she calmly replied. She took a deep breath and decided to explain their situation. She had given Razul bits and pieces of her past but hadn't delved in too deep about her relationship with her former fiancée. She figured now was the best time if she really wanted to get serious with Razul. She knew it hadn't been long, but she really liked him and felt like he may be exactly what she needed.

"Yosohn and I had a beautiful life together." She stared

off. "Basically, he had the money and I had the degree. Not that the money mattered. I loved him. I loved his heart. As tough as his exterior is, he is truly fragile. No family. Just needed to be loved like he'd never been. And I loved him. So very much. And he loved me back because I gave him something he never had. We were a team ... We built a successful business and we were trying to build a life. But he cheated ... Not once, but many times. I looked past a lot. I pretended I didn't see a lot. When I did see it, he would always make it up to me," she said sarcastically. "A diamond bracelet here. A bigger house there. A new car, earrings. Material shit ... But this last time was what ended us ... The girl was obsessed, and she made her presence well known. *Very known*," she said

"A year of drama, and finally, a newborn baby is why I am now sitting beside you." She shook her head sadly. "I couldn't do it anymore. I was good to him. He loves me. I know he does. Always has. And now he won't let go. He says he's changed. But so have I. I have moved forward with my life. Things I went through, things I wound up doing that were completely out of my character ... I just can't."

She basically summed it up as best as she could. She knew she should tell Razul certain things, but she refused to move forward into a new relationship with a bunch of baggage and issues. Some things were better left unsaid. Razul stared at her as she spoke and saw the pain in her eyes. He took his hand and stroked her arm. The light display of affection from him gave her chills.

"You still love him?" he asked. He had to know. He really liked Serenity and knew if he kept dealing with her, he would grow to love her deeply. He could sense a good woman when he saw one --- one who was wounded, but nevertheless, a good woman. He just hoped that even though she had been wronged many times by someone she loved, she was still able to identify a good man.

"Yeah. I do," she responded, without hesitation. Yosohn would always be in her heart.

"I ask you that Serenity because I really like you. I would like for us to be together on a more serious level, but you would have to determine exactly where you want to be."

They had talked about getting serious before, but Razul had never seen Serenity interact with Yosohn before. While he wasn't intimidated by Yosohn himself, he was a bit intimidated by his effect on Serenity. Her entire emotional state changed when he entered that restaurant. He knew love when he saw it. Theirs had been deep, and he just wasn't sure if he could compete with it. He needed her reassurance.

"I love Yosohn, but I'm not going back to him," she said with finality.

She turned to look at Razul. While he still saw pain, he also saw what he felt was sincerity. He hoped her eyes weren't deceiving him and she was telling the truth. He kissed her and she kissed him back briefly before gently pulling away. He smiled and kissed her again on the face before grabbing the remote. Whenever she was ready, so was he. He wouldn't force her. Serenity had decided she would wait. She had a lot of shit to take care of and wasn't going to confuse the situation more with sex. Razul quickly thumbed through the movies that were On Demand.

"The Hills Have Eyes?" he asked with a smirk, figuring she wasn't fond of gory movies.

"Yesss, that's my jawn. I love scary movies," she said. Razul smiled again.

"Bet." They were alike in more ways than one. He was beginning to think he had found his match.

~

Mann quietly sat in his car and continued to wait for Serenity to exit out of the townhouse she had entered several hours before. He had followed her from the restaurant and had witnessed her meet the same mystery man there, and then trail him to this address. He also couldn't help witnessing a desperate-looking Yosohn, stand on the corner and make a fool of himself by begging Serenity for conversation. He hadn't heard the verbal exchange but speculated that was what he was doing. He appeared pathetic if you asked him. She had clearly moved on from everyone, him included. That made no sense to Mann since her favorite excuse for not being with him, was because he and Yosohn were friends. They were no longer friends so she couldn't use that as an excuse. He wanted an explanation. The difference between him and Yosohn was, he wasn't going to beg her.

CHAPTER 41

"Hi, I'm here to see Eva Rodriguez," Bianca said to the front desk receptionist with a warm smile.

"Okay. Sign your name on the clipboard and have a seat over there. We'll have someone to take you back shortly."

This was only Bianca's third time coming to the state center, but she was already becoming a familiar face to the staff at Harbor Haven, a group home for infants.

Bianca signed the board using the attached pen and took a seat in the waiting area. Coming into Harbor Haven always left Bianca with mixed feelings. She was grateful that baby Eva had a place to go but uneasy because she knew before long, she would be sent to a foster home. Her godchild had become a ward of the state since Jocelyn's mother fell ill a few weeks back. With HIV, it was especially important that she take her medicine, and Arima had not been doing so. Without the much-needed anti-viral meds suppressing the monstrous virus ravaging her system, a minor upper respiratory infection quickly led to pneumonia.

Once Bianca received the phone call from a sick and weary Arima, she did her best to step in only to be turned away. Although she had succeeded in getting an apartment, Eva's worker wasn't confident it would be enough to get the judge to allow her to take the newborn home with her. Given the circumstances around her mother's death, they were being cautious with associates other than family caring for the baby.

"Bianca," Eva's worker Stephanie said as she walked over to greet her. She was a plain, professional-looking, brown-skinned woman. Although neat, her pantsuit looked as if it had been washed over a hundred times judging by its ashy, faded gray color.

"Hi, sweetheart. I've been meaning to call you," she continued in a stern voice. She appeared in a hurry and almost irritable. "Come back with me." She waved.

Bianca followed behind her and went to the back of the office building to Stephanie's small space amongst an array of other side by side, drab white cubicles. A foot of space separated Stephanie's workspace from her neighboring cube. Bianca took a seat. She hated coming to the facility or any other government facility. She did her best to get comfortable as she waited for Stephanie to get to the point of why she had brought her back to speak with her.

Normally when Bianca visited, she would go directly back to a large room. She very rarely saw Eva's caseworker. When she did, she would have to catch her unexpectedly and sporadically after making numerous attempts to contact her.

"Listen, the reason I brought you back here is because Eva has been placed with her father. He came and got her yesterday."

Bianca instantly felt faint. "Are you people insane!" she yelled unexpectedly, startling Stephanie. If anything, she thought the young girl would be happy she could get on with her life. It was a surprise to her, as most family members and friends had no real desire to take on the role of caregiver to someone else's child.

"He's the one that killed her mother, and you give *him* the baby. What kind of shit is that?" she demanded to know. "My friend is dead because of him, and she would have wanted me to raise Eva ... And you all give the baby to *him*," she asked in disbelief before breaking down into tears.

She had failed her friend and she was angry. She had done everything she thought she could to get Eva, but despite all her efforts, the judicial system basically pissed on her.

"I understand you're upset sweetie but try to calm down. Please don't forget that this is government," she emphasized, before trying to explain. "At the end of the day we still have to follow the law," she explained. "Mr. Thomas is Eva's father. He has the blood test to prove it. Not only that, but he came accompanied with a hotshot family attorney as well as income and bank statements showing that he is 100% capable of providing for her. Additionally, he was ruled out a suspect in your late friend's murder." Sighing she went on. "Now Bianca, I know you did your best. I don't take that away from you, but the law is the law. She is going to be with her father. I appreciate you coming up here, but I have several dozen cases I need to get to. At this point, baby Eva has been permanently placed."

Naomi stared at the caseworker in disgust and disappointment. She wanted to smack the uncaring smirk off her face. In her eyes, Stephanie didn't give a shit one way or another where Eva went. She was just a case number, and to Stephanie, now one less case that she had to deal with.

"You know what bitch, fuck you! You don't give a shit about these kids. If something happens to Eva, her blood is on your hands," she spat, before getting up and storming out.

Stephanie remained seated. This was nothing new to her. She had no choice but to do her job and, in the process, was unable to make everyone happy. Bianca quickly left the building to avoid assaulting Stephanie. She once again went back to feeling like she had no purpose. Eva had given her a purpose. She had given her the motivation she needed to change her life. However, that was no more. The bad guys always won, and fast money allowed it.

Fuck a job, she thought. It hadn't helped her one bit. She was buying her a quarter of loud and a bottle and going back to doing what she did best: living life in the fast lane. With time, she knew her fate would ultimately be like Jocelyn's. And she was right. She would later be found slain. Raped, beaten, and left in an abandoned building. Sadly, there weren't too many that even cared.

"SO, YOU SAY THE NIGGA IS A COP?" MANN ASKED FOR WHAT seemed like the fiftieth time.

"Yeah, I told you he was. He's like a Captain or Lieutenant or some shit like that in the narcotics department," Naomi replied annoyed. He was asking her the same questions over and over. She sat beside him, half Indian style, with one leg tucked under her and waited for Mann to finish rolling the blunt. He always took forever and would never show her how to roll because he said she would waste his weed. She wished he would hurry the fuck up, so she could get high.

"And she told you that?" he asked, raising his eyebrow, being careful to take his time to join the leafy flaps of the Backwoods.

Lately he wasn't sure if he could believe all that Naomi told him. She seemed hostile at times and he had determined that he was going to have to switch up his approach with her. The manipulation and drugs were no longer enough for

Naomi's feisty, jealous ass. Fear was about to be his new tactic.

"Yeah I told you that already before. She smacked her teeth. "On some real shit, I don't know what that bitch is up to, but I do know that she ain't right ... She knows a whole lot ... Yosohn used to tell her everything, and now all of a sudden, she fuckin' with a top boy from narcotics." She laid it on extra thick to further antagonize him. Mann continued to lay on the rumpled sheets of his bed and let what she had said sink in.

"Here," he said, before finally passing her the rolled blunt. He sat and stared at her. "For some reason Naomi, I'm starting to feel like the information you've been giving me has been ... how shall I say it ... *exaggerated*." He eyed her suspiciously.

"What the fuck does that mean?"

"Exaggerated, like the fuck I said," he restated.

"So, what you're telling me is ... You don't think this bitch is up to something ... Why? You think she Miss Goody Two Shoes?"

Mann just stared at her, disgusted by how much she envied someone who was once one of her closest friends. He was about to say that but then stopped. He knew it would be the pot calling the kettle black.

"You stupid as shit," Naomi began arguing. "This bitch is fucking a nigga from narcotics and you don't think that's fishy, as much drugs as you movin' in this city, *and* as much drugs as you and Yosohn have moved in this city ... You know she thinks you shot Yosohn," she lied. She wasn't slow to anything fast. She knew Mann was up to something and had something to do with Yosohn being injured. "Your dumb, ball-headed ass so mesmerized by this shady, burnt black bitch that you don't know your left from your right ... She doesn't want ya ass, she —"

Before she could utter another word, Mann had sprung up and grabbed her by her neck. He applied enough pressure so that nothing more than a quick gag managed to escape from her. He forced her down and tightened his grip. He didn't shake her, he just held her with all his anger and might. She didn't know when to shut up. But she was going to learn today.

"Just shut the fuck up for once … You fat, miserable ass bitch … Who the fuck do you think you talking to?" he snarled into her ear.

It came out in a whisper and frightened Naomi to the point where she wanted to scream out for help. However, she couldn't. She couldn't breathe, and Mann wasn't letting go. He was strangling her. Her eyes teared up and started to bulge. She did her best to break his grip from her neck by using her free hands to pull at his. Several of her sky blue, acrylic nails broke in the process. She struggled to talk but the sounds she made were inaudible. His eyes appeared coal black and empty as he continued to stare into her eyes while he held her. Just as the pressure became too much and she started to slip into darkness, he let go. She gasped for breath as tears slid down the sides of her face and saliva formed a trail from both corners of her mouth. She immediately began to take in deep gulps of the precious air she had just been denied. Mann continued to kneel over her.

"Next time … I won't let go," he threatened, before getting up and walking into the bathroom.

Naomi touched her sore neck and silently thanked God she wasn't dead. She laid on the bed in the fetal position and continued to cry silent tears. She couldn't believe he had just physically attacked her. She knew the comment about Serenity not wanting him had triggered it. She knew what was going on for quite some time. She wasn't stupid. He was using her. He was getting her high and fucking her to keep her in his back pocket so he could keep tabs on Serenity and Yosohn, mainly Serenity. She had known for a while it wasn't about Yosohn seeking out revenge against him. He wanted Serenity, and although he didn't come flat out and say it, he had made it clear. He also made it painfully clear just now to Naomi, what he thought and felt about her.

She was going to help him learn to love her. She knew sometimes she talked too much. She couldn't help it. She cared about him and was jealous of his infatuation with her former friend. She was going to show him that she could be his down ass bitch. She just wasn't quite sure how yet.

CHAPTER 42

Yosohn lay back on the oversized couch and proceeded to rock his exhausted daughter Eva. She was finally sleep after several hours of crying. Yosohn was tired but he wanted nothing more for Eva, than for her to be comfortable. The bond he was developing with her was undeniable. He loved her dearly and wanted to do right by her. He wished that Serenity would forgive him, come back and get to know Eva. He was certain she would learn to love her the same as he did. He refused to lose hope. Yosohn gently kissed Eva on her pudgy brown cheek before slowly lifting his body up to carry her into her room. She looked so much like him which he was thankful for. The only thing she had inherited from Jocelyn, was her tan, creamy skin. He was glad he didn't have to look at Eva and see her mother every day.

Soon after his lawyer told him he could bring her home; he called a local interior decorator to quickly put together a custom nursery for her. The room was quite lavish, and Yosohn had no regrets; it was perfect. The cream-colored room was draped with expensive, thick pink curtains, a wall lined with stuffed animals and a massive $600 recliner nestled next to a bookshelf that held several dozen children's books, along with bins containing baby care items such as diapers and extra sheets. Yosohn often thought about what he would tell Eva about her biological mother when she was older. He figured she wouldn't miss what she never had. He prayed that was the case. He would take to his grave the truth and vowed to shield Eva from the harmful reality of what and who, her mother really was. Who her father used to be. To make up for their shortcomings, Yosohn planned to focus on being the best father he could be. He planned to take exceptional care of her.

When he first got Eva, it was bittersweet. The circumstances behind her conception were all wrong; however, it was not her fault. Hands down, his daughter was slowly changing his life. He knew who he was. Who he had been. Who he could be. Things were different. Serenity was gone and had appeared to have moved on, while he had been quickly and unexpectedly thrust into a life of single parenting. It was hard.

He did not regret taking his daughter. Had he left her to endure what would be a hard and unfortunate life in the foster care system, he could not live with himself. He knew that world all too well and refused to put her through it when he had the means to provide for her. She would have the best schools and the best care that he could give her for as long as he was physically and financially able.

"YOSOHN ... SHE IS BEAUTIFUL," NIKKI GUSHED AS SHE HELD A cooing Eva. Yosohn had dressed her in a frilly pink dress with bows all over it. He had attempted to put stockings on her but after struggling to pull them over her chubby legs, gave up. She had put on so much weight; no one could ever tell she was a preemie. He figured since it was approaching July, it was too hot for them anyway, so he loaded her up with bare legs and toes and made the trip to Nikki's to see her and the boys.

"Boys come over and meet your cousin Eva," Nikki called.

Eva continued to babble and squirm around happily, her fat legs aimlessly thrashing about. Hakim Jr. and Xavier were in their bedroom playing the Xbox, but pressed pause so they could run out into the living room to see the baby.

"Who's she?" asked Xavier, who was growing taller and taller every day. He hadn't too long turned six and was now missing several teeth on both the top and bottom.

"This is your cousin Eva … This is Yosohn's daughter," Nikki explained. She adjusted the crooked pink bow Yosohn had put in her curly hair. Although she didn't have much, it was enough to hold the bow in place.

"Hi, Eva," Hakim Jr cooed in baby talk with a smile.

He put his finger in her hand and she gripped it tightly while still flailing around. After a couple kisses and holds, the brothers ran back in their rooms to finish playing their game.

"They're going to spoil her," Nikki said, before handing Eva back to Yosohn. "So how are you adjusting? How's everything?" she asked.

It was amazing to Nikki how poor and hasty decisions could alter lives in the blink of an eye. She had seen him only a few times since he had been shot but tried to speak with him regularly.

"It's been tough, but I've been managing." Yosohn admitted honestly. "I mean, when she first came home it was crazy." He laughed. "I see what y'all go through. Up all night at crazy hours, crying nonstop."

"Yeah, nigga. I'm glad you know. Never take the woman's

role for granted." She smiled but decided to go ahead and go in for the kill. "How's Serenity?"

Yosohn looked at her and shook his head. "Man, I don't know. She doesn't return my calls. She doesn't return my texts. It's a wrap. I know I should accept it, but it's hard."

"Well, you did put her through a lot. She tried to hang in there, Yosohn. Being the type of female she is, you kind of left her no choice."

"What you mean by that?" he asked with a frown.

"I mean, she doesn't have to put up with that type of shit, Yosohn. You know that as well as anyone does. She ain't a bum bitch. She's pretty, intelligent, and has the checkbook to prove it. The shit you were doing, is shit you do with young girls … I mean, don't get me wrong … I'm far from a bum bitch, but why do you think I put up with Hakim shit for all those years? Because I knew I wouldn't be able to sustain the lifestyle on my own. Women like me, who just lay up and have the kids with no other title except wifey, tolerate shit like that. You named her co-owner and director of your businesses. She runs it all. She is in graduate school majoring in Finance. She is another level of woman … You've been known this. She put up with you because she loved you. Because she felt like you had potential …"

"I know what she's worth, Nikki," he responded irritated. "And I have changed. But now, I'm like the boy who cried wolf and she don't wanna hear shit. It pisses me off because I was the one who was there before those degrees and shit. I put my hard-earned bread up for those businesses and she just says fuck me. Fuck us … You know she filed legal papers to dissolve our partnership. She wants to either buy me out or I buy her out. That's fucking crazy. I put up every dime to start and run those laundromats. She just sat back and saved her fucking money while she spent mine. It's just hard to accept that she through with me. I mean like, she really trying to finalize the ending of us, even the business aspect."

He shook his head. He didn't know if he was angrier or more hurt by her actions.

"I meant to ask you too. Have you spoken to her?" Yosohn asked. He knew she had but just wanted to see if she kept it real with him.

"Yeah, I did … And that's what I really want to talk to you about … I knew you were gonna be upset, Yosohn, but hear me out first," she said before taking a deep breath. It was now or never. "I had been calling her and checking on her to make sure she was good. She asked me how you were doing, and I told her."

"Ok, what else did you tell her?" he asked. He already knew. He just needed her to confirm it.

"I told her you were doing well, bonding with your daughter," she admitted.

Yosohn dropped his head down and just shook it in disapproval. She had just signed the death certificate to their relationship.

"Why did you tell her that, Nikki?" he asked. "I wanted to tell her my way." He sighed. "What did she say? Be honest."

"I'm always honest, Yosohn. She was pissed. She just lost her baby. You're raising your daughter you conceived with another woman. I am sorry, Yosohn. I honestly didn't think before telling her that."

"So, that basically sealed the deal?" he asked solemnly.

"Yeah it did," she replied solemnly.

"It is what it is. At the end of the day, I fucked up. I gotta live with that, but I'm not gon' let my daughter grow up feeling like I don't want her, even if I didn't initially. I'm not proud of what happened, and I'm not proud of having a baby by no scandalous ass bitch, but I am proud to be the father of

Eva … And that's just how I gotta look at it going forward …
I'm not gon' give up on Serenity though … I just hope that
somewhere, a part of her heart hasn't given up on me."

CHAPTER 43

"No, it's okay, Daddy, you didn't know. I should've told you, or at least gave you a heads up he might call … No, I'm sure … I know … I'll consider that, Daddy, but ultimately, I gotta make the best choice for myself … Ok. I love you too. I'll talk to you later."

Serenity hung up the phone and crept her way through traffic. She was on her way to her new home in Hamilton, NJ, a town about 45 miles outside of Philadelphia. School was nearing and she had decided on a small condo, not too far from her father. Although she was renting to keep her costs low, she didn't plan to move for a while. She didn't want to keep moving Heaven. She wanted to get back to establishing some sense of normalcy for her growing daughter.

"You okay kiddo," she asked her, squeezing at her cheek.

She'd just turned nine and was starting to develop her big girl looks. She was slimming down some from her infamous chubby frame and had Kanekalon-like natural hair that flowed down her back. She was still Serenity's hazelnut beauty.

"I'm okay. Just hot. Can we stop for ice cream?"

"Yeah sure, but if we stop you gotta promise me that you're going to put up all those clothes in your unpacked boxes. We gotta dedicate some time to getting fully settled in."

"Okay."

As Serenity attempted to take a detour to rid herself of the mid-day traffic headache, she decided to call her lawyer to see what the progress was on Yosohn's response to her legal request. She picked up her iPhone and dialed out. After three rings, her lawyer answered.

"Hi, Serenity, how are you?" she asked.

"I'm doing well. Just calling to see if you had any word on dissolving the business." Her lawyer Kristina sighed.

"Well, at this point, he is refusing to do either. He's saying he doesn't see why you two can't both act as co-owners. He's rejected your offer and refuses to make you one either. He's asking for a mediator."

Serenity rolled her eyes. Yosohn was making things diffi-cult just because he could. She hadn't spoken to him nor answered his texts and asking for a mediator was just his way of having a face-to-face meeting.

"I don't want to do this through a mediator Kristina."

"I understand that, Serenity, but if that's the case, then you're going to have to talk to him. Soften him up some, and then we can continue to work out an agreement from there."

Serenity exhaled and shook her head. It wasn't that simple. Her way of dealing with their breakup was by cutting all ties. She had been with him for nearly eight years and moving on was hard. She thought of him every day and wanted to move on with her life completely. She wanted to pretend he didn't exist anymore. Yosohn had even reached out to her father to *"talk some sense into her."* Tate wasn't into meddling and had no intention of being the middleman and politely informed Yosohn of this. He'd just called her to let her know. During the call, he did however remind Serenity that people could change. He often expressed how he wished that when Gina left him the last time, she had given him one last opportunity to change, because when reality set in, he did manage to do just that. He would have made it right and been the man she needed and desired. Her departure humbled him and made him a better man. Unfortunately, it was too late. Although he didn't know Yosohn very well, he couldn't help but detect sadness, yet sincerity in his voice.

"Ok, I'll talk to him," Serenity told her lawyer.

"Great. Let me know how it goes."

SERENITY SIPPED ON A GLASS OF ICED TEA AS SHE WATCHED Naomi walk into the dimly lit steakhouse, with a pair of dark shades on.

"Hey, girl," Serenity said, standing up to give her friend a quick embrace.

"Hey," Naomi replied, with little energy. She didn't really want to be there and had only suggested they briefly meet up because of Mann's insistence.

"So, how've you been … and why you got those dark shades on? It's dark in here *and* it's nighttime." She didn't think nothing of it by asking. She just though Naomi looked a little silly.

"They're prescription," Naomi lied. "The doctor says they're good for day or night. And they're Versace. A little present from my new boo," she bragged, before flashing a forced smile. Serenity couldn't help but notice bright white, plaque-like stains lining her teeth.

"Oh okay, well they're definitely fly and I'm glad you got a new boo-thing … tell me about him," she said merrily.

She was expecting their conversation to be as it always had. They had their disagreements, but they had made up. However, this evening, things seemed strained, almost like she was forcing the conversation with Naomi. She wasn't sure what the deal was, since she was the one that suggested they meet up in the first place.

"Girl, that's a whole phone call. I'll tell you about him on a later date," Naomi said, avoiding any conversation about herself. Serenity found it odd but said nothing.

"So, what's been going on with you?" Naomi asked, changing the subject.

"I've been good. Still settling in at the new house and hanging out with my Dad a whole lot."

"You still running the laundromats way from Jersey?" Naomi asked.

"Yeah, same ol' with that," she said, omitting the fact that she was working on dissolving the business. "It's mostly payroll, paperwork, maintenance issues."

"How's Yosohn doing? He still living at the big house y'all had bought?"

"I don't know; I haven't spoken to Yosohn in a while. Why you ask that?" Serenity asked, doing her best to not sound suspicious of her questioning.

Naomi was shooting off questions and avoiding any talk about herself, which was unusual. That, along with her unusual appearance caused Serenity to immediately put her guard up.

"Just was wondering how he was doing is all ... Excuse me, sir," Naomi called.

She was trying to flag down the waiter who had walked past. She turned her head to get his attention and Serenity discreetly examined her eye in her "so-called" Versace shades. She could easily tell that it was bruised from the side. The black and purple splotches weren't completely concealed at that angle. She immediately grew concerned for her friend. Decaying teeth and a black eye were extreme red flags for someone like Naomi. Although Naomi had some self-esteem issues, she was a pretty girl and did her best to take care of herself and look the part. The woman in front of her appeared slightly disheveled and not as meticulously cared for as remembered. Her Brazilian weave seemed a bit dry and she wasn't fully made-up in her normal M.A.C cosmetics. Naomi loved makeup just as much as Serenity. Additionally, she looked like she had lost over twenty pounds in several months. Things didn't seem to add up, and Serenity didn't want to hold her tongue any longer, especially if she could help her in any way.

"Naomi, can I ask you something?" She sat her menu down on the table.

"Yeah, wassup?"

"Don't get mad, but if something was wrong would you tell me?" she asked.

"Yeah, why do you ask that?" Naomi responded, growing uncomfortable. This was why she didn't want to come. Serenity usually didn't miss anything.

"Well … How do I say it? … Your appearance has changed, and the fact that you have a black eye under those sunglasses, alarms me," she said with concern.

"I'm good, girl … Had a run in with some hoes…But you know how I do."

Serenity didn't comment. Naomi had never been a fighter, and she had known her for years.

"Oh okay. I hear that … So, you've been exercising?" Serenity asked.

"A little bit." She shifted around in her seat uncomfortably. She was ready to go. "Been watching what I eat mostly," she lied.

Part of that was true, considering most days she didn't

have much of an appetite. Just as Serenity was about to probe further, her phone began to vibrate. She looked down. It was Heaven.

"It's Heaven," she said, before quickly answering it. "Hey honey, hold on for a second, okay." She looked back to Naomi. "I'm gonna run to the bathroom. If the waiter comes back just order for me, please ... A Coke, light ice and the rib-eye cooked medium, with mixed veggies and garlic mashed potatoes."

"Sure," Naomi agreed.

She was only half listening, since she too was now looking down at her phone and texting. Serenity hoped she remembered her order. Serenity quickly talked to Heaven, who was just bored and calling to check up on her. After exchanging I love you's, she hung up and used the bathroom. As she made her way back out to her seat, she noticed Naomi was gone. She figured she had stepped out for a minute. She surely hadn't come into the bathroom. After waiting at the table alone for over fifteen minutes, Serenity realized she had been ditched. Naomi hadn't ordered any food because the waiter continuously returned to her table asking her if she was ready to order.

After attempting to call Naomi several times and being sent to voicemail, Serenity determined she was done with her. She understood people went through things, but truthfully, her and Naomi's relationship hadn't really been the same since their argument about her sleeping with Mann. Naomi was distant and often asked a lot of questions, usually pertaining to Yosohn. It was as if she was trying too hard to be the concerned friend. If that was the case, and she was truly concerned she should've been asking how she had been holding up and doing. She'd lost her baby, almost lost Yosohn, and found out he had fathered a child outside of the relationship. Half the time her attention seemed to be elsewhere, and Serenity found herself repeating things.

Serenity wasn't sure what was up with Naomi, but she didn't have time for it. She was getting her life together and if it meant ridding herself of what she felt was another negative, toxic individual, then so be it. She decided to order her meal to-go, making sure to tip the waiter generously since she had been occupying his table for some time.

As she placed her takeout bag in the passenger seat of her truck, she thought about how life had changed. She honestly couldn't say yet whether she appreciated the change. She had loved her life at one point. Things were different— very different. She just wasn't sure if different always meant better.

CHAPTER 44

Mann walked over to the couch and glanced down at Naomi as she lay sleep, the front of her body nestled into the sofa. He scrunched his face up like he had smelled something foul. He used his foot to nudge her. Today was the day. He wanted her out and away from him for good.

"Naomi!" he yelled out to her.

She immediately woke up. She was a light sleeper.

"Yo, get up. I gotta roll. It's 11 a.m. and yo' ass been sleep all morning. I got shit to do and you gotta leave too."

She sat up and wiped at her eyes. She was groggy and her head was pounding. She was several hours late for work but didn't seem to care as she slowly peeled herself away from the couch.

"Make sure you take all your shit with you," Mann stated firmly.

"Mann, if this is still about last night ... I'm sorry," she stammered.

When she had stormed out of the restaurant, Mann told her he was done with her. That of course was after he slapped her around, grabbed her by her hair, and yelled at

her for not listening. He had long ago peeped Naomi's decep-
tion and had followed her to the restaurant where she met
Serenity. He knew it was coming. There wasn't enough slaps
and punches that could make Naomi fully cooperate when it
pertained to his demands regarding Serenity. He watched
her from the parking lot as she walked to her car and drove
off, all the while still claiming to be in the restaurant. She
was painfully jealous of her and it turned him off. She was no
longer of any use to him and he did his best to discard
useless people. The served him no purpose.

"Yo just shut up and get out," he responded to Naomi as
he grabbed his keys from the kitchen counter.

"You gonna call me?" she asked, while putting on her
shoes.

"Na. And don't bother to call me either. I'm good."

"Baby please … why are you doing this?" she whined. She
walked over to him and pathetically dropped to her knees.
She tugged at his jeans. She tried to unbuckle them so she
could give him a good reason to let her stay. She figured that
might change his mind. It didn't. Mann looked down and
shook his head in disgust. Naomi was a mess. Her weave was
wild, and she hadn't even brushed her teeth yet. On top of
that, she had lost a considerable amount of weight and had
loose skin that she showed to the world with her tight
unflattering clothing. In a matter of months, she had let
herself go, and no longer cared about her appearance. She
was a far cry from the spunky Naomi he had met through
Serenity.

Just recently, he even had found out through the streets
that she was copping her own weed way out in South Philly.
It wasn't hard, as he supplied a vast majority of the lower-
level dealers and had driven through the hood plenty of
times with her by his side. It also didn't help that she name-
dropped to get better prices. Her copping her own shit solid-

ified that she was strung out and couldn't be trusted. Naomi would never get the high she was craving since she didn't know Crack is what she truly desired.

Despite being disgusted with her, Mann still fucked her from time to time. However, he would now force her to sleep in the living room instead of his bed.

"I'm good. I'll pass," he told Naomi, who was still in front of him on her knees. He could get head any day from any bad ass hoodrat. He rocked the flyest shit and drove the flyest whip. Naomi was simply no longer up to par.

"Yo move, and get off me," he said, snatching his crotch back from her abruptly.

He was done playing games, and if she knew what was good for her, she would leave willingly, or run the risk of being thrown out. He didn't care about making a scene in the lily-white neighborhood. He had purchased the house for his grandmother and since she was gone, he gave no fucks about pissing off the neighbors.

Naomi stood up shamefully and decided to leave. She knew Mann wouldn't hesitate to hit her. She had been his punching bag for over a month. He needed some serious help. However, she couldn't talk. She had low self-esteem and more recently, suffered from depression. She hadn't been officially diagnosed, but knew it had to be those two things. Why else would she knowingly allow Mann to use, as well as physically and emotionally abuse her?

"I'll leave. But at the end of the day, it's your loss." She grabbed her purse and headed towards the door, but not before doing her best to smooth down her hair. Opening the front door, she proceeded to leave since Mann had made it clear she was no longer wanted there. Before walking out, she stopped and turned around to say one last thing.

"Oh, and by the way," she smirked. "You best hope I don't tell Serenity what ya sick, sorry obsessed ass has planned for her. I heard you several nights ago while you were up and unable to sleep … whispering to yourself about what you were gonna do … fucking self-medicated freak," Naomi spat, mocking his obsessive use of pills, weed, alcohol and pain relievers to function through the day, as well as sleep through the night. "Oh, and I'll also let her know you've been following her."

She had seen him do it. The first night he ran out to Sonix, she went right behind him. Several other times she followed Mann and he always wound up on the side of some street, or in a parking lot tracking Serenity. She found it disturbing, but because of her own self-esteem issues, she stayed. She knew he was borderline obsessed with Serenity, even after she had done her best to taint her image with exaggerations and lies. It wasn't working the way she wanted it to. Mann was still fixated and was becoming more and more violent. Less concerned about being with Serenity and having her as a companion, Mann was now angry and bitter from her rejection.

"You're a weirdo, and you need help," she continued to rant. "You're so busy trying to fill a void in your life with someone who doesn't want cho ass … You're too blind to see what you have in front of you."

Mann just stared at her and Naomi then knew she had struck a nerve. Fury was forming within him. He knew what his issues were. They were like ghosts, haunting him. He didn't want to face them, instead choosing to drown them in drugs. There was truly something wrong in his brain, a real psychological issue. Whatever it was, it had been suppressed until recently. She knew nothing, and her rambling and insults were like adding a lit match to a can of gasoline. Instead of responding, Mann walked off towards his bedroom. Just like he expected, Naomi shut the front door and followed right behind him.

"Oh, you ain't got shit to say now? Cat gotcha tongue? Now you silent?" she taunted loudly, while snapping her neck back and forth, waiting for a response.

Mann reached in his pocket and replied, "Nah, but you will be soon." He flicked open his switch blade that he religiously kept tucked in his pocket and shoved it into Naomi's neck. He grabbed her by her back, pulled her into him and violently twisted the knife. Looking into her eyes, he coldly snatched the sharp bloody blade from her throat and released her with a push. She fell on the bed, eyes wide with terror. To him, her problem was that she never stopped fucking talking. That would shut her up for good. He smiled, while she looked on in terror.

"What did you say you were gonna tell her?"

Naomi immediately reached for her neck while she lost her footing and collapsed on the bed. Blood spewed out of the gaping gash that was long as her thumb. She did her best to keep it closed and apply pressure, but she was going into shock. She knew it was bad and could feel several of her fingers sink into the fleshy wound as she struggled to contain the blood loss.

"Help me," she struggled to mouth before she began to choke on her own blood.

She clenched her teeth and attempted to find air that was now escaping her body. Her bright red blood flowed out like a river, soon forming a circular pattern around her head. A few minutes later, she was dead. Mann looked at her and grinned. She was a grimy hoe anyway. She deserved it. Scenes like the one before him, no longer affected him. He had killed before and would kill again. He was no longer in the right mental state. Naomi was right. He did need counseling. She had told him that on many occasions, mainly after he beat her. He was always a cannon but now he was a loose one. He hadn't been the same since his grandmother died. He also blamed himself for the death of cousin. He lived with guilt.

At first, he tried to reason with himself that Zeke had been a man and that men made their own decisions. However, he knew Zeke was dead because he influenced him and asked him to step outside of his usual crime preference. He hadn't been ready, and no amount of coaching and pep-talks would have helped.

Mann looked back over to Naomi. Her eyes had closed, and her hands were still loosely wrapped around her neck. He closed the door and walked out of the room. He would wrap her up and move her later. He didn't want her soon to be rotting corpse, stinking up his house. In the meantime, there was still money to be made and business to tend to.

CHAPTER 45

"I'm not dissolving *shit*," Yosohn argued. "Shit is fine, just the way it is. I don't see why you wanna fuck it up. You wanna be petty, so I'm gonna be petty."

Yosohn knew he was being childish, but he didn't care. Serenity was trying to force him out of her life, and in his opinion, she was taking it too far.

"What do you not understand?" Serenity asked, from the opposite end of the phone. "We are no longer together, and I feel it's in our best interest to discontinue our business relationship."

Yosohn cut her off. "No! It's in *your* best interest," he said raising his voice. He looked over to his daughter, who was sleeping soundly on the couch and decided to walk out of the room so he wouldn't wake her.

"The laundromats bring in $40k a month. What sense does it make to buy one another out?" he asked angrily. "I'm not giving you shit and I'm not taking your money either … Fuck you think this is? You wanna profit off me. Use my money and go layup with the next nigga. Fuck that!"

Serenity sighed in aggravation. She knew it was pointless

even calling him. She had only did it at the suggestion of her lawyer.

"First of all, don't insult me. I worked hard to build those laundromats from the ground up. You did nothing but finance them. While I was hiring people and handling money so they could be profitable, you sat on your ass! So, you can miss me with the bullshit … Furthermore, any man I decide to pursue a relationship with, will have his own … And let's be clear … I emphasize man because he definitely will be just that. Not some two-timing, fuck-boy."

"Whatever, Ren," Yosohn said shaking his head. She had struck a nerve. "Is that all you called me for? To talk nonsense," he asked.

"You can brush the topic off all you want Yosohn, but at the end of the day we are gonna have to discuss it … Any other time you wanna fuckin talk and blow me up with texts."

"Whatever Serenity. Don't toot your horn sis."

"I guess I'm just making shit up … Bottom line is, it's not going to work. At some point I'm going to be in a serious, committed relationship and us working together is going to be a conflict."

Yosohn paused. She was talking stupid again.

"And you, out of all people … If that is the case, and you wanna be a whore … you gon' let suckin' dick come between ya business, and what you worked hard to build?"

Serenity shook her head sadly. She couldn't believe he just said that.

"Isn't that the pot calling the kettle black? I guess I'll see you in court Yosohn," she said, before hanging up the phone. She was done talking to a self-absorbed, hypocritical idiot.

Yosohn looked down at his phone and knew she was right. However, it didn't dispute the fact that he was still pissed with her. He walked back into his spacious living room to check on Eva. She was still fast asleep with her mouth slightly open. He smiled sadly. He loved his daughter and told himself every day --- rather forced himself to believe, that she was a good thing that had happened to him.

He looked around his junky living room and decided that he would need to call someone to help him out. The house was a wreck and he barely knew how to cook for himself. Eva was now sitting up on her own, so he had tons of stuffed animals and books strewn around where they weren't supposed to be. This wasn't how things were supposed to be. He was a mess, and he knew it. He missed his woman.

SERENITY SAT IN HER TRUCK OUTSIDE OF DUNKIN DONUTS AND waited to go in. She had just gotten off the phone with Yosohn and was reflecting mentally. She had been doing that a lot lately. She let out an exaggerated sigh and peered out the window. If she could wish things back to the way they were, she would. She decided to go in and grab the hazelnut coffee she had come for. Before hopping out, she checked her driver's side rearview mirror. She was parked on the street and wanted to make sure it was safe for her to exit. It was clear, but she noticed a familiar car parked several spaces behind her. It was a white, late-model BMW. She was sure she had seen the car several times around her parking lot. Normally seeing a car one too many times wouldn't have aroused her suspicions. However, it was the frequency of the sightings as well as the locations.

She was sure that was the same BMW parked in the parking lot of her new condo in Jersey. She remembered it because it had Pennsylvania tags and most of the cars that filled the parking spaces were from New Jersey. Despite her suspicions, she decided to go ahead and exit her car. She wanted to take a quick glance and see if she could make out the driver of the vehicle. After all, it could be a coincidence. Many people like herself lived in New Jersey but commuted daily to Philadelphia for work.

Serenity grabbed her signature black and white Chanel purse and got out. She looked to her right and then her left, where the car was sitting. She wanted to act as though she was just checking to make sure the street was clear. The BMW was tinted; however, it wasn't dark enough that she couldn't make out a figure. Whoever it was had a large build, but she couldn't tell if it was a man or woman. Shrugging it off, she crossed the street and went into the store. As soon as she walked in, her phone rang. She quickly unzipped her purse and grabbed it. She didn't recognize the number.

"Hello?" she answered.

"Hi, Serenity." Serenity instantly recognized the voice. The woman on the line had been born and raised in Louisiana, and had a deep, distinct southern drawl that she would always remember. It was Naomi's mom.

"Hey, Miss Cora, how are you?" Serenity asked with a smile. She had always adored Naomi's mom. She was super funny and was one of the nicest people one could meet.

"Hey, baby. I am doing well. I hope you're doing fine yaself … Listen sugar, I don't want to take up too much of you time. I know you're busy, but I wanted to know if you'd spoken to Naomi lately?" she asked. Serenity sensed the worry in her voice, but Cora did her best to conceal it.

"Not today, but a few days ago. I tried to call her, but she didn't pick up … Is everything ok with her?" Serenity asked. She wanted to go into detail about what happened but didn't. Miss Cora paused and decided to go ahead and lay it all out.

"I don't know, sweetie … Naomi's been acting strange lately. She hasn't been to work in several days and I can't get up with her. Her phone is going to voicemail … She hadn't been coming around as much since she started dating that new guy, but last time I saw her ... something was off. She didn't look the same. Like she was stressed and worried."

"I noticed the same thing, Miss Cora, but I do my best not to pry. When I did mention it to her, she got defensive and that's when she ditched me. Do you know the guy's name she was dating?"

"Yeah ... she called him Manny ... Mann, or something like that."

Serenity's stomach immediately formed a knot. She clutched her phone tightly It all made sense to her now. Her random and frequent questions about Yosohn, her distance and standoffishness. It was all so clear. Naomi had no idea who she was dealing with ... Or maybe she did. Serenity glanced back outside, and something immediately clicked. The BMW was now gone, but she now knew exactly who it belonged to. It was the same car Mann drove off in the night he cornered her in the laundromat months ago. She couldn't believe that she had been so wrapped up, that she overlooked critical details of her surroundings. He had been following her. She was usually extremely observant. She immediately thought of her daughter and all the days she'd seen the car while she was with her. Too many to count. He also now knew where she lived. Serenity grew warm with fear but breathed deeply so she could maintain her calm. She was done running.

"Miss Cora, I'm going to try to call her, and I'm gonna ride by her house to see if I see her car. Maybe she's just been holed up in the house."

It wasn't the first time that Naomi had stayed in her house for several days. She had her moments that most people just shrugged off as normal. Serenity, however, knew better. Her girl had issues.

"Thank you so much, baby. If you get up with her, give me a call. I'm worried sick," she admitted.

"I know you are, Miss Cora, and I promise I will." After hanging up from Miss Cora, Serenity skipped her coffee and left. Once she got in her car, she started making phone calls. She immediately arranged to have top of the line security installed for her home, her mother's, and each of her sisters. She didn't care if they lived in a box; if she loved them it would be secured. She was starting to think Mann was missing some screws and was capable of anything. *Following her.* She couldn't wrap her head around it all.

Serenity sat there for a while and decided that she was going to have to take drastic measures to make sure Heaven was safe. She called her mother and asked her if Heaven could remain there for the entire school year. While she was done running from her problems, she would not put her child in harm's way. She was also tired of shifting her around. Since Heaven was already there much of the time, it was easiest and just made the most sense.

She didn't trust Mann. He had shot Yosohn and had turned her friend Naomi into a slithering, slimy black snake. Not only that, but Naomi looked abused and strung out. She wondered what he had been telling her --- or worse, what she had been telling him. She wanted to call Yosohn; he would know what to do. However, she couldn't bring herself to do it.

She decided she was going to drive over to Razul's. She needed his advice. As a police officer, he would know what to do. It was nearly six in the evening and he would be getting off soon. She started her car and drove off. If it wasn't one thing, it was another.

⁓

"DID YOU TRY CALLING HER AGAIN?" RAZUL ASKED FOR THE third time. He had just gotten out of the shower and wasn't sure how to digest all that Serenity had just told him. She had really laid it on him, going all the way back to her sleeping with Mann, to him becoming infatuated.

"Yeah, she's not answering. I rode by there on my way here but didn't see her car in front of her house."

"And you're sure it was his car?" Razul asked again.

"I told you yeah, Razul. Why you keep asking me the same questions over and over?" she snapped. She knew it was probably in his nature because he was a cop, but he was getting on her nerves treating her like someone he was inter-rogating.

"The nigga is a nut. I know this for a fact, and I'm scared Razul. I don't know what to do," she admitted.

Razul didn't bother to ask her for the complete run-down on Mann. He was sure she wasn't telling him everything. It had to be more, judging by how scared she was. She had always been one that offered limited details and that was cool. He figured it was her way of not incriminating anyone, but it wasn't helping him help her.

"Look. Your best bet is to switch up your routine for a little while. You're going to have to lay off going certain places until he eases up."

Serenity looked at him in disbelief. She wasn't sure by what he meant by, *ease up*. Mann wasn't going to ease up. She wasn't sure why she was growing angry, but she was. Razul wasn't really giving her the reassurance that she was hoping for. She honestly wasn't sure what she was looking for. Any problems she had, Yosohn would always swoop in and save the day. She was kind of hoping Razul would do the same.

"Tell me something I don't know Razul." Sensing her frus-tration, he walked over to her and sat beside her. He stroked her arm while he spoke to her.

"Look sweetheart, I know you're frustrated and I'm going to do my best to help you. But if he is how you say he is, then you must be careful. I'll do what I can for you, but at the end of the day, I'm a cop. My hands are kind of tied. If some shit happens and I'm involved, Internal Affairs is gonna be all over my ass and I'll lose my career. I can't risk that," he admitted honestly. "I worked hard to get here. And it's all I have."

Serenity knew what he meant by that, and he was right. While he cared about her, he had a career and reputation on the line.

"It's cool Razul. I understand and respect that."

He kissed her on the forehead, and she smiled lightly in return. It seemed like her problems never ended.

CHAPTER 46

Mann woke up abruptly and wiped the cold out of his eyes. His head was pounding. He used his fingertips to massage his forehead and looked downward, hoping that would help ease the pain. It did not. He was fully clothed and the bright green numbers on his alarm clock told him it was 7 p.m. He had only been asleep for several hours. He was relieved.

He scurried out of bed and checked his phone. He knew he had some money waiting for him, but it would have to wait. He had something far more important to do. He logged into his account on his GPS tracking app to check for updates. After pressing a few tabs to navigate the application, he discovered Serenity was downtown at The Rittenhouse. He figured she would be staying at a hotel after realizing he had been following her. She looked right at him at Dunkin Donuts the previous day. Surprisingly, her little cop friend wasn't with her. He had a tracker on both of their cars and was waiting for the right moment when Serenity was alone so he could confront her. Now was the time. Technology was a beautiful thing.

∽

SERENITY HAD JUST CHECKED INTO THE RITTENHOUSE HOTEL. Razul had surprised her with last minute reservations and she was thrilled. He knew she was frustrated and needed to relax for a few days, so he booked her a room at the luxury hotel and paid for a sixty-minute massage to go with it.

Although excited and very thankful for the gift, Serenity was a bit disappointed that he would be unable to accompany her. His staff was working on a big case and he had decided that he would stay late to help with it. Serenity understood that with no children, his job was his life. She understood, but she wasn't exactly sure where that left space for her in his life. Not one to dwell on silly things, she figured she would catch up on some paperwork after relaxing for a while.

After plopping down on the large bed, Serenity just stared at the ceiling. She had already talked to Heaven and had also informed everyone of where she was at. With nothing to do, she figured she would take a hot bath, order room service, and curl up in expensive Egyptian cotton sheets. Serenity started her playlist on her phone and went to run her water. She decided she would make the most out of her short escape.

After soaking in the tub for thirty minutes, she dried off and ordered room service. A short time later while she was in the process of slathering lotion on her body, there was a knock at the door. She peered through the peephole and saw an older white male in a bright red uniform with gold buttons. It was room service. After receiving her food and tipping him, she went back to applying Pink Chiffon from Bath and Body Works to her skin.

Before she could finish, there was another knock at the door. Figuring it was room service again and they had forgotten something, Serenity ran over and snatched it open. She instantly regretted it.

She quickly tried to shut the door back, but it was too late. Mann forced his foot through the crack and pushed himself in. He drew his gun. He wanted her to know that he wasn't playing with her.

"You better not scream," he yelled.

Serenity froze in fear for a minute, and then made a dash to the bathroom. She clumsily stumbled into an ottoman and tripped over one of her bags. She got into the bathroom and slammed the door. She quickly locked it and grabbed her phone. Mann immediately ran behind her and tried to kick in the door. The force and banging from his foot caused Serenity to jump. She prayed someone heard him in the hotel and called 911. Looking back to her phone, she dialed the first number she saw in her phone. After several rings, Shanita picked up.

"Hello?" Shanita asked.

"Shanita! I need your help. Mann's here. He forced his way into my room and he's kicking in the bathroom door. Oh my God!" she screamed as Mann became more forceful with his kicks. "I think he's going to try to hurt me, Shanita. Please help me. Call 911!" she cried.

"Open the door, Serenity! I just want to talk to you," Mann yelled through the side of the door. She could hear it creak and crack, as he was now using his shoulder to force it in. Suddenly, it gave way and came flying open. Serenity screamed and dropped the phone.

"Hello? Hello? Ren!" Shanita called to her frantically.

Serenity could hear her but wouldn't dare pick up. Mann had his gun aimed at her. The cold look in his eyes scared her and she knew he would shoot. She had no choice but to cooperate.

"Give it to me," Mann demanded. He walked over to her

and she quickly picked up and handed him the phone. He hung up on Shanita and then grabbed Serenity by her arm, forcing her up.

"Get ya ass up and get dressed. You coming with me."

Serenity glanced down at her body and realized she was practically naked. Her robe had flown open and all her dark chocolate flesh was available for Mann to see. She slowly walked out and grabbed the first thing she could find: a black romper.

"Right here. Take that shit off and hurry up and put your clothes on."

He wasn't worried about her being naked. He'd already seen her body. Besides, he had other things on his mind, like getting out of the ritzy hotel before the police arrived. He knew whoever she was on the phone with had probably called 911, plus Serenity hadn't made it any better by running around falling and knocking over shit like a dumb white bitch in a movie.

Although he was pressed for time, he knew it would take the police some time to arrive. In the meantime, whoever decided to be a hero and get in his business, would be knocked unconscious — or shot. It really depended on his mood. Although he had taken the front entrance in, he decided they would take the side out. He had observed the hotel for a while before entering. He always wanted to make sure he had options.

"Mann, please. Why are you doing this?" Serenity sobbed. Tears soaked her cheeks and thoughts of her family flooded her thoughts. He didn't answer. "Where are you taking me?" she asked.

He still didn't answer. He just stared at her. She had no idea what was going through his evil little head. What she did know was that whatever it was, it wasn't pleasant. He looked angry and under the influence of something. His eyes were bloodshot and glassy, while his breathing was heavy, yet methodic. Serenity continued to cry as she led the way out. She quickly grabbed her bag and clutched it tightly in front of her. As they exited from her room and out into the hotel, Serenity's eyes darted around frantically for any sign of help. As expected, the hotel was quiet and nearly empty. It was the middle of the week and most of the people occupying the lobby were old. There was no way they would be able to help her. Mann nudged her side.

"Go through that door over there." He nodded his head in the direction of the side entrance.

As they exited out of the safety of the hotel and into the plush, leather interior of Mann's BMW, Serenity grew worried. Mann had her phone jammed in his pocket and she had no way of contacting her family. She wasn't sure where he was taking her, but wherever it was, he wanted to get there fast. They hadn't long ago left the hotel and they were already on I-76 going well above 80 mph. Serenity glanced at Mann. She hoped her sad face would conjure pity from him. However, he stared straight ahead and never looked at her. His attention was solely on the road and getting her back to his home.

~

"WHOA! SHAMEKA, SLOW DOWN. WHAT ARE YOU TALKING about?" Yosohn asked. He had just lie down in his bed to watch a game, but her call made him sit up immediately.

"I said the nigga Mann just ran down on Serenity! He crazy Yosohn. You gotta help her. We putting on our shit now, and Mommy just called the police," she cried.

"Shameka. Tell me where she is," Yosohn demanded. He knew she called him for help, but she wasn't telling him shit.

"She's at The Rittenhouse Hotel downtown. She went

there to relax, and the nigga just popped up on some crazy shit. Forced himself in with a gun. She ran to the bathroom and called Shanita. From what she could tell, she's still hiding in there with the door locked. She could hear him screaming at her in the background. *Gosh*, she should have bought a fucking gun. He'd been following her. We told her to get one, but you know she don't like shit like that. Now look. You gotta help her Yosohn," she pleaded, her voice cracking.

"Listen Shameka. I'm on my way to her. Call me if you hear anything else," he stated abruptly, before hanging up.

He quickly dialed Nikki. After explaining to her that something extremely important happened, and that he needed to take Eva over there, he ran to his closet and grabbed his gun. He already knew what type of time Mann was on and he wasn't going to give him a second chance when he got there. He decided then and there that he would have to kill him. Pennsylvania had a self-defense law, and he knew Mann was going to force him to use it.

He had determined years ago that he would die for Serenity and wouldn't hesitate to kill for her either. He knew today would be that day.

YOSOHN HAD JUST DROPPED OFF EVA TO NIKKI. SHE HAD sprinted out the house to meet him. Time was of an essence. Now, he was literally racing down I-476 with all kinds of thoughts going through his head. He wondered why Serenity didn't tell him something was up before. He had told her Mann was dangerous. He partly blamed himself. He had become so wrapped up in the problems he'd created, he left the situation with Mann unresolved. He also wondered who the fuck the new nigga she was dealing with that probably knew what was up but wasn't with her. He knew Serenity very well. Although she was a strong woman, she still looked to her man as her protector. Obviously, they didn't know the type of dude they were dealing with.

Mann was not the average cat. That was one of the sole reasons he befriended him. Now it was working against him. He had fucked his girl, shot him, and was now on some obsessed shit. He was a nut. There was no telling what else he was capable of. He just prayed he got there in time. As he continued up the expressway, his phone rang. He quickly grabbed it. It was probably Shameka again. He was wrong. It was Gina.

"Hello," he quickly answered.

"Yosohn, we're tracking her. Don't go to the hotel because she's not there anymore."

"What do you mean, Ms. Gina?" He was confused.

"Serenity just bought Heaven a new iPhone a few weeks ago. They share some kind of locator. We're tracking her now on the computer. It looks like she's in Blue Bell."

"Blue Bell?" he said aloud. Instantly it made sense. "He's going to his house … Listen, tell Shanita, Shyanne, and Shameka to hold off. Do not follow them up there. I'll go alone. You're going to have to call the police … Mann is not the average dude and they will wound up getting hurt or getting Serenity hurt. Call the police and tell them she's been abducted. Tell them she's a wealthy business owner, is a student at Temple --- anything to get them to hurry. I'm not far from where she's headed. She gon' be alright, Ms. Gina." He wanted to promise her, but he wasn't so sure.

"Please, Yosohn. Get my baby. I'm going to call the police now."

Yosohn scanned the highway for the next exit so he could turn around. It was a mile away. He was headed in the wrong direction. However, he was still awfully close to Blue Bell. The home he had just purchased with Serenity was literally ten miles away. Once he turned around, he could get to Mann's house in ten minutes. He had to beat her sisters there. He knew they were still going to go, despite the fact he told them not too. They were riders and wasn't nothing going to stop them from warring over their sister.

CHAPTER 47

Mann forced Serenity through the door with a shove. She stumbled but didn't fall. She clutched her purse and continued into the home. She had been cooperative with him, so she didn't understand why he felt the need to be aggressive.

"Mann, what's going on?" she asked.

She peered around the dimly lit home and grew alarmed by what she saw as well as the foul odor that circulated through the air. She walked a little more into the house and saw he had pushed his dining room furniture all together and had a large piece of plastic covering the floor. That and the smell of rotting meat overwhelmed her. She felt the urge to gag. She figured the smell had to be the trash. Whatever was in there had long ago spoiled and needed to be removed immediately. She began to grow nauseous but took a deep breath to contain it.

"You tell me?" he asked. He sat on the arm of his large Victorian-style couch and waited for her to respond. One foot dangled, while the other rested on the floor.

"You the one playing games. Out here being a whore, right?" he asked. His gun was tucked in his pocket.

"What are you talking about?" she cried.

"You left Yosohn right? You said you couldn't be with me because I was friends with Yosohn. Yet, you left him, cut ties with him, and said fuck me. Went out and got a cop for a boyfriend. Am I right?"

"Mann, I'm sorry ... but there's something wrong with you. You need to get help."

"Yo stop fucking saying that!" he yelled. He jumped off the arm of the couch and stood up. He was tired of hearing people say it. Serenity jumped in fear and slowly backed up. She stared at Mann. She wanted him to see her fear, let him know that he was in control, so he would let his guard down some.

"Mann." She spoke quietly and carefully. "Sweetie, I know you're upset with me, and I don't know what Naomi has told you, but some things are wrong ... Yes, I left Yosohn. Yes, I tried to cut ties with him, and yes, I was seeing a cop. But I had not completely moved on. I never had sex with him ... You and I just weren't right. You know that."

She did her best to explain. She knew Mann was borderline crazy and his mind was giving him feelings of infatuation with her, so she emphasized that she had not been intimate with anyone.

"Bitch! You're fucking lying!" he snapped before snatching his gun from his waistline. "I saw you at his house. And if you cared so much about me, how come you never called me, returned a call or text? Reached out in any way? I lost my grandmother. You never called! Never texted! Nothing!"

"Mann, I couldn't," she pleaded. "And me and Razul never had sex," she reiterated desperately. "I'm so sorry about your grandmother. You're right, I should have reached out."

She looked to his side where his gun was now resting. She was terrified. She prayed that God would send help while Mann ignored her lies and excuses.

"I wasn't good enough for you. I wasn't rich enough. I could have given you everything you wanted if you had given me time ... but you used me and then dismissed me. Yosohn was more important. It was fuck me. Even during my lowest point." His image of her had been forever tainted. Serenity shook her head back and forth and cried.

"I'm so sorry you feel that way, but you're wrong. Please let me leave," she begged.

"I can't. Everybody leaves me. I won't let you do that again."

Serenity now knew what the plastic was for.

"Oh my God, Mann, please don't," she screamed.

He went to lift his gun, but the door flew open. It was Yosohn with his gun drawn. Emotions overwhelmed Serenity. Her sister must have called him. She had no idea how he found her. God had answered her prayers.

"Mann, let her go," he stated firmly. Mann smiled at him and smiled in satisfaction.

"Fuck you pussy —" he said, before firing at Serenity.

Serenity saw him squeeze the trigger and the bullet flew past her face. She immediately screamed and hit the floor in fear. The sound was loud, and her ears were ringing from it. She could have sworn she'd been hit. She was sure she had saw a spark and a bright light.

As soon as Mann put his finger on the trigger, Yosohn squeezed his and proceeded to unload his clip on him. The shots caused his body to jerk, as he took one after another until he hit the floor with a hard thud. He gasped for air as he automatically fought to hold onto the life that was escaping him. The bullets hurt but Mann prayed they would end his life. He had nothing left to live for.

Serenity lay on the ground and covered her ears. She continued to scream even after the sounds of gun fired stopped. Soon, she felt Yosohn's hands pull her stiff body up from the floor and embrace her. She knew it was him and proceeded to cry into his shoulder. She kept her eyes closed as she sobbed. She refused to open them because she didn't want to see the aftermath of what had just happened.

Several minutes later, the cops arrived, along with Gina and Serenity's sisters. Her nightmare was finally over. Yosohn's was just beginning. The cops placed him under arrest, and everyone watched as he was hauled away. Even after Serenity had explained the situation, they still had to charge Yosohn with murder. She sobbed into her mother's arms while her sisters stood by helplessly and watched.

SEVERAL DAYS LATER, YOSOHN WAS CLEARED OF ANY wrongdoing and released. John successfully convinced police and prosecutors that he acted in self-defense and speculated that Mann would have killed Serenity had he not come to her defense.

Naomi's body was soon found in the home after cops entered to carry Mann out, further adding to Yosohn and Serenity's claims that Mann was a cold psychopath and had to be taken down with deadly force.

EPILOGUE

Serenity didn't care about ruining her expensive patterned tights or her $400 Vince Addie booties as she knelt in front of Jahkee's tricycle shaped headstone.

"This is your brother," she said with a smile to her twin boys Isaiah and Christopher. Heaven, who was now eleven and standing nearly the same height as her, put down Isaiah and he walked over and touched the stone. Christopher, a mama's boy wouldn't budge, choosing to remain attached to his mother's chest.

"Come get your flower, baby. We're gonna lay them down for Jahkee," she said to Isaiah, who was a busy bee and liked to wander off.

It had been two years and she would never forget her late baby boy. Even when he had passed, she still shared a bond with him. She would come out as often as she could to visit him, and while she never would get over the pain of losing a child, she thanked God for what he gave her in return for passing him along to Him.

Yosohn, who was holding a sleeping Eva, allowed Isaiah, Christopher, and Heaven to pick out their flowers from the fresh, mixed bouquet. He laid what was left on top of the grave. Serenity stood up and kissed Yosohn and quickly looked over her beautiful family. She was blessed.

She knew people looking in on her situation would call her stupid, but she didn't care. Her decisions were hers and hers only. She told herself that if her decisions made sense to her heart, then that is what she would base it on. Yosohn had changed. With therapy and lots of forgiveness, they had made it. Every tear she had cried, every blow she had thrown, every prayer she had prayed was not in vain. She was happy and nothing could take away what she had.

Walking away from Razul wasn't easy. He was an awesome guy. Serenity concluded that she would let someone else experience what Razul had to offer. She felt that God had another plan for her. She genuinely believed that she and Yosohn were soulmates, destined to be together.

Yosohn too, felt blessed. The day that Serenity decided to cut ties with Razul and allow him back into her life, he was overjoyed and relieved. He loved her with every fiber of his being. He agreed to give up all things in his life that weren't good. He had a good woman. A woman that had been his rock and his guide, a woman that had prayed beside him when she thought he was dying, and finally, a woman who had opened her chest and gave her fragile heart to a child that was not hers. He wanted to live with her, grow old with her, and eventually die with her. He loved her and he knew that he was a lucky man.

Yosohn knew that he didn't deserve her or anything he had. He had selfishly taken a life. He knew he was wrong and would end up in Hell behind it. He prayed that God could forgive him for all his wrongs. If he didn't, he would understand. He had given him everything he had now, and it was certainly worth an afterlife in Hell.

"Come on, babe," Yosohn said. "They're all tired and need

naps. We'll see him again soon. He leaned in and kissed her on the cheek, and they prepared to leave. She hated saying bye.

"Baby, grab Isaiah for me before he takes off," she said to Heaven with a smile.

Isaiah had just gotten some new walking shoes and he was all over the place. As they walked over to their new Mercedes G Wagon, she now knew the answer to her question from several years ago. Things had changed a lot. Things were different. Gone were the people she had once loved. New people were in their place. Children. Friends. *Was different always better?* She had asked herself. To her, it depended on what and who was different ... and for her, yes it was. Yes, it was.